D1090364

602

BEYOND RECALL

Oxford University Press, Amen House, London E.C.4

GLASGOW NEW YORK TORONTO MELBOURNE WELLINGTON
BOMBAY CALCUTTA MADRAS KARACHI LAHORE DACCA
CAPE TOWN SALISBURY NAIROBI IBADAN ACCRA
KUALA LUMPUR HONG KONG

THEODOR FONTANE

BEYOND RECALL

(UNWIEDERBRINGLICH)

———

Translated with an Introduction by
DOUGLAS PARMÉE

LONDON
OXFORD UNIVERSITY PRESS
NEW YORK   TORONTO
1964

THEODOR FONTANE

Born: Neuruppin, near Berlin, 30 December 1819
Died: Berlin, 20 September 1898

Unwiederbringlich, *first published in* 1891, *was
included in* The World's Classics *under the title*
Beyond Recall *in an English translation by Douglas
Parmée in* 1964

English translation and Introduction
© *Oxford University Press* 1964

PRINTED IN GREAT BRITAIN

INTRODUCTION

IT is paradoxical that the German novelist with the greatest claim to a European reputation, excepting perhaps Goethe, was, through both parents, of French origin, as was his wife. At the same time, no novelist was ever more solidly anchored in his homeland than Fontane; yet, although his series of 'Journeys through the Mark of Brandenburg' offers a charmingly discursive tribute to its historical interest and scenic beauty, Fontane was no rustic provincial bound narrowly to his native heath. Most of his life was spent in Berlin, the bustling capital of the new Reich created by Bismarck, and some of his best novels are accurate studies of specifically Berlin milieux, ranging from the lower-middle class of a Lene (in *Irrungen Wirrungen*) to the Prussian nobility. Indeed, Fontane saw it as one of the most important tasks of the novelist to examine the individual in society. *Unwiederbringlich (Beyond Recall)* is particularly interesting as being a novel in which the interest centres perhaps more on individuals than on society, even though, as in many of Fontane's novels, it is plain that these individuals have qualities which give them value as types, human or social, while retaining specifically personal qualities.

Theodor Fontane was born in Neuruppin near Berlin in 1819 and after private schooling finished his studies at a Berlin technical school where he learnt his father's trade of apothecary and for some years exercised it in various parts of Germany, including Leipzig and Dresden as well as Berlin.

However, he early started frequenting literary circles and in 1844 he became a member of the well-known Berlin literary club *The Tunnel over the Spree*, where he read his first literary productions, which were ballads.

In 1849 he gave up dispensing and took to journalism, an excellent school of worldly experience and unsentimental tolerance for any novelist. In 1850 he married and lived, for a time, rather miserably, from his pen. After short earlier visits to England he was from 1855 to 1859 a foreign correspondent in London; among the fruits of these stays were his travel books *Ein Sommer in London* (1854) and *Aus England* (1860). He also spent some time in Scotland, on which he wrote a further travel book; and Scottish ballads had already attracted his attention, as well as the works of Walter Scott. In 1860 he at last obtained regular employment on the staff of the conservative *Kreuzzeitung*, which gave him leisure to pursue his own literary activity. In 1864, 1866, and 1870 he wrote books on the three wars waged by Prussia against Denmark, Austria, and France respectively. The step to the historical novel was a short one and in 1878 there appeared *Vor dem Sturm*, set in Germany at the end of the Napoleonic domination. From now onwards Fontane's life is the story of his works, especially as in 1870 he at last found congenial appointment as dramatic critic to a Liberal newspaper *Die Vossische Zeitung*, which provided at least a reasonable income for himself and his family. After a further historical novel he moved over to the contemporary scene in *L'Adultera* (1880)—the theme of adultery or of extra-marital love was a constant in most of his works, nor indeed was there a better theme to combine Fontane's chief concern: the study of individuals as free moral beings in relation to society, a conflict in which, even although the conventions of society usually triumph, the defeated individual gains a greater sympathy. In 1887, when Fontane was already sixty-six, appeared his first masterpiece, *Irrungen Wirrungen*, the story of an affair between a young lower-middle-class Berlin girl and a rich young officer; a potential tragedy which Fontane resolves with gentle understanding and typical lack of sentimentality when the two protagonists go their own ways, to appropriate and not unhappy marriages within their respective classes. Later novels included in 1891, *Unwiederbringlich*, the subject of the present translation; then in 1892, *Frau Jenny Treibel*, where with an increasingly accurate depiction of milieu Fontane studies the attempts of a schoolmaster's daughter to marry into the new wealthy industrial class and her final realization that marriage within her own sphere is, if not better, at least an acceptable *pis aller*. In 1894 came *Effi Briest*, an ironical study of the conventions which demand that a wronged husband must seek 'satisfaction' even when the adultery took place many years ago and this satisfaction will lead to the destruction of a not unhappy marriage as well as to divulging an affair that could easily have remained secret. Fontane's last great novel *Der Stechlin* was published in 1898, the year of his death at the age of seventy-eight.

Fontane may be described, roughly, as a realist. At an elementary level, this means that he took great pains to ensure factual accuracy in details, especially of milieu. In *Unwiederbringlich*, for example,

Fredericksborg was a Renaissance castle actually destroyed by fire in 1859, the Hermitage park existed and so did Vincent's Restaurant in Kongens Nytor in Copenhagen; Wortsaae and Thomsen were real antiquarians and Melby and Marstrand well-known Danish painters; Tersling, Bülow, du Plat, General Schleppegrell, and others were real soldiers; there was a famous Dutch doctor called Boerhave (p. 214); Fritz Reuter and Klaus Groth were contemporary poets and Lucile Grahn a well-known ballerina; the communities and schools of Gnadenfrel, Gnadenberg, and Bunzlau existed; and so on.

All this lends a great air of verisimilitude, but as Fontane himself wrote: 'It is not the purpose of the novel to describe things which happen or at least can happen every day; the modern novel's purpose seems to me to depict a life, a society, a *milieu* which is the undistorted image of the life we lead.' Thus the novelist's work overflows into life and we must have the feeling, when reading, that we are continuing our real life; at the same time, the life imagined by the novel must have 'the intensity, clarity, lucid arrangement, roundness and resulting heightened intensity of feeling achieved by the transfiguration which is the task of art'. Realism is not mere accumulation of naturalistic details but the careful composition of a story by which the heightening of effect can give a more general validity to normality.

Thus, one of Fontane's most striking devices to achieve apparent objectivity—the lack of intrusion of an omniscient author—conceals deeper purposes. Again in Fontane's own words: 'the author's intrusion is almost always wrong and at least superfluous. But it is difficult to ascertain where such intrusion begins, for the author must, as such, do and say a lot . . .; but he must only refrain from judging, preaching, being clever and wise.' Hence, in *Unwiederbringlich*, the wide use of dialogue, conversation, and letters; we learn about Holk and Christine and Ebba largely through their speech and actions or through the speech and actions of others, and although motives are sometimes not untransparent, there remains an uncertainty, an ambiguity, a mystery about the core of their being—if core there be; for this, too, is left undetermined—which gives them the living and fascinating quality of real human beings. It is hardly necessary to point out the great opportunities of delicate irony offered by this method of allowing characters to reveal and indeed betray, if not to condemn, themselves out of their own mouth. If any analysis occurs, it is often sincere and splendidly muddled self-analysis that, even in moments of tension, is not without its humorous side. Fontane himself writes of the need to show things in a humorous light or at least to give them an interesting grotesque shape; again, examples are not lacking in *Unwiederbringlich*.

Fontane is well aware how little people frequently know about themselves and about others; and by letting his characters thus think and act for themselves, he is able to unfold his story in such a way that it takes place before our eyes. Thus he ensures that, as in life, the fate that overtakes his characters is never inexorable, at least not until it has taken place. At the end we may look back and see how everything, including chance, has had its role to play in any character's lot, but while reading, we are left guessing, from one event to the next, how the apparently casual adventure will develop. *Ars est celare artem*, and the great art of Fontane is always to leave scope for interpretation and imagination.

Similarly, when a fate is finally decided, there is no question of its being a last judgement. Fontane is too wise, tolerant, and, above all, too skilful an artist to condemn. His purpose is not to embody a message but to tell a story. If he has any message, it is that all messages are contradictory and thus it is false to think that anything or anybody can be wholly right or wholly wrong. Indeed, in *Unwiederbringlich*, it might well seem that the only thing that is plainly and whole-heartedly disgraceful is just the lack of a sense of humour which prevents self-awareness, an ironical view of oneself, although even here one or two of the minor characters, e.g. Schwarzkopf, pompous though he is, seem exceptions to such a rule. Ultimately, we can only feel that Fontane has achieved his object of creating a work of art that retains the exasperating yet fascinating ambiguities of life.

Since *Unwiederbringlich*, as well as a psychological novel and a novel of *mœurs*, is something of an histori-cal novel, a few historical notes may be appropriate to help the English reader, particularly on the Schleswig-Holstein question. As Palmerston once remarked, only three people had ever understood it, of whom one went mad, the second had died and the third, Palmerston himself, had forgotten! Briefly, the nineteenth-century history of the duchies con-cerns their attempts to remain united and, in spite of certain personal links with the Danish monarchy, relatively autonomous, in accordance with the declara-tion of 1460 (referred to by the Princess on p. 100) that they should remain undivided in perpetuity—*uf ewig ungedeelt*. A second obvious factor was the desire

of some Danes to incorporate parts of Schleswig-
Holstein into Denmark; in particular the so-called
Eiderdanes (of whom the politician Hall, also mentioned in the novel, was one of the leaders) wished the
whole of the area north of the Eider to become
Danish. The German *Bund* or Confederation, with
Prussia in the forefront, was equally determined to
maintain rights, at least in Holstein which, since
1815, was a member of the *Bund*.

In 1848, Frederick VII, of whom we hear a good
deal in the novel, proclaimed Schleswig a Danish
province. The Schleswig-Holsteiners appealed to
the Bund and their forces under a Prussian general
achieved considerable success until, in 1849, they
were at last decisively defeated at Fredericia, in north
Schleswig. The Prussians then concluded an armistice
and when the Schleswig-Holsteiners tried to fight on
they were defeated at Idstedt by the Danes under the
command of de Meza, a Dane of Portuguese extrac-
tion who also appears in Fontane's novel. Finally in
1853, by the so-called London protocol, Schleswig
remained in loose union with Denmark while Holstein, although largely administered from Copenhagen, remained a member of the German *Bund*—
an explosive situation which forms the historical
background throughout *Unwiederbringlich*.

Fontane, who was the author of a book on the
Danish war of 1863, took great care to ensure accuracy,
both in the general background and in political events
as well as in personal details, for example concerning
Frederick VII. Frederick who lived from 1808 to
1862, first married in 1836, married a second time in
1841 and divorced five years later. His mistress Luise
Rasmussen, later Countess Danner, of whom so much

is heard in the novel, had been successively a governess and a ballerina before being set up as a milliner with the help of the King's private secretary Berling, who then withdrew in favour of the King. One of the undoubted charms of *Unwiederbringlich* is the way in which Fontane's imagination has been stimulated and entranced by the setting of the novel on the Baltic coast as well as at the Copenhagen court and in the Danish country-side, which he visited to obtain local colour. Fontane has thus been able to give a wider resonance and a freer rein to his imagination in his treatment of the *fait divers* (actually occurring in Mecklenburg-Strelitz) which provided him with the starting-point of his novel; and it is relevant both to his obvious depth of understanding and to his powers of moral and emotional detachment that the relationship between his own father and mother and his own wife and himself seem to have provided material for the relationship between Christine and Helmut in the novel. Be that as it may, the combination of so many factors—the accuracy and vividness of the background and setting (not forgetting some very comical secondary characters), the skilful narrative technique, the sureness of purpose, the brilliantly aphoristic style, the pervasive irony, the importance and modernity of the theme, make *Unwiederbringlich* one of the outstanding novels of the nineteenth century.

This translation is dedicated to my wife.

DOUGLAS PARMÉE

Queens' College, Cambridge
1963

CHAPTER 1

HOLKENÄS CASTLE, the family seat of Count
Holk, was built on a dune sloping down to the sea,
a mile south of Glücksburg: an impressive sight for
the occasional visitor to a district at that time quite
off the beaten track. It was an edifice in the Italian
style, reminiscent in so many ways of classical Greek
architecture that the Count's brother-in-law, Baron
Arne of Arnewieck, could well speak of a *latter-day
temple of Paestum*. Ironically, of course, yet with some
justification, for seen from the sea it looked like an
oblong cluster of columns which concealed the living
and reception rooms on the ground floor of the building, while the upper storey broke sharply back, rising
a bare six feet above the columns which extended all
around the four sides of the building to form a
veranda; and it was these columns which gave the
building its markedly Mediterranean appearance.
Along the veranda stood stone seats spread with rugs,
used all day and every day throughout the summer
months, unless it was pleasanter to move up on to the
flat space, more terrace than roof, which ran all round
the top floor. On this roof-terrace supported by the
ground-floor columns stood pots of cactus and aloes;
here, even on the warmest day, the air was relatively
cool and if a sea-breeze sprang up, the flag drooping
from its mast would start flapping loudly, adding to
the breeze as it fluttered to and fro.

The castle of Holkenäs had not always stood upon
this dune and the present count himself, after his

marriage sixteen years before to the beautiful baroness Christine Arne, youngest sister of the owner of the neighbouring estate, had moved with his bride into the modest rooms of the original old castle of Holkenäs further inland in the large village of Holkeby, exactly opposite the old village church, built of stone and possessing neither chancel nor tower. Both buildings dated from the fourteenth century and a new castle had already been planned under the count's grandfather. But it was the present count who, possessing amongst other fads a passion for building, had taken up the idea once more and soon afterwards had built the much-discussed castle on the dune which, scoffed at by some, admired by others, was not only more elegant but more comfortable. In spite of this, the countess had never ceased to prefer the old castle; and so strong was her preference that she never passed it without a pang of melancholy at the thought of the pleasant time she had spent there. For her, those years had been the happiest of her life, when all was love and no differences between herself and her husband had yet appeared. Her three children had been born in the old castle opposite the church, and the death of the youngest, who had been christened Estrid, had only brought the handsome young couple closer together and strengthened their sense of belonging to each other.

Nothing had remained quite the same since they had moved into the new castle and the countess, who had been brought up by Herrnhuter[1] and was, in any case, of a highly emotional nature, had had such a

---

[1] A strict pietistic Protestant sect founded in the eighteenth century, of which the English equivalent, very roughly, would be the Plymouth Brethren.

strong premonition of this change that she would
have much preferred to see the old castle renovated
and enlarged so that they might have continued to
live there. The count, however, was obstinately set
on his 'castle by the sea'. On the first occasion
when he mentioned the subject to his wife, he de-
claimed:

> *'Hast Du das Schloss gesehen,*
> *Das hohe Schloss am Meer?*
> *Golden und rosig wehen*
> *Die Wolken drüben her—'*[1]

a quotation which had exactly the opposite effect on
the countess whom it was intended to impress and
thus win over to the new building, for it merely
aroused in her a somewhat malicious bewilderment.
Holk was not a very literary man and no one knew
this better than the countess.

'Where did you unearth that quotation, Helmut?'

'At Arnewieck, of course. There's an engraving
hanging on the wall in your brother's house and it
was written underneath. And I must confess,
Christine, that I was very much taken by it. A castle
by the sea! I think it would be a splendid thing and
make us both very happy.'

'If people are happy they should not try to become
any happier. And do you realize how strange it is
that you should quote that? I think you only know
the beginning of that song which, by the way, is by
Uhland, I hope you don't mind my telling you . . .

---

[1] Have you seen the castle? It towers by the sea. The clouds above
drift by, all golden and pink.

but it does not go on at all in the way it begins. At the
end, it becomes very sad:

> *Die Winde, die Wogen alle*
> *Lagen in tiefer Ruh',*
> *Einem Klagelied aus der Halle*
> *Hörte ich mit Tränen zu . . .*[1]

Yes, Helmut, that is how it ends.'

'Excellent, Christine. I like it too,' laughed Holk.
'And it is by Uhland, you say? Highest regard for
him. But you surely don't expect me not to build my
castle by the sea merely because "a song of mourning"
resounded from the hall of an imaginary castle by the
sea—even if it was imagined by Uhland?'

'No, Helmut, I hardly expect that. But I confess
that I would rather stay down here in the old stone
house in spite of its lack of comfort—and its ghost.
The ghost doesn't affect me but I do believe in
premonitions, even if the Herrnhuter refuse to have
anything to do with them and are probably right.
Nevertheless, we are all subject to human weakness
and so we're often anxious about things that we cannot put out of our minds, however hard we try.'

After this conversation, the subject was not raised
again except on one occasion when, after sundown,
the couple had climbed on to the dune to look at the
new building which had been started meanwhile.
When they reached the top, Holk smiled and pointed
at the clouds which were, at that very moment,
'golden and pink'.

'Yes, I know what you mean,' said the countess.
'And?'

---

[1] The winds and the waves all lay in deep peace. In tears I listened to
a song of mourning from the hall.

'In the meantime, I have resigned myself. When you first spoke to me about the new building, I was feeling sad; you know why. I could not forget our child and I wanted to be near the spot where he was buried.'

He kissed her hand and then confessed that what she had said on the last occasion had upset him as well. 'And now you are so good and kind. And how lovely you look in this beautiful evening light. I think that we are going to be very happy here, don't you, Christine?'

She hung tenderly on his arm. But she made no reply.

All this had taken place the year before the completion of the building and soon afterwards, because the old castle in the village was becoming less and less habitable, Holk agreed with his brother-in-law to send Christine and the children to Arnewieck and to leave them there until the following Whitsun when everything should be ready; and now Whitsun was drawing near and the day had come to move into the new castle. True, the garden which sloped down at the rear of the dune was only half-planted and there was still much left uncompleted. But one thing had been finished: the narrow façade facing seawards. Here, there were already small shrubberies and circular flower-beds and in front, where the dune sloped downwards, a flight of steps led from the terrace to the beach and was continued by a pier built out to sea, which was also intended as a jetty for the steamers plying between Glücksburg and Copenhagen.

Christine was filled with admiration and joy far beyond her expectations and when, after going round the house, she walked up on to the flat roof and looked out over the splendid view spread before her, she forgot all the worries and forebodings that had continued to plague her even after she had accepted the idea of the new building; she called to the children still standing on the terrace to come up and share her pleasure. Holk saw how deeply she was moved and was just about to speak and thank her when she forestalled him: 'Helmut, it's almost a year since we last stood here on the dune and you asked me whether I would be happy here. I didn't want to reply then.'

'And now?'

'Now I say yes, I am.'

CHAPTER 2

SOME weeks later, an old friend from her boarding-school days at Gnadenfrei, Julie von Dobschütz, also arrived. She was a young woman in somewhat straitened circumstances, originally invited to stay the summer. Soon, however, the countess felt that it would be pleasant to have her as a companion, friend, and governess, a feeling shared by Holk, since he was rather concerned at Christine's isolation in the new castle. So Fräulein Dobschütz stayed on as governess to Asta and Axel, the two children. Asta was left entirely in her charge; but Axel changed his teacher when a young ordinand, by the name of Strehlke, joined the household.

All this had taken place seven years ago. The count and the countess had settled in at the new castle and were enjoying in actual fact the 'happy days' that they had hoped to spend there. The love and affection that had bound them together over the years continued and although they sometimes had differences of opinion over educational and religious matters, they were not of so serious a nature as to endanger the peace of the household. It is true that recently, since the children had grown older, there had been no lack of such differences, which was hardly surprising in view of the diversity of character of the count and his wife. Holk, though a kind and excellent husband, was none the less a man of rather ordinary gifts and in any case markedly inferior to his wife, who was a far more talented woman. Of this there could be no doubt; but that it was so—and no one saw it more clearly than Holk himself—was nevertheless somewhat galling for him and there were times when he suffered from Christine's virtues and wished for a rather less outstanding wife. At first, this had been only an unspoken feeling, one which he hardly admitted even to himself; but for some time now this feeling had been put into words; frequent disputes arose and although Julie Dobschütz had great diplomatic gifts and did not find much difficulty in smoothing things over, the fact remained that Christine, who had foreseen all this, began to think nostalgically of the old days when such things never, or hardly ever, occurred.

It was now the end of September 1859, and the harvest had long been gathered in. The swallows that nested round the arcades had left, a breeze was rising and the flag on the flat roof fluttered lazily to and fro. They were sitting under the front terrace overlooking the sea, with the big dining-room behind them; Julie was preparing the coffee. The countess was sitting at a near-by table talking to Schwarzkoppen, the principal of the seminary at Arnewieck, who had walked over, half an hour ago, with Baron Arne, to take advantage of the beautiful day and partake of Holk's hospitality. Arne himself was strolling to and fro on the paved floor with his brother-in-law, stopping every now and then entranced by the scene before his eyes: fishing-boats were setting out, the sea was gently rippling and overhead the sky hung blue, without a cloud to be seen, unless it were the black plume of smoke of a steamer on the horizon.

'You were right after all,' said Arne, 'when you moved up here and built your "temple" on this spot. I was against it then because moving and changing house seemed to me something improper, something modern that . . .'

'That was only suitable for the proletariat or a petty civil servant, you said.'

'Yes, I imagine that I must have said something of the sort. But meanwhile I have undergone conversion in many things, including that. However, be that as it may, one thing I do know is that, even if I am the same in politics or religion or agriculture, which are after all the most important things for people like ourselves, I still have to admit that it is quite delightful up here, so airy and healthy. I really think, Holk, that when you moved up here, you must have added fifteen years to your life.'

At that moment coffee was handed round by an old retainer wearing gaiters who had been in service with the count's father. Both of them took it and drank.

'Quite delicious,' said Arne, 'to tell you the truth, almost too delicious, especially for you, Holk. Coffee like that will take five years off the fifteen that I just promised you and those dull dogs who believe in homeopathy—highly respectable people, of course, but strongly against either Moka or Costa Rican— would perhaps subtract a little more. Apropos of homeopathy, have you heard of the homeopathic veterinary surgeon who has been in Lille-Grimsby for the last few weeks?'

And walking slowly up and down, the two brothers-in-law continued their conversation.

Meanwhile the countess was discussing quite another matter with Schwarzkoppen, who had left his parish in Wernigerode many years ago to come to Schleswig-Holstein on appointment as principal of the seminary. He had the reputation—and appearance—of a solid churchman, but—what was of almost greater importance for the countess—he was at the same time an authority on educational matters, matters which had recently become burning questions for the countess, as Asta was sixteen and Axel almost fifteen years old. Schwarzkoppen was now being consulted yet again on these delicate questions—and was making the most circumspect replies. When the countess perceived that, perhaps out of consideration for Holk, he was not prepared to give her his whole-hearted support, she let the matter drop and turned to another of her favourite projects, which she had also frequently discussed with the Principal, the erection of a family vault.

'What is happening about it?' asked Schwarz-koppen, glad to leave the question of education.

'I still haven't dared discuss the matter,' said the countess, 'because I am afraid my husband will refuse.'

'That is a mistake, my dear countess. Such a fear is always wrong, because, although it is intended to foster good relations, it always leads to discord and conflict. And there is no need for either. If you can't find better motives, you must play on his foibles. After all, as you have yourself often told me, he has a passion for building.'

'That is true enough,' replied the countess, 'and this castle is living proof of it, for it was hardly necessary; rebuilding the other would have been quite sufficient. But however much he likes building, he still has his own preferences and what I'm planning to do is not likely to appeal to him. I am quite sure that he would rather build a badminton court or one of those fashionable roller-skating rinks or anything rather than a building connected with the Church. And as for building a vault, well, he hates the idea of death and he always wants to postpone what the Scriptures call so beautifully "setting your house in order".'

'I know,' said Schwarzkoppen. 'But you ought not to forget that all his likeable qualities as well depend on just such weaknesses.'

'His likeable qualities,' she repeated. 'Yes, he has plenty of those, almost too many, if you can ever have too many likeable qualities. And he would certainly be an ideal husband—if he had any ideals at all of his own. Forgive my play on words, but I cannot help it, because it is the truth and I must say it again, he thinks only of the present and never of the future. He refuses to face anything that might remind him of it. Ever since Estrid's funeral he has not once been back to the vault. That is why he doesn't even realize that it is completely dilapidated, although it is, and

a new vault will have to be built. I say "have to be",
and if I did not make every effort to avoid personal
or offensive remarks, I would point out to him that
it's not a question of fearing that he might be the
first, that I should like to be . . .'

Schwarzkoppen tried to interrupt, but Christine
paid no attention and went on: 'I want to be the first;
but I insist, for my part, that my last resting-place
must be one that I like and not a crumbling and
tumble-down. . . . But there's no point in surmising
what I would or would not say. For the moment I'm
more interested in showing you some water-colour
sketches of my design which Fräulein Dobschütz
recently did for me, at my request. She is so good at
drawing. It is a small covered forecourt with Gothic
arches and the paved floor forms the roof of the vault.
What I think most important, although this little
sketch doesn't, of course, show it properly, is the
paintings to decorate the walls and ceiling. The side-
walls with a Dance of Death, possibly in the style of
the one in Lübeck, and angels and palm-leaves on the
curved surface of the groins. The lovelier the better.
And if we can't afford the best artists, then we shall
have to be content with ones who are less good: after
all, it is the thought that counts. Dear Julie, excuse
my troubling you but will you please fetch us that
sheet of paper . . .'

Meanwhile, Holk and Arne had continued their
stroll and eventually reached the gravel path which
wound its way to the near-by steps of the terrace
leading down to the sea. Here there was a bower of
cypresses and bay-trees with a marble seat in front
and the two men sat down to smoke their cigars in

peace, something which the countess did not really
allow indoors, although she never forbade it. Surprisingly enough, their conversation was still about
the amazing veterinary surgeon, which can only be
explained by the fact that Holk, in addition to his
love of building, possessed a passion for fine cattle.
He was not a great farming man like his brother-in-
law and, indeed, made a point of not being one; but
he was fond of his cattle, almost as a sort of hobby,
and enjoyed seeing them admired and telling stories
of fabulous yields of milk. For this reason, the new
veterinary surgeon was an important person for him,
but he was continually being assailed by doubts as
to the latter's homoeopathic methods. Arne was re-
assuring him: the most interesting thing was, he
said, not that the new man was making successful
cures—others were able to do that—but how and
with what methods he was achieving such cures. It all
amounted to nothing more nor less than the final
triumph of a new principle and, through the treatment of animals, the success of homoeopathy had at
last been proved beyond all doubt. Until now, all
the old quacks had always been able to talk of the
power of the imagination, meaning, of course, that
it was not the minute doses themselves that were
effecting the cure; but, thank God, a Schleswig cow
could hardly be accused of possessing any imagination and if she were cured, it was by the drugs and
not by faith. Arne enlarged on this point, at the same
time emphasizing that there were other factors, not
directly connected with allopathy or homoeopathy, in
the cures effected by this new surgeon who had
recently arrived from somewhere in Saxony to stay in
Schleswig for a while. Amongst these factors was the

most meticulous cleanliness, verging on luxury, so that one must have modern cow-sheds and in some cases one even needed to use marble mangers and racks made of nickel. Holk was almost in ecstasies at hearing this and was so anxious to tell Christine all about it that he threw away his cigar and rejoined the others.

'I have just been hearing the most interesting things, Christine. Your brother has been telling me about the homoeopathic cures of the new veterinary surgeon from Saxony who studied in Leipzig. I stress Leipzig, because it is the stronghold of homoeopathy. Really marvellous cures! Tell me, Schwarzkoppen, what's your opinion on the matter? Homoeopathy has something mysterious about it, something mystic. It is certainly most fascinating and by its *mystic* quality, just the thing for Christine.'

Schwarzkoppen smiled: 'As far as I know, homoeopathy has nothing to do with anything mysterious or even very wonderful. It's simply a question of small or large quantities and whether you can do as much with a grain as with half a hundredweight.'

'Obviously,' said Holk, 'and then there is the expression "similia similibus" which everyone can interpret as he likes. And a lot of people refuse to interpret it at all—our enlightened sly old vet included, I have no doubt. He merely dispenses his tiny doses and apart from that he is mainly concerned with cleanliness in the cow-sheds and marble mangers—I dare say even that the troughs have to be kept as clean as a font.'

'Helmut, I do think that you might show more consideration in your choice of metaphors, even for my sake but particularly as Dr. Schwarzkoppen is here.'

'I agree. Incidentally, they were the exact words

used by your brother when he was quoting the wonder doctor himself, although no doubt it cannot be denied that even a doctor is ill-advised to use such expressions, especially if he is a Jewish convert —his name, by the way, is Lissauer.'

Schwarzkoppen and the countess exchanged glances.

'If he happens to come up to the farm, incidentally, I shall invite him to lunch in the bailiff's house. His presence here in the castle . . .'

'Can easily be dispensed with.'

'I'm well aware of that and you have no need to worry. But I give him credit for having his own ideas and the courage to express them. As far as the marble mangers are concerned, it's rather stupid and I think we need only give him credit for a rather charming oriental metaphor. But he's completely right in his insistence on general cleanliness. My cow-stalls date from the end of the last century and they must go. I'm only too pleased to have an excuse for putting an end to that dreadful state of affairs at last.'

The countess said nothing and merely poked her needle in the ball of silk lying on the table in front of her.

The count was annoyed by her silence. 'I thought that you would agree.'

'You know that those are estate matters in which I have no say. If you think mangers of marble or something similar are necessary, then we shall have them, even if they have to be fetched from Carrara.'

'Why do you talk like that, Christine?'

'I'm sorry, Helmut, but you happen to have chosen the wrong moment. I have just been talking with Dr. Schwarzkoppen about matters much closer to my heart, building matters as well, incidentally, and at this very moment you come and talk of building cowsheds . . .'

'Of course I want to build them. You always forget, Christine, even if, as you've just said, you have no say, you always forget that first and foremost I am a farmer and that a farmer has, in fact, to be interested in farming, that it is the main thing for him.'

'No, Helmut, it is *not* the main thing.'

'Then what is?'

'It makes me very sad and unhappy that where you're concerned, I always have to point out the obvious.'

'Oh, now I understand. The church needs rebuilding or is it a convent or an orphanage? And after that it will be a Campo Santo and then we shall have to buy up all the pictures of Cornelius and have them made into frescoes for the walls . . .'

The count rarely descended to the use of such forceful language, but there were some subjects that had the effect of making him lose his temper and forget the good manners on which he normally prided himself. His brother-in-law knew this and so quickly intervened to change the subject, which his imperturbable good humour always enabled him to do.

'Sister, Helmut, my view is that we must do the one and not forget the other. There's wisdom for you—and peace too. Particularly as you have no idea what the question is about, my dear brother-in-law.'

Holk laughed good-humouredly.

'You have no idea,' continued Arne, 'and I have no idea either, although Christine normally lets me into all her secrets. No doubt this will give us the

key, unless this is all meant merely to mislead me.'
He picked up the water-colour which Fräulein
Dobschütz had meanwhile fetched. 'Charming, whoever the author of it may be. Gothic arches, angels,
palms. May a man not walk unmolested even in such
surroundings? And our poor unfortunate veterinary
surgeon was the cause of all this trouble, a man who
walks about in top-boots and the only comic thing
about him is that he speaks with a Saxon accent. He
ought really to speak Low German or even Mecklen-
burger. Which reminds me, did you know that in
Rostock and Kiel they have founded a school of Low
German poetry, or rather, two schools, because when
the Germans start anything they always split into
two at once? Hardly was the Low German school
started than we had another *itio in partes* and so the
Mecklenburgers are parading under their leader Fritz
Reuter and the Holsteiners under Klaus Groth. But
Klaus Groth has stolen a march on the other because
he is a lyric poet who can be set to music and everything depends on that. Before twelve months, no,
before six months are out, there won't be a single
piano without a song of his perched on it all the time.
I saw something on your piano, Asta, can you sing
anything of his?'

'I'm not very fond of Low German.'

'Well then, sing something in High German as
long as it is nice and cheerful.'

'I'm not very fond of cheerful things.'

'All right, if it can't be cheerful, then it will have
to be sad. But then I shall have to be sad, too, to make
it worthwhile. Something about a page who dies for
his Lady Asta or about a knight who is killed by his
rival and is buried by the road-side. And his faithful

hound keeps watch over the knight's grave and three ravens sit on a black poplar and caw and stare.'

Asta was used to her uncle's teasing and would not have been at a loss to answer had her attention not been distracted at this moment by something else.

'There's Elizabeth,' she cried, pleased and excited. 'And old Petersen with her, and Schnuck, too.'

And with the others she went into the garden at the front and they all called down to the new-comers.

CHAPTER 3

PASTOR PETERSEN and his granddaughter failed to notice their welcome, perhaps because the light was shining in their eyes, but those standing on the terrace could see them all the more plainly as they approached along the beach. The old man, hat in hand so that the wind was ruffling his long, thin, white hair, was a few steps in front, while Elizabeth was picking up small pieces of wood and bark and throwing them into the sea so that Schnuck, a splendid black poodle, could retrieve them. Now, however, she had stopped playing and was picking a few flowers which were growing among the wild oats at the edge of the beach. Slowly sauntering, they eventually reached the pier and turned left towards the terrace.

'Here they come!' shouted Asta delightedly. 'And Elizabeth has brought her grandfather with her.'

'Yes,' said Arne. 'And one might almost say that her grandfather has brought Elizabeth with *him*. But you are all the same: youth is everything and when you are old, you are merely an accessory. Youth equals selfishness. But I suppose we older ones are hardly any better. When *I* saw the old gentleman *my* first thought was, here comes our game of whist. I know that Schwarzkoppen is not in favour of gambling but, thank God, he's not against it either and if he were a Papist he would probably call it only a venial sin. And those are my favourite sins. By the way, I rather like that poodle, what's his name?'

'Schnuck,' said Asta.

'Oh yes, Schnuck. More a name for a character in a comedy than for a dog, don't you think? He has already been up and down here three times. He's obviously enjoying himself immensely. And now tell me, Asta, what is he pleased about—you or the tricks he is going to show off or the sugar you are going to give him for doing them?'

Two hours later all was quiet on the terrace; evening had come and only on the sky-line could a red glow still be seen. Everyone had retired to the drawing-room, which was the same size as the dining-room and situated immediately behind it; and from here, they were able to look out on to the well-kept garden, with its greenhouses adjoining, which sloped away towards a large park.

The drawing-room was richly furnished but there was still space to move freely about. Beside the grand piano, in the most secluded corner, was a large round table on which stood an oil lamp. Here the countess sat with her friend Julie Dobschütz, who was about to read to her, while Asta and Elizabeth were sitting beside them on two foot-stools alternately chatting quietly to themselves and putting the poodle through his tricks, to its great and manifest delight. At last, however, tired by its efforts, it overbalanced and its paw struck one of the piano keys.

'Now he is trying to play the piano as well,' laughed Asta. 'I think that if he wanted, Schnuck could play better than I can; he's so clever and Aunt Julie will bear me out. They tried to make me play earlier on and even sing; Uncle Arne wanted me to very much but I took good care not to, because, although I quite like it, I'm no good at all. Have you brought anything with you, Elizabeth? You always have something new and I saw that you had a music-case under your arm when you came in. Let's see.'

The girls continued to chat whilst in the corner diagonally opposite the four men sat playing whist, Arne as usual blaming Petersen for playing so slowly, as slowly, he was complaining, as at the time of the Congress of Vienna.

Petersen laughed: 'Yes, exactly as I used to play at the time of the Congress of Vienna; people used to play slowly then, because it was considered distinguished to do so and later on I must tell you a story about that which is not very well known and as far as I know came from Thorwaldsen,[1] who had it from Wilhelm von Humboldt . . .'

'Alexander von Humboldt,' corrected Arne.

'Oh no, please allow me, Arne, from Wilhelm von Humboldt. Wilhelm was particularly . . .'

'Careful, Petersen.'

The game proceeded without further interruption and even the girls lowered their voices, for Fräulein Dobschütz had started to read from a big newspaper which the postman had brought that afternoon. She

---

[1] A well-known Danish sculptor of the nineteenth century. W. von Humboldt was a philologist, Alexander a scientist.

had not yet properly started her reading but was trying to find one or two matters of interest. The Italian war was still struggling in its death-throes, so first of all she chose the headlines and read in a querying voice: 'Archduke Albrecht and Admiral Tegethoff?' The countess shook her head. 'On the march to Magenta? . . . Bonnemain's Brigade of Cuirassiers? . . .' Another shake of the head. 'Our correspondent reports from Charlottenburg on the state of health of King Frederick William IV of Prussia? . . .'

'Yes,' said the countess, 'read that, my dear Julie. The piece from Charlottenburg. I'm not interested in all those stories about the war, they are all the same, someone is always collapsing fatally wounded and dying so that something or other called Poland or France or for all I care Schleswig-Holstein may live. But it's always the same. This modern cult of nationalism is not my sort of worship. I prefer something with purely human interest—and that includes religion, at least for me. . . . That poor unfortunate king in his palace at Charlottenburg; . . . such a clear-sighted man and now his mind is all in darkness. Yes, that interests me. Is it long?'

'One column.'

'That is rather long. Anyway, please start and we can always stop.'

So Fräulein Dobschütz read: 'All reports are agreed that the king's state of health is deteriorating; his power of understanding is weakening and his periods of lucidity are becoming less and less frequent. Naturally the sick man's condition has now started to have repercussions on matters of state and certain considerations that have hitherto been possible can now no longer be taken into account. The fact can no longer be hidden that a complete change in the system of government is impending and that this change will show itself in foreign policy. The link with Russia and Austria has weakened and a *rapprochement* with the Western Powers, and certainly with England, seems increasingly likely. All these events may recall the period from 1806 to 1813 which, following upon the previous humiliation, was a period of preparation and rearmament. The Prince Regent is incessantly concerning himself with such rearmament and when Prussia has reached the state of military preparedness which he is striving to achieve, we shall be in a position to see what will happen. This policy will show itself nowhere more plainly than in Schleswig-Holstein.'

'That will do,' cried the countess, 'I thought that the article would be giving anecdotes about the court, and all the trivialities that are their main concern most of the time; and instead, he's making all sorts of political prophecies that are always being made by those least qualified to make them. . . . But what is that picture on the back-page, the castle with towers . . .?'

Julie ran her eye over it and said: 'It is an advertisement for a Swiss boarding-school, on Lake Geneva, naturally. That little building there is the school and the big hotel in the foreground is for show.'

'Read it to me. Advertisements about schools interest me.'

'Our school at Beau-Rivage is now entering its twenty-fifth year. During this period, young ladies from every part of the world have been pupils here and, to the best of our knowledge, have always left with very

pleasant memories of us. This we doubtless owe, in
addition to God's blessing, without which we could do
nothing, to our strong guiding principles: complete
cosmopolitanism and non-sectarianism. A clergyman
of the Calvinist persuasion is the leading spirit of our
community but, in full acceptance of the spirit of
toleration, he allows the parents and guardians of the
pupils entrusted to our care to decide whether or not
they should take part in this religious instruction . . .'

The countess was visibly amused. She possessed the
characteristic, common to most devout churchgoers,
not only of suspecting the piety of others but of considering them, on the whole, rather comic; as a result,
reports from the Catholic or, even more, from the Calvinist camps were usually a source of amusement to her,
even when, as now, her amusement had not been directly aroused by a blatant piece of commercialism.
She took the paper in order to finish the rest of the advertisement, but the servant who had been watching the
whist-table for the last quarter of an hour, waiting for
the rubber to end, now announced that tea was served.

'Just at the right moment,' said Arne. 'When you
have just won, a partridge—and I hereby warn you
that I am relying on having one—a partridge is the
best possible meal. When you have lost, it's different.'

With these words, he offered his arm to Fräulein
Dobschütz, while Schwarzkoppen preceded him with
the countess.

'Well, Petersen,' said the count, 'We must make
do with each other.' And as he passed Asta and
Elizabeth, he called to them: 'Now, ladies.'

But Asta merely stroked his hand and said: 'No,
Papa, we are staying here, Mama said we might; we
still have all sorts of things to talk about.'

CHAPTER 4

THE table was laid in the dining-room, the double doors were open and bright lights met them as they went in. The countess sat down between the two clergymen while Julie sat opposite with Holk and Arne. A moment later the tutor and Axel appeared.

'I have just been highly amused,' said the countess, turning to Schwarzkoppen.

'Really?' interpolated Holk, in a tone of voice that would have been more charming had it been less sarcastic. Arne, who noticed the irony only too plainly (for Christine was incapable of being really amused), chuckled to himself.

'Yes, I have just been highly amused,' repeated the countess, with a certain hauteur, and went on: 'It really is a most peculiar thing about those Swiss boarding-schools, the way they seem to combine their Calvinism so well with their sense of business. Its worldliness has always seemed to me the unpleasant side of Calvinism . . .'

Schwarzkoppen, to whom this second remark was also addressed, inclined his head; but her brother said: 'That is the first time I have heard that, Christine. As far as I know, Calvin was ruthless and uncompromising and so was John Knox, too. And after all, Coligny can't have been as worldly-wise as all that or he might have lived a little longer. And then there was la Rochelle and the ten thousand believers who went into exile for their faith. Lutherans would be hard put to it to match that or improve on it. I appeal for justice: Schwarzkoppen, you mustn't leave me in the lurch against my sister. Nor must you, Petersen.'

Holk, who was, in any case, very fond of his brother-in-law, was delighted to hear him talking like this. 'That's quite right, Alfred. The absent must be defended.'

'Even when it is Prussia,' added Arne with a smile. 'And that reminds me of the article that was being read a moment ago. What was it saying exactly? You know that I have the faculty of winning at whist and at the same time following, more or less, all that is being read or said. I heard something about the court at Charlottenburg and rearmament and 1813. Was I right? I certainly heard 1813 and rearmament as well.'

'Do tell the Baron what it was all about, my dear Julie,' said the countess.

'It was exactly as the Baron was saying. In general, the article seemed to think that Denmark was finished unless the language question can be satisfactorily settled.'

Holk laughed. 'Denmark finished? Oh no, Mr. Prussian, things haven't yet reached that stage and whatever happens we must not forget the fable of the stork and the fox. The fox couldn't reach the water because it was in a bottle and the latest fox, the Prussian, cannot reach Denmark because it is all islands. Yes, water, thank God! It is always the same story, what some people can do, others can't, and however good the Prussians are at their goose-step, you can't march across the Baltic, even if Klaus Groth did write: "The Baltic is nowt but a puddle." '

Arne, who used regularly to start his dinner, until sometime in late autumn, with a spoonful of sour milk and was just putting bread and sugar on the bowl in front of him, calmly completed his task, took his first spoonful and then, wiping his beard, replied:

'Now there we differ. Our only difference. And let me add, fortunately, because one can wage all sorts of war against one's sister but not against one's brother-in-law. I appeal to Petersen who has seen more of life than we have.'

Petersen nodded.

'You see, Holk,' continued Arne, 'you were talking about the fox and the stork. Well, I have nothing against moving into the animal world, nothing at all. There happens, however, to be another fable about a bird—the ostrich. My dear Holk, you're hiding your head in the sand, like the ostrich, and refusing to see the danger.'

Holk shifted to and fro in his chair and said: 'Ah well, Alfred, who can see into the future anyway? Not you nor I. At the end of the day, everything is a matter of probability, and danger from Berlin or Potsdam is the most unlikely thing of all. The days of parades at Potsdam are over. I have nothing against old Fritz. He has no more fervent admirer than me, but everything he did seems to me a mere episode which has somehow become fatal to his country.'

'And so a country's fame or even its greatness can be fatal to it?'

'I know it sounds strange but all the same, my dear Alfred . . .'

Holk broke off as Asta was heard in the next room endeavouring to pick out the accompaniment to a song on the piano. But silence fell again and Holk repeated: 'Yes, Alfred, it sounds strange that fame should be fatal but such things do happen and when

they do, it's because of the natural order of things.
It is just possible that a new race of world-conquerors
might have flourished on those sandy marshlands of
Brandenburg, where after all, the Semnonians[1] and
other red-headed world-conquerors once lived, that
I can admit, but to achieve this, the country would
have had to undergo a long and slow process of
development. And it was Frederick the Great who
disturbed that process. Prussia went to bed a province
and woke up a state; that was abnormal and caused by
the fact that overnight or, more exactly, over a period
of some forty years, Prussia was racked and torn.'

'Those aren't your own ideas,' said Christine.

'No, and nor do they need to be; it's sufficient to
have made them my own. So please let me continue
with my borrowed ideas. With all due respect to
Frederick the Great, he was unique, *sui generis*. But
I cannot admire what we can call, if you like, the
posthumous Prussia, Prussia after him, always in
tow to some other country. Today it's Russia,
tomorrow perhaps it will be Austria. Everything that
it ever succeeded in doing was done in some sort of
double harness, not under its own eagle, whether red
or black. I can understand people who refer con-
temptuously to the Prussian cuckoo. For a state to
be more than a day's wonder, it must have frontiers,
it must represent a nation.'

'There are other ingredients needed to make a
state,' said Arne and both Schwarzkoppen and
Christine nodded approvingly.

'Certainly,' retorted Holk. 'Money, for example.
But who's joking now? Prussia and money!'

'No, not money; another trifle—a trifle that is

[1] A tribe of the Suevi who penetrated as far west as Portugal.

called an idea, a faith. With the Russians, the idea still lives on that they must possess Constantinople and one day they will possess it. History is full of such examples and something similar can be found with the Prussians. It's unwise to laugh about such things, too. Ideas like that are a force. Someone once wrote that our fate can be read in our hearts and what that inner voice says will be fulfilled. In Prussia—which, incidentally, you have been unable to tolerate ever since you were a boy—in Prussia, for the last century and a half, everything has been directed towards one great purpose. It was not old Fritz who was an episode but the period of weakness that you mentioned which was an interregnum. And now this interregnum is over. That newspaper article was right; the recruiting sergeant's drum is moving gently through the whole country and "old Denmark", when the time comes to call the tune, will have to pay the piper, if I may mix my metaphors. Petersen, you must say something. At your age, you have second sight and can see what is going to happen.'

The old man smiled gently. 'I should like to pass the question on, because what men have when they are eighty or more—and I am not quite that yet—women have from birth; they are born prophets. Certainly the countess must be.'

'And I want to reply, too,' said Christine. 'At first, I was only half listening to what Julie was reading, because I only wanted to hear about the dear King and Queen and not about rearmament and such things. But what they were saying was right . . .'

Arne threw a kiss to his sister while Holk, who was now beginning to feel himself the victim of a certain animosity, began to busy himself with his plate.

'The report in the *Hamburger Nachrichten*,' continued Christine, 'was obviously written by someone who is in close touch with the new ruler and knows his plans. And even if they are not plans as yet, they are at least aspirations. But I must agree wholeheartedly with what Alfred has just said about the power of certain ideas. The world is governed by such things, for good or evil, according to the nature of these things. And with the Prussians everything is based on . . .'

'Duty,' interpolated Arne.

'Yes, duty and trust in God. And if that is saying too much, then at least it is based on Luther's catechism. They still have that. Thou shalt keep holy the Sabbath day, thou shalt not commit adultery, thou shalt not covet thy neighbour's man-servant nor his maid-servant nor his ox nor his ass nor anything that is his—yes, such things are still believed in Prussia.'

'And, apart from Prussia, have otherwise entirely disappeared from the world,' laughed Holk.

'No, Helmut, not entirely but from the little corner of the world in which we live. I do not mean from our dear Schleswig-Holstein, because God in his mercy has not let us sink so low, I mean everything that is going on across the water in Denmark where the government is that we have to obey—and which I am prepared to obey as long as law is law. But for me to approve everything that goes on over there, that you cannot expect, that is impossible. In Copenhagen . . .'

'Your *bête noire* again. What do you have against them?'

'In Copenhagen everything is worldly pleasure

and sensuality and intoxication and that doesn't give strength. Strength belongs only to those who are sober and self-controlled. Tell me yourself, do you think that can still be called a court and a monarchy over there? A monarchy, if it stays as it should, has something compelling about it, it can make us ready to sacrifice ourselves body and soul and give up everything for it, belongings, family, everything. But a king who is only good at divorcing and is more interested in seeing a low farce or drinking Acquavit than thinking of his country or of justice, a king like that is completely without strength nor can he give any strength, and he will succumb to those who can.'

'And so we shall all become good little Prussians and a spiked helmet will be stuck on a pole and we shall have to bow down and worship it.'

'Heaven forbid. German, not Prussian, that is what we must become. I am a Schleswig-Holsteiner through and through and I ask you gentlemen to drink to it with me. You too, Helmut, if your position as gentleman-in-waiting permits you to. And see over there, Dr. Schwarzkoppen, the moon is rising as if it wanted to bring peace to the whole world. Yes, peace is the best thing of all; ever since I was a child, I have always believed that. My father used to say that we are not merely born under a certain star but, in the book of heaven, against our names, there is always a special sign written, ivy or laurel or palm. I hope there is a palm against mine.'

Old Petersen took her hand and kissed it: 'Yes, Christine. Blessed are the peace-makers.'

He had spoken quietly and casually, with no thought that his words might affect the countess in any way deeply, yet this is what in fact occurred. She

had been almost boasting of her peacefulness or at
least expressing her firm belief in it and yet, at the
very moment that old Petersen seemed to be almost
promising it to her, suddenly she became aware that
she did not possess it. In spite of having the best of
husbands whom she loved as much as he loved her,
she yet did not possess that peace for which she
longed; in spite of all their love, his easy-going
temperament was no longer in harmony with her
melancholy, as recent arguments had proved to her
more than once to an ever-increasing degree and
even though she would strive with all her might to
resist her tendency to disagree. Hence Petersen's
well-meant words found no response amongst the
others, indeed they all stared silently in front of them
and only Arne dared to look down the table through
the high french-windows out over the sea, shimmering and silvery beneath the moon.

At this moment full of uneasiness and oppression,
Asta suddenly came out of the next room and
whispered to her mother: 'Elizabeth wants to sing
something. May she?'

'Certainly she may. But who is going to accompany
her?'

'I shall. It's very easy and we have just been
through it. I think it will be all right. And even if
I break down, it won't be a disaster.'

She went back to the grand piano, leaving the big
dividing doors open. The music was already open on
the piano, the lights were on, and they both began.
But what they had feared happened: voice and
accompaniment failed to keep pace and they both
burst out laughing, half embarrassed. However, they
started again at once and Elizabeth's high, clear

voice, still almost that of a child, rang through the two rooms. Everyone listened in silence. The countess seemed particularly moved and at the end of the last verse, she rose from her chair and went over to the piano. Then, picking up the song still lying open on the music-rest, without saying a word to anyone, she left the room. This did not cause undue surprise, since everyone knew how sensitive she was. Holk merely asked Elizabeth who had written the words.

'Waiblinger, whom I had never heard of till now.'

'Nor me,' said Holk. 'And the title?'

' "The churchyard".'

'That must be why.'

A quarter of an hour later, the Arnewieck carriage arrived and Arne insisted on Petersen's accompanying him as far as the vicarage; Schnuck would be able to keep up alongside. After some discussion, the offer was accepted and Arne took the back seat while Elizabeth, who was fond of chatting with the coachman, climbed up on the box. Barely was she ensconced than she found herself being told at length about his sick wife and the 'sympathy' which had proved once again to be more help than the doctor who always merely prescribed things without looking properly to see what was wrong and particularly without discovering whether her spleen was in order. For the trouble definitely lay in the spleen.

This conversation was short-lived, for in less than ten minutes they pulled up in front of the vicarage. Schnuck vigorously voiced his delight at being home again and Arne moved over to sit beside Schwarzkoppen. Then, after a further exchange of greetings and thanks, they both drove on towards Arnewieck.

CHAPTER 5

THEIR way lay between high quickset hedges with the sea close by on the left; but it could only be heard since a low line of dunes obscured it from view. Arne and Schwarzkoppen had both wrapped their feet in plaids and rugs for, after the lovely warm day, it had become cool and autumnal, cooler than usual for September. This only increased the liveliness of their conversation which, naturally enough, concerned the evening they had just spent together.

'That Petersen girl has a charming voice,' said Arne. 'All the same, I wish she had sung some Weber rather than that gloomy song.'

'It was a very lovely song.'

'Certainly it was and we two can both listen to it without coming to any harm. But not my sister! You must have seen how she took the music and left the room. I feel sure that she immediately learned it by heart or cut it out and stuck it in an album. You know, although she is thirty-seven years old, she is still in many ways the little schoolgirl from Gnadenfrei, particularly now that she has Fräulein Dobschütz living with her. Of course, Fräulein Dobschütz is an excellent person and I have all possible respect for her character and her learning. But the fact remains that, as far as my poor brother-in-law is concerned, she is a mistake. You're surprised but it's true. She is far too intelligent and far too good-hearted, too, to try to come between them, either wilfully or through vanity, but my sister is forcing her into a false position. Christine always needs someone to complain to, some soulful figure straight out of the works of Jean-Paul Richter, someone perpetually worrying about the fact that life is real, life is earnest. . . . The only thing that is capable of relieving her gloom is gossip about the affairs of the heart of heretics—a heretic being anyone who is not an Old Lutheran, a Pietist, or a Herrnhuter. And it is a miracle that she can at least tolerate those three. She is so obstinate and unapproachable. I keep trying to persuade her and explain to her that she ought to be more adaptable and be prepared to listen to her husband if he tells a joke or a story or even makes a pun.'

Schwarzkoppen nodded: 'I was telling her as much today and pointing out all the count's amiable qualities.'

'A suggestion which she no doubt rather haughtily denied. I know her. Always some question of education or reports from some missionary in Greenland or Ceylon, or a harmonium or church-candles or an altar-cloth or a crucifix. It's quite intolerable. I am mentioning all this to you so frankly and fully because you are the only one who can help. Mind you, I'm not certain that she finds you completely satisfactory because, thank God, you lack the necessary pietistic tinge of "little blossoms, little angels". The temperature of your religion is not quite high enough for her, but she at least accepts its form and because of that, she will not only listen to your advice but will follow it as well. Which is something.'

While Arne was speaking, they had reached the place where the dunes opened out towards the sea. The surf could now be seen and, further out, fishing boats lying with furled sails in the moonlight. A rocket shot up on the horizon and stars of light slowly descended.

Arne ordered the coachman to stop. 'Enchanting. That's the steamer from Korsör. Perhaps the King is on board and wishes to spend a few weeks more in Glücksburg. I have already heard that they have dug up something else in the bog near Süderbrarup or somewhere, a Viking ship or King Canute the Great's pleasure yacht or something. Personally I would sooner read *David Copperfield* or *The Three Mus-keteers*. It all leaves me quite cold, these combs and needles they keep digging out of the bog or else some tangled mass that sets Thomsen and Worsaae at loggerheads because they can't decide whether it is a bundle of roots or some sea-king's head of hair. As for the royal luncheons where the chief item on the menu is crates of schnaps or else Countess Danner herself, of humble memory—a former mil-liner, I believe—well, I find all that quite repugnant. In everything else, I try to differ from my sister, even when she is right and makes such a fuss about it, unfortunately; but where this is concerned, I can only agree with her and I cannot understand why Holk persists in keeping on with all that business over in Copenhagen and seems to enjoy strutting about in his gentleman-in-waiting's uniform. I grant that there is no reason why his feelings as a Schleswig-Holsteiner should stand in his way, since as long as the King is living, he is, after all, our King and Duke. But I think it inexpedient and unwise. After all, life with Countess Danner is hardly conducive to longe-vity—I mean for the King, of course—and overnight it may be all over. In any case, he's an apoplectic. And what will happen then?'

'I think that Holk doesn't ask himself that question. He lives only for the moment and consoles himself with the saying: *Après nous le déluge.*'

'Very true. He lives only for the moment and the fact that he does this is another thing my sister cannot forgive and here again I must take her side. But let's not talk about this any more; today I don't feel like making a list of all my sister's virtues but rather of *les défauts de ses vertus* which, my dear Schwarzkoppen, we must combine in opposing or else we are going to witness something very unpleasant, of that I am certain. The only thing of which I am not certain is, who will take the first step—the first step to disaster. Holk is easy-going and modest almost to a fault—he is too respectful and chivalrous and he has become used to playing second fiddle to his wife all the time. It's natural enough. In the first place, he is impressed by her beauty—she really was very beautiful and still is, in fact. Then he is impressed by her intelligence or what he takes to be intelligence. Finally, and perhaps most of all, he is impressed by her piety. But recently and, I'm afraid, all too rapidly, there has been a change and he has become impatient and touchy and sarcastic. Only this afternoon, it struck me how much his tone has changed. Take that question of the marble mangers. My sister took what was intended more or less as a joke with deadly seriousness and replied half in anger and half sentimentally. Now, three years ago, Holk would have let that pass but today he took it up sharply and made fun of her because she is only happy when she is talking of graves and chapels and painting angels on walls.'

Schwarzkoppen had punctuated all this with an

occasional 'only too true' and left no doubt as to his agreement. But when Arne, who wanted something more explicit than mere agreement from Schwarzkoppen, stopped talking, the Principal betrayed little desire to expatiate on the subject, being reluctant to take the bull by the horns. Pointing towards Arne-wieck, he said: 'How lovely the town looks in the moonlight! And how well the dyke there makes the roofs stand out and the gables between the poplars and willows! And now St. Catherine's: listen to the sound across the bay. I bless the day that brought me here to your beautiful country.'

'And I must thank you for those kind words, Schwarzkoppen, because we all like to hear someone praising our own country. But may I point out that you are evading the issue? Here am I, begging you to stand by me in a very difficult matter, much more difficult than you imagine, and all you can do is to admire the landscape. Of course it's lovely. But I'm not going to let you get away like that. With the influence you have over my sister, you must approach her through the Bible, and convince her, with half a dozen examples from the Gospels, that things cannot be allowed to continue as they are, that her attitude is nothing but self-righteousness, that real love has nothing to do with this hidden pride that is merely parading as humility, in other words, that she must mend her ways and fall in with her husband's wishes instead of making the house unbearable for him. Yes, and you can add, too—and there is some truth in this as well—that he would probably long since have given up his post in Copenhagen if he wasn't glad to escape now and again from the depressing effect of his wife's virtues.'

'Ah, my dear Baron,' replied Schwarzkoppen, 'I'm not really trying to evade the issue, not in the least. I have all the goodwill in the world to co-operate, within my powers. But goodwill is not enough. If your sister were a Catholic instead of a Protestant and I were a Redemptorist or even a Jesuit father instead of the principal of a seminary in Arnewieck, the matter would be very simple. But that is not the case. There's no question of authority. Our relationship is purely a social one and if I were to try to play the father confessor or healer of souls, I should be intruding and doing something that lies outside my competence.'

'Intruding?' repeated Arne with a laugh. 'But my dear Schwarzkoppen, I cannot accept the idea that you should feel troubled by thoughts of Petersen when he is nearly eighty years old and has reached the point where any idea of rivalry or any possibility of misinterpretation must be out of the question.'

'I don't mean Petersen,' said Schwarzkoppen. 'He has long ago left all those petty jealousies behind that are normally only too common with my pastoral colleagues. He would certainly approve my role of reformer and miracle-worker. But we must not always take advantage of what chance offers us. In this case, there are so many adverse factors and difficulties that I feel bound to be cautious.'

'So you refuse?'

'No, I'm not refusing. I shall do everything that lies in my power but it can only be very little. If only for physical reasons. I have work to do and the distance to Holkenäs is not so very short, so that the opportunities that you spoke of will not occur very often. But the chief difficulty is the countess herself.

I have rarely met any woman whom I admire more. She combines all the advantages of being a lady, a noble lady, with all the virtues of being a Christian and a woman. At all times, she endeavours to do what she thinks best, to do her duty, and it is extraordinarily difficult to lead her conception of duty into another direction. As you know and as I was suggesting only too plainly, our Church doesn't permit anything more than counsel, exhortation, and request. Everything depends, more or less, on textual interpretation and this naturally opens the door to controversy. What is more, the countess not only knows her Bible very well, she also possesses the great strength of all those who look neither left nor right, make no concessions, and through their inflexibility, which is almost remorselessness, are far better armed than those who rely merely on gentle and loving faith. She will not be affected by contradiction and even less by my assuming an air of superiority.'

'Certainly. I can only repeat that it must all be made to appear accidental.'

'The only thing I can do is to act prophylactically, if I may be allowed a rather pedantic expression, since I'm half a schoolmaster at the moment. Precautions, prevention; I shall look around for stories from my past experience as a pastor—and what complications and aberrations does one not meet with and learn to understand!—and I shall try to make these stories do their work in secret. Your sister is both imaginative and thoughtful and her imagination should lend vividness to what she hears while her thoughtful nature will force her to face the matter squarely and perhaps lead to a change of mind and then to a change of heart. That is all I can promise. It will be a slow process and the effort may well be quite disproportionate to the result. But at least I intend not to evade the issue because I realize that something must be done, even if it must be kept within very carefully defined limits.'

'All right, Schwarzkoppen. I have your word and that is sufficient. What is more, it's a favourable moment to put our project into execution. Holk is expecting to be summoned to Copenhagen by the Princess in about four weeks' time and he will be away until Christmas. In the intervening period, I shall frequently come over to see to the administration and accounts of the estate, as I always do whenever Holk is away in Copenhagen. I shall let you know each time I am driving over, to discover if you can come with me. I should also mention that, every time he is away, she is in a much more gentle, almost tender mood and she always recovers her earlier fondness for him, which at the moment is more a hope than a reality. In a word, while he's away, her mind is like a field all ready to receive the good seed. It is merely a matter of trying to show her everything from another, as it were equally legitimate, viewpoint. If we succeed in doing that, then we shall have achieved our purpose. With the seriousness and conscientiousness with which she approaches everything, she will certainly be able to reach the right conclusion herself, once she has seen reason.'

They had now reached the dyke which stretched out along the other side of the bay and on which the roadway continued to run for a short distance. The town lay below them and in the distance towered St. Catherine's church in which the seminary was incorporated, while dominating the further end of the town stood the ancient castle that was Arne's home. As the carriage drove down the slope into the town, Schwarzkoppen said: 'What a strange sort of melodrama! Here we are, like a couple of conspirators, hatching plots by night and I suppose that I shall be playing the part that should have been taken by Petersen. And it is all the more strange because the countess really has a passionate admiration for him and the only thing she can find to blame in him is his rationalism. His rationalism! Nothing but a word and if you look at it closely, it is not really as bad as she seems to think, at any rate now. He has reached the limit of our allotted span and his eyes see more clearly than ours, perhaps in all things, and certainly in those pertaining to this world.'

CHAPTER 6

THE lovely autumn days seemed reluctant to depart. Next morning, too, dawned bright and sunny and the count and countess took their breakfast in the open on the front veranda with Julie. Asta was practising the piano in the adjacent room while Axel and his tutor had gone shooting on the dunes, taking advantage of the Michaelmas holidays which the countess, as with holidays in general, was rather loth to recognize as a rule. In town and at school, holidays might be justified, but in the country amongst all the freedom of God's creation, they were, she felt, to say the least, superfluous. The countess had long held this view on principle and smiled in a condescending manner when the count attempted to defend the opposite opinion; but although not having changed her views, she had, as an exception, not objected to this year's Michaelmas holidays because she had still not abandoned her plan of sending the two children to boarding-school at the beginning of the winter term. So a few days were not important. The count for his part continued to show the same lukewarmness which the countess was continually criticizing: he was not really against it but he was also never really for it. In any case, he denied that there was any need for haste, to which the countess made the vexed reply that that, at least, she refused to accept; it was not only time, it was high time. Asta was sixteen, Axel rising fifteen, and they were both at an age when character was being formed. They were, in fact, at the parting of the ways: were they to go left or right? 'And are they going to be black sheep or white,' interrupted Holk maliciously and picked up the paper.

This mocking tone should have warned the countess that she was once again taking things too seriously; instead, it merely made her more serious. Paying no attention to the presence of Julie, who in any case knew all about the matter, the countess said: 'I do beg of you, Helmut, to stop taking this serious matter as a joke. I enjoy being amused . . .'

'Sorry, Christine, but that seems to have become a favourite expression of yours since yesterday.'

'I enjoy being amused,' she repeated, 'but there is a time for everything. I am not asking you to agree, I only want a firm answer and you need not even give your reasons. If you tell me that Strehlke is adequate and that you prefer Elizabeth Petersen to a whole

boarding-school of young ladies, I shall not agree
with you but I shall accept your decision and say
nothing. It is true that I hardly call that education . . .'

'Ah, my dear Christine, here comes your hobby-
horse again or one of your long list of them. If you
had not been born Baroness Arne, you would certainly have been called Basedow or Pestalozzi and
replaced Schwarzkoppen as principal of the seminary.
Or perhaps even have become its inspector. Education, education, nothing but education all the time.
To be quite honest, I find it impossible to believe all
these stories about education. Even in education, the
most important factor is predestination and grace.
In this respect I am prepared to follow Calvin, however good a Lutheran I may be in other ways. And in
case the mention of Calvin annoys you at the moment,
since you happen to be in one of your high-minded
moods, then let me simply remind you of the old
proverb: What's bred in the bone comes out in the
flesh. Education has not really much to do with it;
and if we are going to talk about education, then let
me remind you that it comes from the home.'

The countess gave a slight shrug of her shoulders
which Holk ignored as he continued: 'The home
sets the example and example is the only thing which
I think has the power to educate. Example and
natural love. I love the children, in which I hope I
have your full approval at least; and I feel the need to
see them every day.'

'It is not a question of us, Helmut, or of what you
need but of what the children need. You see the
children only at breakfast when you read *Dagbladet*
and at tea when you read the *Hamburger Nachrichten*
and you lose your temper if they ask you a question

or even if they talk. It may be that it gives you a certain feeling of satisfaction to have the children around but it is not really very different from the sugar-basin that must be at your right-hand side for you to be happy. You say that you need the children. Do you think that I don't need them too, surrounded by all this quietness and loneliness with nobody but Julie? But the happiness of my children means more to me than my personal comfort and duty has nothing to do with one's own well-being.'

Holk stroked the table-cloth with his left hand while with his right he snapped the lid of the sugar-basin open and shut three or four times until the countess, who was always irritated by this sound, pushed the basin to one side. Holk made no effort to prevent her, for he fully appreciated that such a bad habit must be difficult to bear. What is more, this petty incident completely restored his good humour. 'All right then, as far as I am concerned. Talk it over with Schwarzkoppen and your brother and of course with our dear Julie. And then do what you think best. It is absolutely pointless to turn all this into a feud and I am most annoyed with myself for having said so much on the subject. After all,' and he took her hand and kissed it, 'after all, it is only a piece of play-acting on your part, a sweet, charming piece of play-acting. Why it is I cannot conceive, but you seem to want to continue making me believe that what takes place in Holkenäs depends on me. Now, Christine, not only are you a much stronger charac-ter than I, you are also much cleverer. However, I am clever enough to know who is master here and who gives the orders. So if one morning you say to me: "Last night I made up two parcels and sent one to

Gnadenfrei and the other to Schnepfental and in one of the parcels I put Asta and in the other I put Axel," then you know as well as I do that I might be taken aback for a second but that I certainly would not attempt to contradict you or even go so far as to blame you.'

The countess smiled, half placated yet half sad.

'There now,' said Holk, 'I see that you agree with me and if you hesitate one second longer I shall call on our friend Julie to decide. Isn't it right, my dear Julie, that it is foolish and even unkind to talk of a husband's contradictions or indecisiveness when his indecision is never an obstacle because the decisiveness of his better half immediately makes his own indecision a matter of no moment whatsoever. And there is the *Dronning Maria* coming round the point. Another five minutes and she'll be in. I suggest that we go down to the landing-stage and collect the Copenhagen mail.'

'No, I will,' cried Asta who had heard the news of the arrival of the *Dronning Maria* from the next room and immediately closed the piano at which she was practising. 'No, I will, I'm quicker.'

Without giving time to answer yes or no, she flew down the terrace towards the pier, reaching the end just as the boat arrived. The captain, who knew her very well, saluted her and personally handed her a bundle of papers from the bridge. A moment later the ship set off again for Glücksburg while Asta hurried back to the terrace. When still only half-way there, she held up a long envelope which the count and countess had no difficulty in recognizing as an official communication by its large size and seal. A

second later, Asta placed the papers on the table and
handed the letter to her father. He hastily scanned
the address and read: 'The Honourable Count
Helmut Holk of Holkenäs, Acting Provost of the
Noble Company of St. John in Schleswig, Gentleman-
in-Waiting to Her Royal Highness Princess Maria
Eleanor.'

'There's only one man who is so punctilious and
thorough,' said the countess. 'The letter must be
from Pentz. I always have to laugh when I think of
him, half Polonius and half Rosencrantz and Guilden-
stern. Asta, you ought to go back to your practising.
I think the *Dronning Maria* arrived rather too con-
veniently.'

Asta went back to her piano.

Meanwhile Holk had opened the letter and began
reading it aloud, knowing that he would not be
betraying any state secrets.

Copenhagen, The Princesses' Palace,
September 28th, 1859.

My dear Holk,

First of all, our baronial greetings! And hot on the
heels of my greetings, my most humble request for
indulgence, since I am about to disturb the family
life of Holkenäs castle. Our friend Thureson Bille
who was to have started his term of duty with the
Princess, alternating with Erichsen, was laid low
three weeks ago by the measles, a childish complaint
that, in the words of H.R.H., whom I quote, has
addressed itself to the right victim. Now it is true
that we still have Baron Steen but he happens to be
in Sicily where he has been waiting for Etna to erupt
for the last five weeks. Since Steen has found himself

unable to continue his eruptive life in person, he has turned to the eruptions of fire-belching mountains. I wonder what his own past seems like in comparison! I have only known him for thirty years myself. In spite of all his efforts to be a Don Juan, he was fundamentally a Sir Andrew Aguecheek, which, judged by his own standards—and pretensions—makes him about as ridiculous as can be. But let us leave all these eruptions and *revenons à nos moutons*: Steen and Bille are not available and so you must step into the breach. The Princess herself wishes me to express all her regrets to you and to the charming countess and commands me to add that she will spare no effort to make your sojourn as easy and pleasant as possible and I have no doubt that she will succeed. The King intends to spend the late autumn in Glücksburg— with the Danner woman, of course—so that you will find our *serenissima* in the best of humours since, as you know, she is not over-fond of breathing the same air as that lady. The position of Hall, who is, as always, the Princess's favourite *in politicis*, has been badly shaken but even that has helped to improve her good humour since everything suggests that the "Peasants' Ministry" which is impending has an expectation of life of not more than a month and if Hall returns to power—and he will be begged to do so —he will be more firmly in the saddle than ever. Moreover, my dear Holk—and I am more than delighted to be able to tell you this—it is not at all necessary for you in any way to rush and jump on the first steamer; the Princess asks that you be so instructed, an especial mark of favour, since punctuality is rather essential in your office and something on which the Princess is normally most insistent—indeed, in some

circumstances, she can be quite touchy about it.
Here I must stop and not make any premature
revelations from my store of secrets which I am saving
for your arrival. Moreover, the Princess is vexed if
anyone reveals beforehand any gossip that she would
have liked to tell herself. Just one really dainty
morsel: Adda Nielsen is leaving the stage to become
Countess Brede, after hesitating for a fortnight as to
whether she would not rather continue in her freer
and financially more advantageous position with the
wholesaler Hoptrup. But legitimacy has its charms,
too, and after all, this will make her a legitimate
countess while Hoptrup, even if he were to become
a widower, of which there seems at the moment no
likelihood whatsoever, will never be anything more
than a State Councillor, in spite of all his millions.
And that is not enough for the pretensions of our
leading tragic actress. De Meza has become aide-de-
camp. Thomsen and Worsaae are quarrelling again,
naturally enough over a hollowed-out petrified tree-
trunk which Worsaae wants to date only from Ragnor
Lodbrook while Thomsen, not satisfied with this,
wants to go back as far as Noah. I personally am all
for Noah; it holds pleasanter associations for me: the
ark, doves, rainbows but, above all, the grape-vine.
Let me have a note or better still a telegram to let me
know when we may expect you.

> *Tout à vous*, Your
> Ebenezer Pentz.

Holk read this letter with great amusement; but
the countess was not amused.

'Well now, Christine, what do you think? Pentz
all over, wasn't it? Full of good humour, malice, and,

fortunately, poking fun at himself as well. Court life does produce some extraordinary characters.'

'It does indeed. And particularly over there in our dear Copenhagen. Even at court, its fundamental nature cannot be hidden.'

'And what is its *fundamental* nature?'

'Dance-halls, music, and fireworks. It's a town made for ships' captains who have been drifting around for six months and now are only thinking of making up for lost time and throwing away all the money they have saved. Copenhagen is a town of drinking and pleasure.'

Holk laughed. 'Presumably including in your description the Thorwaldsen Museum, the Norse antiquities, St. Olaf's Cross, and the Church of our Lady, with Christ and the twelve Apostles as well?'

'Oh Holk, what a question! You could easily make a longer list and of course I am not blind to all the lovely things to be found there. They are certainly a highly civilized people, very intelligent and talented, endowed in many, many ways. But if they have all the virtues of social intercourse, they have all its vices as well. They are all completely worldly; they have never had to worry or exert themselves and wealth and good fortune have just fallen into their laps. They have never known what it is to have a thrashing and that is what sets their whole tone and gives them their taste for pleasure. What is more, not content with merely drifting along with them, the court even sets the pace, instead of having the sense to realize that whoever wants to govern must first learn to control himself. But they don't understand that, in Copenhagen, and even your Princess does not know it and least of all our good Baron Pentz who seems to imagine that the Tivoli pleasure gardens are one of the pillars of society. And he writes in that way, too. I cannot bear that tone and I feel bound to say that, in my view and with my upbringing, I think that it is heading straight for disaster.'

Holk dissented. 'Believe me, Christine, however much royal and less than royal junketing takes place, it is really not like Balthazar's feast and the writing will not be on the wall for my dear friends from Copenhagen for a long time yet. But what shall I do about this summons from the Princess?'

'Obey it, of course. You are in her service and as long as you think fit to continue in it, you will continue to have certain duties that you have to fulfil. And in the present case, the sooner the better, at least in my view. I shouldn't believe all that he says about there being no hurry and, in any case, I shouldn't take advantage of it. I have always avoided having anything to do with courts and I have a horror of princesses, old or young, but I do know enough about the life there and its laws to realize that you cannot show too much deference and that there would be something rather improper about calmly accepting any liberties that you are offered. And then, even if you were to stay here, you would only be restless, and so should I, too—we all should be. So my advice to you is to leave tomorrow.'

'You're right; that is the best thing to do, not to think about it too long. But you should come with me, Christine. Frau Hansen has a whole house to let over there, which is more room than we should need, and she is the best of landladies. And you would have the company of your friend Countess Schimmelmann and the daughter-in-law of our good friends the Brockdorffs and Helen Moltke. I mention those three because I know how much you like them. And then there are all the churches in Copenhagen, and Melbye is your favourite painter, and you have always had the greatest admiration for old Grundtvig the theologian.'

The countess smiled and said: 'Yes, Helmut, that is just like you. Only a moment ago we were talking about the children and our arrangements for them and you have already forgotten every word about it. One of us must be here to make sure that we do the right thing. I should like to know what is on your mind. Your memory seems to miss all the good grain and keep only the chaff. Forgive me, but I must speak the truth even if it seems a little harsh. I think that if my brother Alfred were to die, or perhaps someone even closer to you, and you happened to be going shooting, you would forget to go to the funeral.'

Holk bit his lips. 'I see that I've failed to put you in a better temper or prevent you from brooding and being so serious all the time. I wonder whether it's my fault or yours.'

At these words, Christine was suddenly touched. Taking his hand, she said: 'We are both to blame and perhaps I more than anybody else. You are easy-going and indecisive and changeable and I am sad and take life too seriously, even when it would be better to take it less seriously. You've been unlucky in your choice, you need a wife who is better able to laugh. I try now and then and even feel proud of having tried but I'm never quite successful. Solemn I certainly am and perhaps sentimental as well.

Forget what I said to you a moment ago, it was hard and unjust and I allowed myself to be carried away. Certainly, I often criticize you, I cannot deny it but I can also say that I blame myself as well.'

At that moment Asta came out of the drawing-room into the hall with a hat under her arm.

'Where are you going?'

'To Elizabeth's. I want to take back her music-case which she left behind yesterday.'

'Excellent,' said Holk. 'I shall go part of the way with you.' Asta, who saw plainly that a serious conversation had been going on, after greeting Fräulein Dobschütz, kissed her mother on her forehead. Then, taking her father's hand, she walked with him down the hall towards the front of the castle.

When they had left, Julie said: 'I almost thought that you would have liked to keep the music-case here for a few days, Christine. I noticed the effect the song had on you yesterday evening.'

'Not the music, only the words. And in the first flush of my enthusiasm, I copied them out straight-away yesterday. Please fetch them from my bureau, will you, Julie? I should very much like you to read the whole poem to me again or at least the first verse.'

'I think I know that one by heart,' said Julie.

'I think perhaps I do, too. But I should like to hear it in spite of that; recite it really slowly.'

So Julie slowly recited in a quiet voice:

> *'Die Ruh' ist wohl das Beste*
> *Von allem Glück der Welt,*
> *Was bleibt vom Erdenfeste*
> *Was bleibt uns unvergällt?*

Die Rose welkt in Schauern
Die uns der Frühling gibt,
Wer haßt ist zu bedauern
Und mehr noch fast, wer liebt.'[1]

The countess stopped her sewing and a tear fell on her hand. Then she said: 'A wonderful verse. And I am not sure which is the lovelier, the first two lines or the last two.'

'I think they both belong together,' said her friend, 'and one couplet enhances the beauty of the other. "Who hates, is to be pitied and almost more, one who loves." Yes, Christine, it is true. But because it is so true . . .'

'The other couplet which begins the verse is all the truer:

"Die Ruh' ist wohl das Beste . . ." '

CHAPTER 7

WHILE Christine was having this conversation with Julie Dobschütz, Holk and his daughter walked down the hall and then parted a hundred yards further on beside the round patch of lawn where they used to play cricket when there were visitors. Holk went to speak to a gardener busy in front of a greenhouse, while Asta continued on her way along the well-kept park drive which sloped gently down until it turned sharply left into a wide, level chestnut

[1] Peace is surely the best of all earthly happiness; what earthly joy remains free from bitterness? The rose withers beneath the spring shower; who hates, is to be pitied and almost more, one who loves.

avenue leading to Holkeby village. Chestnuts were lying all over the ground or bursting their husks and falling at Asta's feet. She kept bending down to pick them up but when she reached the pastor's house, which was inside the precincts of the churchyard, she threw them all away and hurried on to the house. The door had an old knocker that seemed to be failing in its task, for no one came. Only after repeated knocking was the door opened by the pastor himself, who had obviously been disturbed. But when he caught sight of Asta the look of annoyance quickly vanished from his face and, taking her hand, he led her through the open door into his study. The windows looked out on to the churchyard which sloped slightly upwards, so that the tombstones seemed to be looking over each other's shoulders. Here and there aspens and weeping-willows were planted and, in spite of the season, the scent of reseda was wafted through the windows.

'Sit down, Asta,' said Petersen. 'I had just fallen asleep. At my age, sleep no longer goes by the clock. At night it refuses to come and then in the middle of the day it comes and takes you by surprise. Elizabeth is over at Schünemann's to take some grapes she picked this morning to the poor old lady who, I fear, is not long for this world. But she will be back immediately. Hanna is lending a hand in the fields. And now you must have a glass of Malmesey with me. That is a proper ladies' drink.'

So saying, he pushed his open Bible away to the right, a box of archaeological specimens to the left— for like most Schleswig-Holsteiners, he was a keen antiquarian—and placed two wine-glasses on his desk.

'Let us drink a toast. What shall we drink to? Shall we say a happy Christmas?'

'Oh, that's a long way off.'

'For you it is but my way of counting is not the same as yours. . . . So I drink that Christmas will see all your wishes come true.'

As they touched glasses, Elizabeth came in and said: 'I must drink as well, even if I don't know what you are drinking to.'

The two girls greeted each other affectionately and Asta handed over the music-case, telling her at the same time how much her mother thanked her for her beautiful song of the other evening. She said all this rather absent-mindedly because her attention had already been caught by the various objects, all numbered, which littered the specimen box. One of them seemed to be of gold wire, formed into a large spiral.

'Why is it made of gold?' inquired Asta. 'It looks rather like a sofa-spring.'

The old man smiled at this and explained that it was something rather better than that, a sort of bracelet which a previous young Asta had worn two thousand years ago.

Asta nodded delightedly at this and Elizabeth who knew more about such things than she would have liked, since she was more or less the custodian of the collection, added: 'And if your horseshoe brooch is found in another two thousand years from now, I can assure you that it will also give rise to all sorts of suppositions and theories. . . . But come now, Asta, we must not disturb grand-papa any more.'

She took Asta's arm and led her across the hall to a door leading directly out into the churchyard. A few paces further on there was a broad path which ran diagonally between the tombs to the old stone church, an early Gothic building that could easily have been mistaken for a barn except for the pointed windows over which small-leafed ivy was climbing thickly right up to the roof. The bell hung down from some weather-boarding on one side of the church gables while on the other side there stood a low brick pent-house building with small windows, each protected by two iron bars. Some of the graves, particularly near the church, had their headstones right against this pent-house vault and on one of these Asta climbed to peer curiously through the small grilled window. To do this she had to lean against a loose brick which slipped backwards, loosening another half-brick which crashed noisily down into the vault.

Asta started back and jumped down from the tombstone on which she had been standing. Elizabeth was equally scared and it was not until they had run quickly away from the eerie vault and out of the churchyard that they recovered their courage and were able to speak. Outside along the cemetery wall lay great heaps of cut planks and baulks of timber, because parallel to the wall and separated from it only by a broad lane, there lay a long carpenter's yard overgrown with short grass where Norwegian timber was always being cut. At this very moment a roughly hewn tree-trunk was lying on two tall wooden trestles and two carpenters, one standing above and the other below, were sawing along the trunk with a saw that became brighter and brighter as they worked. Both girls looked eagerly towards them and the presence of the men and the lively sound of the sawing cheered them up after the chill of horror that they had felt beside the crumbling vault.

It was an attractive spot because the nettles, so thick and high everywhere else, had been trodden down and so the two friends could sit comfortably and cosily on the high pile of planks, using the baulks as a footstool and the cemetery wall as a back-rest.

'You know,' Asta said, 'Mama is right to have nothing to do with the vault and to be afraid of going down into it. Almost every stone is loose and it all seems ready to collapse at any minute. However, twice a year she does go there to lay a wreath on the coffin, on his birthday and on the day he died.'

'Can you still remember your brother?'

'Oh, certainly I can. I was already seven years old.'

'And is it true that he was called Adam as well as Estrid?'

'Yes. Mama really wanted him to have Helmut as his second name, like Papa, Estrid Helmut—Aunt Julie has often told me about it; but Papa insisted on Adam because he had heard that children with that name never died, and then Mama said—all according to Aunt Julie—that such ideas were pagan and superstitious and they would be punished because God would not allow himself to be dictated to and it was blasphemous and wrong to try to do so.'

'I can just imagine your mother talking like that. And the punishment did come, too. But Asta, I still feel that your mother is too strict about that sort of thing. Even Grandpa, who really loves her very much and married her—which is supposed to have upset the vicar of Arnewieck very much, by the way—and who cannot imagine anyone nicer than his "dear Christine", as he always calls her, and who knows your father very well too—even Grandpa says that she is too sure of herself and too strict towards other people . . .'

'Yes, everybody says that, your grandpa and Principal Schwarzkoppen and Uncle Arne. And even if Axel and I ought not to listen, we still do and so we talk about it between ourselves . . .'

'And whose part do you take?'

'Always Mama's.'

'That surprises me rather. I thought that you were your father's darling and loved him best of all.'

'Oh, I do love him very much; he's so kind and lets us have everything we want. But it is still Mama who thinks of our real good and because of that, she's stricter. Just because she loves us.'

'That's not what you always say, Asta. Only a week ago you were complaining bitterly and saying that it was hardly possible to live with your mother any more, she kept on saying "no" to everything and everything always seemed so important for her just as if life and death and salvation depended on it.'

'Yes, I may have said that. But everyone complains sometimes! And then it's often so quiet here and that makes you sad and you want something else. You see, I look at it like this. Mama often scolds us but she does care for us whereas Papa is amusing all the time but he doesn't really trouble himself about us very much. He's always thinking of something else and Mama is always thinking of us. If things were to go on as Papa wanted, then everything would go gently on until someone came along and wanted to marry me. Asta Holk, auburn hair, no physical defects, some money—I think that is all he has in his mind and he thinks that everything will turn out for the best. He doesn't stop to imagine that I have a soul as well, perhaps he doesn't even think that I have.'

'What awful things you say! He must surely think that you have a soul.'

'Perhaps he does, I don't know. But that is the difference between him and Mama. She *definitely* thinks that I have and wants me to learn things and have firm beliefs, "an anchor for the storms of life" as she puts it, and I should be very happy about it if it didn't mean leaving you. I shall never find a friend like you again.'

'But surely you don't want to go away, Asta, do you? What will you gain? Surely Fräulein Dobschütz is clever as well as being good and kind? And you can *parlez-vous français* so well that it's a pleasure to listen to and Strehlke has won two prizes, one in Copenhagen on coastal plants in North Schleswig and one in Kiel on jelly-fish and starfish. And I am sure he knows all about geography because quite recently he knew what the summer castle of the king of Naples was and even your uncle Arne congratulated him. What more do you want to learn? It's really not kind of you to want to learn so much more than me and when you come back you'll not want to see me any more. And I do so want to see you because I'm so fond of you. And your mama, if she does send you away, will certainly send you to some big Swiss boarding-school.'

'No, to quite a small Herrnhuter school.'

'Ah, that's different, Asta. I know the Herrnhuters. They are good people.'

'I think so, too. Mama went to a Herrnhut school.'

'Has it already been decided?'

'As good as decided. Papa has given in and in any

case he is going off tomorrow to Copenhagen to the Princess, which was quite unexpected, and Mama will certainly take advantage of that to have everything arranged as quickly as possible. I imagine in a fortnight or less . . .'

'Oh Asta, if it weren't for Grandpa, I should ask your mama to let me go with you. What shall I do here when you have gone away?'

'I'm afraid I have to go, Elizabeth, and I shall go. It will be hard for me as well. And Mama will be all alone, too, with nobody here but Aunt Julie, and in spite of that she is sending me away. And Axel is going too. What Mama was saying yesterday is right: we must not live for our own pleasure and enjoyment but to do our duty. And she begged me always to remember that, because in that way we shall always be happy and blessed.'

'All that is true, Asta, but it doesn't help me very much.' Elizabeth's eyes were glistening as she said this. 'I cannot just keep on walking up and down the beach looking for amber and making lists and copying numbers. And just think of the winter when everything is covered in snow and the crows are sitting on the crosses and then at twelve o'clock the clock strikes . . .'

And at that very moment the bell started striking. The two girls jumped up. Then they laughed and realized that it was time to go.

'When are you coming again?'

'Tomorrow.'

They parted and as Asta was passing the place where the bell hung, it struck for the last time and the little boy who was tolling it raised his cap and disappeared among the graves.

CHAPTER 8

AFTER Holk had left Asta by the cricket pitch, he went to the nearest greenhouse in front of which his gardener was hard at work. Holk greeted him and then, tearing two leaves out of his memorandum pad, he wrote a couple of telegrams to Pentz and Frau Hansen, announcing to both his arrival in Copenhagen the following evening. 'Ohlsen, these telegrams must be sent from Glücksburg or from Arnewieck, if you like. You may take the brake.'

The gardener, a lout like most of his kind, was plainly annoyed, so Holk added: 'I'm sorry to have to interrupt your work, but I need Philip to help me pack, and your wife's brother, who seems quite promising, doesn't know his way about yet, and anyway I'm not sure that he is reliable enough.'

At this the gardener quite recovered his good humour and said that if the count did not mind, he would prefer to go to Glücksburg: his wife had such an itch all over her body, which certainly must come from her spleen, because she lost her temper so easily, and so he would like to go to the doctor's for a prescription.

'All right,' said Holk. 'And while you are there, will you at the same time make sure that the ship definitely calls here tomorrow morning, as once or twice it has failed to put in here. And also ask whether the King has already arrived in Glücksburg and how long he is expected to stay.'

The count then returned to the castle, where Philip had not only got out all the trunks but had also started packing.

'Excellent, Philip. I see that your mistress has already told you that I have to leave. Well, you know what I need; but not too much because the more you take the more you need. If you take a full trunk, in the end you expect to have everything that you have at home. Don't forget one thing—my fur boots and galoshes. You lumber about in them like an elephant but they warm the cockles of the heart and that is the main thing. Don't you agree?'

Philip did agree, whereupon the count, visibly pleased, sat down at his desk and wrote a few letters, including one to Arne, while the old servant continued packing his bags.

'What books does the count require?'

'No books. The ones we have aren't suitable for Copenhagen; but put in a couple of Walter Scott's; one never knows and he is always suitable.'

At noon, while Asta was still down in the village, Baron Arne came over from Arnewieck and as they were chatting with the ladies in the hall, Holk handed him with a laugh the letter he had written him that morning. 'There, Alfred; but read it when you're at home. There is no hurry about it and I think you probably know what is in it. It is the old, old story: I'm handing over Holkenäs castle and all its arrangements to you, as I have already done so often, and I appoint you major-domo for the period of my absence. Advise your sister, discuss with her' (he added in an undertone) 'the building of a new chapel with a vault or anything else she wants, and have plans drawn up for the cow-sheds. Do the one for the shorthorns first. Ask the advice of the homoeopath of whom you were telling me such extraordinary things

the other day and send the drawings over to Copenhagen. Pentz also knows something about it and the
much-travelled Bille even more; after all, his measles
cannot' (he turned back to the ladies) 'go on for ever.
When he has peeled—it's funny to think of him in an
isolation hospital—I shall go and see him and show
him the plans. Invalids are always glad to hear something more than the tinkle of a medicine spoon or the
sound of a doctor's stick.'

Holk continued to speak in this tone, leaving no
doubt as to his very great pleasure at being able to
go away from Holkenäs for three months. It was,
indeed, somewhat offensive for the countess and she
would certainly not have failed to mention the subject
had she not detected a rather similar feeling in herself.
The Holks were like many other married couples.
When they were not together, they felt closer to each
other, for then not only did all their differences of
opinion and bickering disappear from their memories
but they also found themselves recovering their
former feelings of affection for each other and even
used to write each other loving letters. As no one
knew this better than the brother-in-law, he now
began to pass a few jocular remarks on this subject,
which were not well received; apt though they were,
his sister had no desire to hear any reference, however slight, to such matters at this moment. Observing
his wife's hauteur, Holk invited Julie to come for a
walk in the park, as 'he had one or two things still to
discuss with her'.

When Christine was left alone with her brother,
she said: 'You ought not to have said such things,
Alfred, while Helmut was there. You know that in
any case he has a tendency to take things lightly, and

if you lead the way, you only encourage him in his pretence of being frivolous.'

Arne smiled.

'You are smiling but you are quite wrong. I didn't say "being frivolous", I said "pretending to be frivolous". He is not able to be a real free-thinker because he is not fitted for it either by character or intelligence. And that is what is so wrong. I could live with an atheist or at least I think I could, yes, I think it might even stimulate me to have serious discussions with him. But that would be impossible with Helmut. Serious discussions! He doesn't know what it means. You may say what you like to me, but with him, all you are doing is confusing him and encouraging him in his weakness and vanity.'

Arne said nothing and merely threw a few crumbs to some finches which had appeared while they were talking.

'Why don't you say something? Do you think I'm being too "churchy" again? I have not *once* mentioned the word church. Or am I being too strict for your liking?'

Arne nodded.

'Too strict? Amazing. You seem to have become quite incapable of understanding me any more, Alfred, and if that is a reproach and you mean it as such, then you must allow me to return the compliment. I *cannot* understand you any more. You know how fond I am of you, how grateful I have always been to you since I was a child and how grateful I still am. But I still cannot help pointing out that it is you who have changed your opinions and principles, not I. One day you find me too strict in my morals, the next you find me too inflexible in my religion, the third day too

Prussian and the fourth not Danish enough. I'm never right. And yet, Alfred, it is you who made me everything I am, or most of what I am. It was you who showed me the way. You were already thirty when I was left an orphan and I was brought up according to your ideas, not our parents'. It was you who found the Herrnhut school for me, you introduced me to the Reckes and the Reusses and all those pious families, and now that I have become what you intended, you find it wrong. And why is it wrong? Because in the meanwhile you have changed sides. I don't reproach *you* because when you were thirty your ideas were hide-bound and aristocratic and now you are sixty you suddenly see the world through liberal spectacles. But have you the right to blame me if I have remained what you used to be and what you yourself made me?'

Arne gently took his sister's hand. 'Dear Christine, you may be whatever you like. I no longer have the heart to despise anyone's views. That is the one thing that I have learnt in my second thirty years. It is not the opinion that matters but the *way* you defend it. And there, I feel compelled to say that you are holding the rein too taut, you're making too much of a good thing.'

'Can you make too much of a good thing?'

'Of course you can. Any excess is wrong. Ever since I learned it, I have always been most impressed by the idea that in antiquity they valued nothing so highly as moderation in all things.'

At this point Holk and Julie came back from their walk and Asta came up from the beach on the other side and immediately hurried towards Arne, whose favourite she was and who was always ready to listen to her. With her mother she was reserved but when Uncle Alfred was there, she always had to pour out everything that was on her mind.

'This morning I was sitting at Pastor Petersen's desk and on the right-hand side was the Bible and on the left his box of antiquities and there was really not an inch of space left to show me what was in all the boxes. It was mainly stones. But finally, after he had pushed the Bible out of the way . . .'

'Then you had room,' laughed the countess. 'Dear old Petersen is always pushing the Bible out of the way and is forever busy with his old stones and he even has a tendency to give stones instead of bread . . .'

Arne was tempted to contradict but, remembering the conversation he had just had, quickly changed his mind and was glad when Asta went on: 'And then I went with Elizabeth outside into the churchyard beside her mother's grave and I saw that Elizabeth is really Elizabeth Kruse and only her mother was a Petersen and that we really ought not to call her Petersen. But she told me that she had never known her father and her mother had always been known as old Petersen's daughter when people talked of her down in the village, and so she was called Elizabeth Petersen as well, and that it was really all right. And then we went further along the cemetery up to the church and climbed up on a tombstone that had half fallen over and tried to look through the iron bars of the window into the vault and a brick fell in with a crash and I almost had the feeling that I had killed someone. Oh, I can't tell you how scared I was. I don't ever want to go in there now and if I die you must all promise me that my grave will be in the open.'

The countess's eye fell on her husband who was

plainly moved as he nodded in a friendly fashion to his wife: 'We must see to all that, Christine. I have already spoken to Alfred and also to Julie a moment ago. We shall turn it into an open courtyard with Gothic arches to enclose the burial ground, and anything else that needs doing you can arrange for yourself.'

The count and countess discussed this matter for a few more minutes while Arne talked with Asta and then, when the conversation became general again, the latter led it on to other matters; this was not difficult as the gardener Ohlsen had just come back with the news that the King was arriving the next day and Countess Danner as well, and he intended to stay four weeks excavating a barrow on Brarup moor; and the ticket had been bought and the steamer would arrive at the pier below tomorrow morning at ten o'clock or thereabouts. It was the best ship of the line, the *King Christian*, with Brödstedt as skipper.

Before Ohlsen had finished making his report, Axel came in with his tutor and pulled out of his bag the partridges that he had shot.

'Many thanks, Axel,' said Holk, 'that will give me some lunch on the way. You'll be a decent shot yet, like all our family, and frankly that is what I should like best. Learning is for others.'

As he said this, Holk's glance fell briefly and quite unintentionally on poor Strehlke who, while his pupil had been shooting partridge, had been content to take a dozen fieldfare out of the snares.

CHAPTER 9

THE *King Christian* was as good as its word; punctually at ten o'clock it came in sight and ten minutes later moored at the landing-stage. The count was already there, his cases beside him, on which Axel and Asta were sitting, with shot-guns over their shoulders. He said good-bye to his children and climbed on board behind two of the crew carrying his luggage. Captain Brödstedt called down to the engine-room, the quartermaster let the wheel run through his fingers, and with heavy thuds, for it was still a paddle-steamer, the ship left the jetty and headed east towards the open sea. Meanwhile Holk had climbed up to the captain on the bridge and was watching the pier where the two children were still eagerly waving while Axel even fired a farewell shot from his gun. The countess and Fräulein Dobschütz were standing on the top step of the terrace and then moved up to the tall colonnaded gallery to follow the ship more easily. At the same time they were able to look down on to the pier where the two children were now coming back in lively conversation. When they reached the beach they parted, and while Axel turned off into the dunes, bent on some gull-shooting, Asta climbed up to the terrace.

When she arrived, she pushed a footstool close to her mother's chair, took her hand and tried to joke: 'It was the handsome Captain Brödstedt on the boat who, according to Philip, has a very pretty wife whom he is supposed to have taken from the Bornholm lighthouse. It really is a shame that just because of prejudice one can't marry a man like Captain Brödstedt.'

'But Asta, how can you say such a thing?'

'It's quite simple, Mama. After all, everybody has eyes in their head and hears all sorts of things and makes comparisons. Now just take Dr. Schwarz-koppen who married into the aristocracy; it's true he's a widower now. But you must admit, Mama, that the Principal is not half as good-looking as Brödstedt. And Schwarzkoppen might be a possi-bility, but Herr Strehlke . . .'

They both laughed, and as her mother said noth-ing, Fräulein Dobschütz said: 'Asta, you are behaving just like a young filly and I see to my horror that you need some schooling. And what were you saying exactly, as if there was a difference socially speaking between a man like Brödstedt and a man like Strehlke.'

'Certainly there is a difference. That is to say, not for me, quite definitely not for me, I assure you. But for others there is a difference. Just look around us. And I have never heard of a marriage between a ship's captain and the daughter of a count; but if I were to add up all the tutors and curates around here who . . .'

'Please let us try to avoid comparisons, Asta.'

'All right,' she laughed, 'but to be a lighthouse-keeper's daughter and then be taken from a lighthouse by Captain Brödstedt is very charming and really a sort of real-life fairy story. And I adore anything to do with fairy stories, I have a passion for them and I like Andersen's tale about the brave tin soldier much, much better than the whole of the Seven Years' War!' And with these words she jumped up from her foot-stool and went off to play the piano, leaving the two women alone. Immediately afterwards, one of

Chopin's *Études* could be heard, played rather un-
evenly and with many mistakes.

'How did Asta come to make such a remark? Is it
just high spirits or what? What put such strange
ideas into her head?'

'Nothing that you need to be afraid of,' said
Fräulein Dobschütz. 'If that were so, then she would
keep quiet about it. I spend more time with her than
you and I can guarantee her commonsense. Asta has a
lively mind and a lively imagination.'

'Which is always a danger . . .'

'Yes. But often a blessing as well. A lively imagination can often turn ugliness into something else and
then it is a shield and protection.'

The countess stared straight ahead without replying and when, a little later, she looked out again over
the sea, there was nothing to be seen of the ship
except a thin wisp of smoke along the horizon,
growing paler and paler. She seemed very pensive
and when Fräulein Dobschütz gave her a furtive
glance, she saw that her eyes were full of tears.

'What is it, Christine?' she asked.

'Nothing.'

'And yet you seem so moved . . .'

'Nothing,' repeated the countess, 'or at least
nothing definite. But I have a vague fear and if I
didn't dislike fortune-telling and interpreting dreams
as being something godless and a source of trouble,
I would tell you of a dream that I had last night. And
it wasn't even a particularly horrifying dream, merely
sad and melancholy. It was a funeral procession, just
you and I and Helmut in the distance. And then all at
once it was a wedding procession and I was in it and
then it was a funeral procession again. I cannot put

it out of my thoughts. The strange thing about it was that I was not frightened by it during the dream, but only when I woke up. It was for that reason that I was so disturbed by what Asta said. Yesterday I should merely have been amused at it, for I know the children and know that she is exactly as you said. . . . And then, frankly, this journey makes me afraid. Look, the smoke has disappeared now . . .'

'But Christine, you will get over it; it's like being afraid of falling off a chair or of the ceiling falling in. Ceilings do fall in and houses as well, and ships founder too, between Glücksburg and Copenhagen but, thank God, only once every hundred years . . .'

'And when it does happen, someone suffers and who can say who that someone will be? But it is not that, Julie. I'm not afraid of an accident on the way. What is worrying me is quite different. As you know, I was looking forward to this period of quiet that was going to be such a busy time as well, yet ever since this morning I'm not looking forward to it at all.'

'Have you changed your mind about the children?'

'No, I shall do what we decided long ago between us and my only uncertainty is where to send Axel. But it will not be difficult to settle that either. No, Julie, what has been preying on my mind since this morning is simply this: I ought not to have let Helmut go or, at least, not alone. I have always been uneasy and unhappy about this strange situation and even although he was compelled to go this time, otherwise it would have seemed an insult not to appear, then all the same I should have gone with him . . .'

Julie had difficulty in suppressing a smile.

'Jealous?' And as she asked, she took the countess's hand and felt it trembling. 'You don't reply. So I have guessed right and you really are jealous, otherwise you would have said something and laughed at me. One never stops learning, even about one's best friend.'

A silence followed, painful for them both but especially for Julie who had aroused all these emotions quite unwittingly and unwillingly; but the embarrassment on both sides could now only be removed by continuing the conversation that had caused it.

'May I say something?'

Christine nodded.

'Well then, Christine, I have been in many homes and seen many things that I would rather not have seen. Ancient families often leave much to be desired. But on the other hand, if I have ever found a secure home, it is yours. Like all beautiful women who are good as well as beautiful, you are an angel, which is something truly rare and I know that, personally, I have never met anyone better than you. But your husband is a really good man, too, and in the matter that we are discussing, he is a paragon. If I had to show a stranger what a German home and German morals can be, I should take his hand and lead him to Holkenäs.'

The countess's face lit up.

'Yes, Christine, all things considered, you are a very lucky woman. Holk is straightforward and trustworthy and even if one out of every three women in Copenhagen was a Potiphar's wife, you could still be sure of him. And after all, Christine, even if in spite of everything you still had doubts . . .'

'Yes?'

'Then you ought to suppress them and use all your affection and common sense to persuade yourself that it is not true. It is trust that makes people happy and kind and restores their confidence, whereas horrible suspicions can spoil everything.'

'Ah, my dear Julie, you can talk like that because, although you know so much about our life and our home, you still don't properly understand—you were only saying so yourself a moment ago—you don't understand what is happening inside me. You know everything and yet not enough. I think that only husbands and wives themselves can ever know what a marriage really is and sometimes even they do not know. An outsider sees every moment of pique and hears every argument, for strangely enough married couples don't generally hide all their disagreements and quarrels from others, yes, it sometimes seems almost as if others are meant to hear them, as if all the most violent things were intended especially for them. But that gives quite a false picture, because as long as some love still remains, marriage always has another side to it. You see, Julie, when I want to talk to Helmut about something and go and look for him in his room and see that he is writing or working on something, I pick up a book and sit down opposite to him and say: "Don't let me disturb you, Helmut, I can wait." And then, while I'm reading or pretending to read, I often look over the top of the book and it makes me so happy to see his dear, kind, face and I want to run over to him and say: "My darling husband." You see, Julie, that happens as well but no one ever sees or hears it.'

'Ah, Christine, I can't tell you how glad I am to hear that out of your own mouth. I have often been worried for you both and for your happiness. But if everything is as you say . . .'

'It is, Julie, exactly—and sometimes even in spite of myself. But because it is like that, you are still wrong to advise me always to think nothing but good and sometimes even to close my eyes. If you love someone, that is impossible. And then, Julie dear, you are also wrong or half wrong at least, in what you said about Helmut. He is kind and loyal, the best husband in the world, that's all quite true, but he is still weak and conceited and Copenhagen is not the sort of place to give strength to a weak character. You see, Julie, I know that you are defending him and that you believe in him, but even you spoke of certain possibilities and it is just these possibilities that are preying on my mind at the moment.'

Fräulein Dobschütz was endeavouring to reassure her further when Philip brought a letter which had just arrived by messenger from Arnewieck. The countess assumed that it was from her brother but, glancing at the address, she saw that it came from Schwarzkoppen. She read:

My dear Countess,

Since our meeting of the day before yesterday, I have been examining in greater detail the question that we were discussing and have been studying the educational institutions that might be suitable for Axel. Some of the best are too strict, not only in their discipline but also in their doctrinal position and I have reached the view that the *Pädagogium* at Bunzlau corresponds most closely with our requirements. I know the headmaster and would consider it an honour to be allowed to write him a few words

of introduction. In addition, Gnadenfrei is relatively
near so that brother and sister will be able to see each
other quite frequently and travel back together for
the holidays.

> I remain, my dear Countess,
> Your sincere and devoted,
> Schwarzkoppen.

'Now Julie, this has come just at the right time.
I rely implicitly on our friend in this question and
my husband has given me a free hand. What a good
thing it is that we now have some definite plans. We
must make a list this very day of what each of the
children needs. There will be so many things. And
then there will be the journey and of course you must
come with us. I am looking forward immensely to
seeing my beloved Gnadenfrei again and I know that
you will enjoy it, too. And when I think how my
brother came and fetched me, oh, so long ago, with
Helmut. . . . It was almost like the lighthouse from
which Captain Brödstedt brought home his girl from
Bornholm. Yes, it certainly was a lighthouse for me
and for you, a real beacon for life and, I hope, till
death.'

CHAPTER 10

THE crossing was smooth and it was not yet nine
o'clock in the evening when the *King Christian* turned
into Copenhagen harbour between Nyholm and Tol-
boden. Holk was standing on deck enjoying the
magnificent scene; overhead, the stars were twinkling

almost as brightly as in winter, and the harbour lights were reflected beside them on the shimmering surface of the water. Shipping agents and harbour officials pushed forward, the coachmen raised their whips and waited to be beckoned. However, Holk preferred to walk the few hundred yards to Dronningens-Tvergade, and so, rejecting all offers of service, he merely asked the chief steward to send his luggage as soon as possible to Frau Hansen's. Then he went off along the quayside as far as St. Anne's Square, where he turned off towards Dronningens-Tvergade in which stood his landlady's two-storeyed house immediately on the left-hand side of the street. In a few minutes he came in sight of his lodging and he was delighted to see how clean and attractive it all looked. The first floor, where his two rooms were, was already lit up and the sash-windows open to let in the fresh air. 'And I bet there's a fire as well. The perfect landlady.' And with this reflection, he crossed the street and knocked on the door, not too loudly and not too softly. The door was opened at once by Frau Hansen, a widow of close on fifty, still handsome, who greeted the count with great cordiality and said how pleased she was to see him again so soon, after not having expected him again until the New Year at the earliest. 'Fancy Baron Bille catching measles! But such is life and it's an ill wind that blows nobody any good.'

As she was speaking, the widow had retreated into the hall to show the count up to his room. He followed her but at the foot of the stairs he stopped for a moment, with every justification in view of the sight that met his eyes. The back of the rather narrow hall lay almost in darkness but at the far end a door stood open,

presumably leading to the kitchen, and in the light
shining from it into the hall, a young woman was
standing, perhaps in order to see but more probably
in order to be seen. Holk, a trifle embarrassed, said:
'Is that your daughter? I have already heard of her
and was told that she had not sailed with her husband
this time.' Frau Hansen replied affirmatively but
briefly, presumably not wanting to spoil the effect
of the tableau by a lengthier explanation.

In his room upstairs, thickly carpeted and richly,
though not extravagantly, adorned with vases and
other *orientalia*, everything was as Holk had imagined:
lamps were lit, a fire blazed in the hearth, and there
was fruit on the sofa-table, no doubt rather to enhance the still-life effect than to be eaten. Beside the
fruit-dish lay the visiting cards of Baron Pentz and
Baron Erichsen who had called an hour ago to ask
after the count. 'They would be back.'

At this moment voices were heard in the hall. 'That
will be my things,' said Holk and, still preoccupied
by the vision of the young woman below, was half
expecting her to appear together with his luggage.
But instead in came the two barons. Holk greeted
them both, Pentz cordially and jovially, Erichsen
formally and with some reserve. Frau Hansen made
as if to go, stopping merely to ask what the count
would like for his supper. Holk was about to reply
when Pentz interrupted: 'Dear Frau Hansen, for this
evening Count Holk desires nothing further than to
come with us to Vincent's. You must allow us to
drag him from you straightaway, from you and your
lovely lady daughter. And that reminds me, is there
any news of Captain Hansen, that most enviable and
foolhardy of husbands? If I had such a wife, I should

have chosen a career that kept me at home twenty-four hours a day. In any case, ship's captain would have been my very last choice.'

Frau Hansen was visibly amused, but drawing herself up with some difficulty, she replied, rather solemnly and with an attempt at maternal dignity: 'Ah Baron, when you are always thinking of your husband, you never have time to think of anyone else. My late lamented husband was a captain too, and I never thought of anyone but him . . .'

Pentz laughed: 'Well, Frau Hansen, we are taught to believe everything a woman tells us, are we not? So I shall try to do so now.'

So saying, he took Holk by the arm to lead him off to supper and the inevitable gossip at Vincent's restaurant. Baron Erichsen followed with an expression on his face that seemed to disapprove of Pentz's banter with the landlady, although he knew well enough that Pentz always behaved in this way. Frau Hansen for her part had already removed the shade from one of the two lamps and was holding it up for them until the three men had left the house.

Pentz and Erichsen were contrasts, which did not prevent them from being on excellent terms with each other. In any case, everyone was on good terms with Pentz because not only did he wholeheartedly follow the proverb, 'Be surprised at everything and angry about nothing' but he had pushed this precept even further and ceased being surprised at anything either. He believed above all in *ride si sapis* and saw everything from its funny side. In life, politics, and religion he gave the broadest possible interpretation to Pontius Pilate's words: 'What is truth?' and to become heated over moral questions—in the discussion of which he used regularly to quote the Greeks, Egyptians, Indians, and Circassians as representatives of *every* trend in life and love— seemed to him merely proof of an inadequate education and lack of familiarity with the 'changing forms of human association', as he liked to put it, holding up his gold-rimmed spectacles. Every time he did this you would see his tiny eyes gleaming quizzically and with a look of superiority. He was a bachelor in his sixties and, of course, a *gourmand*. The Princess liked him because he never bored her and because he discharged his functions, which were no sinecure, as if they were child's play, yet with the greatest punctilio. This made it possible to disregard many other things about him and principally the fact that, in spite of all his merits, he was, in appearance, a figure of fun. As long as he was sitting at table, it was all right; but when he stood up, it could be seen that nature had treated him, in one sense, too meanly and, in another, too generously. His pedestal left much to be desired or, as the Princess expressed it, she had never seen a human being 'who was less stilted than Baron Pentz'. As she never made this statement except when he had just said something that was, morally speaking, most 'unstilted', she was thus able to enjoy the double pleasure of ridiculing him and flattering him at one and the same time. He was an extremely nimble man and might, for this reason, have seemed destined for a long life but for his stoutness, his short neck, and his ruddy complexion, three things which betray the apoplectic. Erichsen could be considered Pentz's exact counterpart: if the latter was an apoplectic, the former was a born hectic. He sprang from a consumptive family which, being very wealthy, had furnished the cemeteries of every health resort in the world with memorials in marble, syenite, and bronze. On these memorials the symbols of immortality were always the same: in Nice, San Remo, Funchal, and Cairo, yes, prosaically enough, even in Görbersdorf, a butterfly could be seen soaring heavenwards as if it were the armorial bearings of the Erichsens. Our present Erichsen, the gentleman-in-waiting, who had been in the Princess's service for some ten years, had undergone the full treatment but with more success than others of his ilk. From the age of forty onwards he had settled down to live a restful life, a principle that he observed with such thoroughness that he hardly ever left Copenhagen. He had had enough of travel but at the same time, from his long periods of abstinence under doctor's orders, he had acquired a dislike of all excess which he had carried over into his life at court. Accustomed to living on milk, breast of chicken, and Vichy water, his lanky figure, shaped rather like an exclamation mark, had, as Pentz used to say, only one role to play at any feast or banquet: 'a dreadful warning against Bacchic indulgence'. 'Erichsen the Conscience' was one of the many nicknames that Pentz had bestowed on him.

It was only five minutes' walk from Frau Hansen's house to Vincent's restaurant in Kongens Nytorf. Pentz sent Erichsen ahead to prospect because 'as a six-footer, he would be better able to survey the seating position at Vincent's'. There was good reason for these cautious instructions, however jokingly made; for when Pentz and Holk followed Erichsen into the restaurant a minute later, it seemed impossible to find a free table. Finally, they managed to discover quite a pleasant corner that not only had comfortable seats but was a good point of vantage to survey the room.

'I think we'll start with a medium-full Rüdesheimer. Dr. Grämig, at the moment one of the most cheerful men alive, was saying recently how remarkable it was that I still hadn't got gout, for which I have every medically and historically justified qualification, not only through my way of life but also my attitude to life. But the more he seems likely to be right, the more I'm determined to make good use of what little time remains. Erichsen, what may I order for you? Some Vichy or soda—or perhaps a little iron phosphite? . . .'

A waiter came and soon they were all three drinking together out of their magnificently cut hock-glasses, for even Erichsen had taken some of the Rüdesheimer, having first made sure that he was provided with a decanter of water.

'Here's to "Old Denmark",' said Pentz, to which Holk, touching glasses, replied: 'Certainly, Pentz, *Gamle Danmark*. And the older the better. For the only thing that could ever part us—and may that day be far distant—is new Denmark. Old Denmark, there I'm with you, and I drink to Frederic VII and our Princess. But tell me, Pentz, what has come over my good friends the Copenhageners and particularly those in this cosy little restaurant? Just look over there how excited everyone is, snatching newspapers out of each other's hands; and Colonel Faaborg, yes, it is Faaborg, I must go and say good-evening to him later, is as red as a turkey-cock and waving his paper about like a sabre. Who is it he's talking about?'

'Poor Thott.'

'Poor? Why?'

'Because as far as I can tell, Thott is suspected of being in the plot.'

'What plot?'

'But Holk, you're at least a generation out of date. It's true that as you were packing all day yesterday and travelling all today, you may be half excused. We have something of a conspiracy on here. Hall is being relieved of his post.'

'And you call that a plot? I remember, by the way, that you said something about it in your letter to me. Why don't you want to let the poor man go? He can't be very eager to pull Denmark together if it really is falling to pieces, which, incidentally, I do not believe for one moment. Hamlet didn't want to, so why should Hall?'

'Well, *he* certainly doesn't want to, you are quite right there. But our Princess *does* want him to and that settles the matter. The less she trusts the King— and this is not unconnected with her dislike of Countess Danner—the more she trusts Hall. Only Hall can save us and so he must stay in office. And a good many people think like the Princess, so I beg you not to mention your own opinion if you don't agree. Hall must stay. And that is why you see Faaborg brandishing his paper like a gladiator.'

Erichsen had also been following this animated scene across the room. 'Fortunately de Meza is sitting at the next table,' he said. 'He will restore order.'

'Oh my dear Erichsen, please spare me your "restore order". As if Faaborg, that quintessential Dane, were the sort of man to allow himself to be calmed down once he has been excited. And by de Meza of all people!'

'De Meza is his superior officer.'

'What does that mean, superior officer? He's his superior officer when he's inspecting the brigade but not here in Vincent's or anywhere else, particularly when it's a matter of politics, and Danish politics at that, about which de Meza understands nothing, at least in Faaborg's view. For him de Meza is just a foreigner and there is something in what he says. De Meza's father was a Portuguese Jew, like all Portuguese really, who many years ago, as Holk may perhaps not know, came over as a ship's doctor to Copenhagen. And even if it were not completely vouched for, you can look it up in any book and de Meza himself makes no secret of it, you can see his origin in the shape of his nose. And then there's that swarthy complexion.'

Erichsen was highly delighted at all this and was nodding in agreement.

'And it's not only his complexion,' went on Pentz. 'Everything about him is southern European or even oriental. The most important thing for him is the weather-vane and the barometer. He is always feeling chilly, and what other people call fresh air, he calls a draught or a wind or a hurricane. I should like to know what King Waldemar the Conqueror, who used to spend fifty-three weeks of every year at sea, would have thought of de Meza.'

Up till now Erichsen had been in agreement but these last remarks were as incautious as they were tactless, applying as they did much more to the lanky gentleman-in-waiting than to de Meza.

'I can't understand you, Pentz,' he said touchily,

forgetting his usual taciturnity. 'Next you'll be trying to prove that it's impossible to be a good soldier if you wear anything made of wool. I know that de Meza wraps himself up in flannel because he feels the cold, but that didn't prevent him from accomplishing a great deal at Fridericia in 1849. And at Idstedt the year after, it was he who was responsible for practically everything. As for me, I am quite certain that Napoleon kept looking at the thermometer as frequently as anyone else, though I imagine that in Russia it was hardly necessary. Incidentally, I notice that in the officers' corner over there they have gone back to their newspapers and have left us to go on arguing. Shall we go over and speak to de Meza?'

'I think we had better leave it,' said Holk. 'He might ask questions about this and that which I shouldn't like to have to answer today. I'm not particularly anxious about de Meza because he respects everyone's opinion, but I am far less sure of some of the others there, although I don't know them personally—but I think I can recognize some diehards. For example, Lieutenant-Colonel Tersling on the left by the window. And I must also think of the Princess who because of her interest in politics is bound to be kept informed of everything straightaway. In any case, I'm dreading the interrogation that I shall have to undergo tomorrow or the day after.'

Pentz laughed. 'My dear Holk, I hope that you know what women are like . . .'

Erichsen's eyes were twinkling, because he was well aware that Pentz, in spite of his own conviction that he knew, most certainly did not.

'Women, I was saying. And if not women, at least

princesses, and if not princesses, at least *our* Princess. You are quite right, she is greatly interested in politics and you must not approach her with a programme for Schleswig-Holstein's future. In that matter, there has been no change in her view and certainly no change for the worse, because with all her interest in politics, she remains completely *ancien régime*.'

'All right. But what advantage is that to me personally?'

'Every advantage. And I am surprised to have to enlighten you on the subject. What does *ancien régime* mean? Under the *ancien régime*, they were also interested in politics, but for them it was all a matter of sentiment, certainly for the women, and that's perhaps the best way. In any case it was the most amusing, and there you have the important word. What was *amusing*—and that is always equivalent, in politics at least, to *chronique scandaleuse*—what was amusing was always the most important, and it is exactly the same thing today with our Princess. So if you are afraid of a political interrogation, all you need to do is to talk about Berling or Countess Danner or Blixen-Fineke and just hint at the pastoral or bucolic comedies that are being played in Skodsborg or in the villa of the worthy Frau Rasmussen, and every political topic will be immediately dropped and you will have escaped the horns of the dilemma. Am I not right, Erichsen?

Erichsen nodded.

'Well gentlemen,' laughed Holk, 'I shall make use of your information but I can't agree that my own situation is very greatly improved by it. The difficulties merely cancel each other out. What is supposed to protect me from a political discussion is almost more difficult than the political discussion itself, at least for me. You forget that I'm not an initiate and that in spite of my occasional visits, I only know Copenhagen quite superficially from *Dagbladet* or the *Flyveposten*. Countess Danner and Berling or Danner and Blixen-Fineke—it seems that I'm supposed to be able to talk about them impromptu. But what do I know about them? Nothing but what I have learnt from the latest review, and the Princess knows that too, because she reads reviews and papers all day and all night. I have nobody but Frau Hansen who is hardly adequate as a source of information.'

'You are quite mistaken, Holk. When you say that, you have no idea of Frau Hansen—or her daughter. They are a complete work of reference for everything that happens in Copenhagen. Where they learn it all is a mystery. Some people talk of Dionysus' ears, others of an underground passage, others of a special Hansen telescope that is able to extract from their hiding-place things hidden to mortal eye. And last of all, there are those who speak of a chief of police. To me, this seems the most likely supposition. But whatever it is, one thing is certain and that is that those two women—or ladies if you like, since their social status is difficult to ascertain—both know everything that there is to know, and if you appear on duty every morning with ammunition supplied by Frau Hansen, then I guarantee that you will be proof against any tricky political discussions. The Hansens —especially the younger one—know more about Countess Danner than she does herself. You see, police officials have, as it were, something of a diviner's or a poet's skill in this most fascinating sphere, and if nothing can be discovered, then it has to be invented . . .'

'You are making me see our good Frau Hansen in quite a new light. I had assumed the very greatest respectability . . .'

'And so there is, in a certain sense. . . . When there's no prosecution, there's no case . . .'

'And in those circumstances, I shall have to be extremely cautious . . .'

'Now there I venture to disagree. The disadvantages of such a course are obvious and the advantages highly questionable. In that house, nothing can be concealed, even supposing your character made it possible. The Hansens can read into your very soul and the best thing that I can advise is to be completely free and natural and to talk as much as possible. Talking a great deal is an excellent thing and in some cases it is by far the best diplomacy, because if you talk a great deal, then the details can never be properly ascertained, or better still, one detail cancels out another.'

Erichsen smiled.

'You're smiling, Erichsen, and smiling becomes you. In addition, however, since a smile, being rather vague in its effect, always suggests all kinds of veiled criticism, it warns me that it is time to release Holk. It's already a quarter past eleven and the Hansens are respectable folk who don't like staying up after midnight, at least not if they can be seen from outside and with the hall light on. Moreover, the tables over there have already dispersed. Let me see to the bill you can wait for me outside.'

Holk and Erichsen strolled up and down until Pentz rejoined them and all three went off to Dron-

ningens-Tvergade where they parted opposite the
Hansen's house. The house was in complete darkness and only the moonlight, between the clouds,
was shining on the top-floor windows. Holk lifted
the knocker but before he could let it go, the door
opened and young Frau Hansen stood before him.
She wore a matching skirt and jacket of some light
material, simple in cut yet skilfully calculated for
effect. In her hand she held a hanging lamp as shown
in pictures of ancient Greece. All in all, it was a
remarkable *mélange* of *frou-frou* and Lady Macbeth.
Holk, somewhat taken aback, was speculating how to
address the young woman when she anticipated him
and, with drooping eyelids expressive of the greatest
lassitude, explained that her mother asked to be
excused as, although she was quite robust, she needed
some sleep before midnight. Holk expressed his
regrets at having stayed talking so late, adding at the
same time that, next time, there was no need for
anyone to wait up for him. The young woman,
without saying it in so many words, indicated that
they could not allow themselves to be denied the
privilege of waiting up for their guest. At the same
time, she slowly led the way with her lamp, but
stopping at the foot of the stairs, she rested her left
hand on the bannisters and held the lamp high in her
right hand to show the count upstairs. As she did so,
the wide sleeve of her loose coat fell back, baring her
very beautiful arm. When Holk reached the top of
the stairs, he said good night to the young woman
once more, and as she slowly and quietly withdrew
along the passage, he saw the play of light and shadow
in the hall and staircase gradually diminishing. For a
minute or two he stood listening at his half-open door

and then, when all was quite dark downstairs, he quietly closed his own door.

'A lovely young woman. But rather uncanny. I must certainly not mention her in my letter to Christine, otherwise she will reply with dreadful reminders about all the dubious females from the Old and the New Testaments.'

CHAPTER 11

BEFORE going to sleep, in spite of his tiring journey Holk found his thoughts more preoccupied by the younger Frau Hansen than with politics and princesses. The following morning, however, all this was forgotten, and when he chanced to remember the apparition with the lamp, he merely smiled. He tried to think what goddess or lover was usually depicted in antique wall-paintings as carrying such a lamp but, unable to remember, he finally ceased searching and, pulling the latch, he opened the window to enjoy a breath of fresh air before breakfast. He glanced into the street. There were few people passing through Dronningens-Tvergade at this comparatively early hour but everyone of them was brisk in bearing, blooming and fresh, and he felt that he understood the Danes' pride at thinking themselves the Parisians of the north, the only difference being that they felt superior to their model. At this moment the curtains billowed out and, looking round, he saw that the widow had come in with a heaped breakfast tray. They exchanged greetings and after the routine inquiry as to how the count had slept and what his dreams had been, 'because first dreams always come true', Frau Hansen laid the cloth and placed everything from the tray on to the breakfast table. Holk studied the magnificent array and said: 'There certainly is no better place than Frau Hansen's. Everything so cheerful, so spick and span, and, most of all, Frau Hansen herself. And the lovely China tea-service! It's obvious that your late husband was on the China run and, as Baron Pentz was telling me yesterday evening, your son-in-law does the same and is also called Hansen. The same name, the same rank, one could easily find oneself confusing mother and daughter!'

'Ah, Count,' said Frau Hansen, 'nobody could confuse us. Me, an old woman who has had such a long and difficult life . . .'

'Come, come . . .'

'And Brigitte who will not be thirty until tomorrow! But you mustn't give me away, Count, and tell her that I told you that it is her birthday tomorrow.'

'I, give you away? Please, Frau Hansen. . . . But you keep on running round all the time, you're making me feel giddy. Do you know what you must do? You must sit down and talk to me, always assuming that I am not holding up your house-work or something more important.'

Frau Hansen pretended to be uncertain whether to stay or to go.

'Really, you must make this the first of your kind visits and I hope that you will be making them regularly from now onwards. In any case, I have so many questions on my mind. Please sit down here, here in this chair where I can see you best, and if you can *see* well, you can *hear* well. I used to hear very well but in recent years my hearing has let me down now and again. It's the first sign of old age.'

'You'll have difficulty in finding anyone to believe that, Count Holk. I believe that you hear everything you want to hear and see everything you want to see.'

'I hear nothing and see nothing, Frau Hansen, and when I do see something I forget it again. Not quite everything, of course. Yesterday I saw your daughter, Brigitte I think you said her name was; a lovely name into the bargain. Now, nobody could forget her again. You must be proud to have such a beautiful daughter, and what I cannot understand is her husband calmly leaving her here while he sails to and fro between Singapore and Shanghai. At least, I assume that's what he does because most of them sail between those two ports. Well, I think that a beautiful wife like that ought to be taken everywhere, from the North Pole to the South Pole, don't you, Frau Hansen? And if not for love, then just because you're afraid or jealous. And this much I do know, if it were I, I would always say to myself, you mustn't expect too much from a young woman and you certainly shouldn't expect miracles. I think we agree on this, don't we, Frau Hansen? Why does he expose her to such a risk? And, of course, expose himself as well . . .'

'Ah, that's a long story, Count Holk . . .'

'All the better. A love-story can never be too long and I imagine that it must be a love-story.'

'I don't rightly know if I can call it that; it's something of a love-story but it is not a proper love-story . . . only it might easily have become one.'

'You're making me more and more curious.

Incidentally, this is most excellent tea and I can recognize once again the result of all those trips to China. If you want to give me a real pleasure, let me pour you a cup of your own tea.'

He stood up and from a cabinet standing near the window took out a cup on which was written in gold letters: 'To the happy couple'. 'To the happy couple,' repeated Holk. 'Who were they? Perhaps you were one of them, Frau Hansen? You're laughing. . . . But one's never too old to be wise and the wisest thing for a widow . . .'

'Is to stay a widow.'

'Well, if you like; you may be right. But how about this story. . . . Captain Hansen, your son-in-law, must certainly be a fine-looking man, all captains are fine-looking men, and Frau Brigitte must certainly have married him for love.'

'That she did, at least she never said the contrary, except on one occasion. But that was later and I'm talking now of the early days when they had only just married. She was very affectionate and loving then, and wherever he went she went with him on board, even where there was yellow fever, and when she came back to Copenhagen . . . in those days she had her own place, because my husband, whom the count will remember from Glücksburg, was still alive then . . . now what was I saying, whenever she came back from a long trip, she was always wanting to be off again straightaway because she used to say that she didn't like the people here, and it was much nicer in the big outside world.'

'But that's amazing. Was she really as modest and bashful as all that? Didn't she enjoy being flattered and courted as she certainly must have been here in

Copenhagen? They showed her what they thought
of her here by the time of her confirmation, I'll be
bound!'

'Indeed they did, but Brigitte paid no attention and
she remained the same, even after she was married.
Only now and again she seemed a little wild. Everything stayed like that until 1854; I remember exactly,
because it was the year the English fleet came here on
its way to Russia. And that same summer we had a
very young Guards officer here in Copenhagen, who
spent all his time in and out of the Rasmussen's
house—I mean Countess Danner but we still always
call her Rasmussen—and he got so heavily in debt
that he couldn't be kept on any more and had to
leave. But since he was very clever and knew everybody—because he went into all the wealthiest houses
and especially those where there were ladies—Baron
Scheele, who was Minister in those days, said he
would take the lieutenant on with him. And so he
took him into the Ministry for Home Affairs, where
he still is, and has become very important, too. But
in those days, he was still just a young cub, nothing
but a very good-looking young man, and when
Brigitte saw him, it was the very same day we had
news of the bombardment up there, I can't remember
the name, I'm afraid, anyway, she confessed that
she was fond of him. And she showed it at once, too.
And when Hansen had to go off to China that same
autumn, she told him bluntly that she didn't want to
go and she told him the reason, too, or perhaps other
people did. The long and the short of it was that when
the time came for the ship to leave, Hansen became
very serious and refused to take no for an answer and
said to her, Brigitte, you must come with me. And

though up till then he had been taking her with him for love, now he wanted to take her as you said, Count Holk, as a precaution or because he was jealous.'

'And was it any help? Did the trip cure her of her love? I mean, of her love for the man in the Ministry?'

'Yes, she was cured, although with Brigitte you can never be quite sure, because although she talks a lot, she still keeps a lot to herself. And anyway it doesn't matter very much because it turned out all right by and large.'

'And how did it turn out by and large?'

'My son-in-law got back his trust in his wife completely. Hansen is really a very good man and he's quite calm and sensible again now and goes off quite happily to China.'

'I'm delighted to hear that. But in these matters we must be careful not to leave anything out or forget anything. I think, my dear Frau Hansen, that you were going to tell me exactly how it came about that your son-in-law recovered from his jealousy.'

'Yes, I was going to do that and I always say that man decides and God provides and the greater the need, the nearer the help. I must say that I was very worried; a mother is always worried about her child and it makes no difference whether she is married or not; yes, I was worried about Brigitte because I thought there would be a divorce, for she is very strong-willed, you could almost call her obstinate, and very excitable, although she seems so quiet and dreamy at times . . .'

'Ah yes,' laughed Holk, 'that's often the case, still waters run deep.'

'So I was worried. But it all turned out quite differently and it was just at the same time that Brigitte had, so to speak, been compelled to go away with her husband. This is how it happened. In the course of the trip, Hansen had to take a cargo back to Bangkok, a big town in Siam that I had visited myself many years ago with my husband. When Hansen arrived and had been lying moored in front of the Imperial Palace for a couple of days—the Siamese have an Emperor, you know—a Minister came on board and invited Hansen and his wife to a big official banquet. The Emperor must have seen her. Brigitte sat next to him and talked English and the Emperor kept on looking at her. And after the banquet, he was most gracious and respectful and never took his eyes off her, and when they were leaving, he said to Hansen that he was most anxious for the captain's wife to come to the palace next day, so that all his friends and intimates and particularly all his wives—he had a great number of wives—could meet the beautiful German lady again face to face. For a moment Hansen was afraid that this flood of honours might mean treachery, for all around the palace there were heads stuck up on sticks just like pineapples; but Brigitte, who had heard them talking, just bowed to the Emperor and said with a proper air of deference, because she has always been very dignified and self-possessed, my Brigitte, she said that she would come at the time he had mentioned.'

'That was very bold.'

'And she really did go and she was placed on a high seat that had been especially erected in front of the palace gates, so that she would be in the shade, and she sat on this throne with a peacock fan and the Emperor put a pearl necklace round her neck. She said that the necklace was a marvellous one. And all the important people of Bangkok filed past and then the ordinary folk and they all kotowed to her and finally there were all the wives, and when the last one had gone Brigitte stood up and walked over to the Emperor to return the peacock-fan and the necklace which she thought had only been lent to her for the ceremony; and the Emperor took them both but gave her back the pearl necklace, so that she could wear it in memory of him always. And then with the Ministers leading the way and the bodyguard lined up on each side, she was taken back to the landing-stage where Hansen had been watching the whole scene.'

'And then?'

'From that day onwards there was a great change in Brigitte and when she came back here the following winter and the man who had nearly caused her to make a fool of herself tried to see her again, she refused to have anything to do with him, as far as I could see. And when Hansen set off again six months later, Brigitte said that if he had no objection she would rather stay at home because after having received such an honour from an Emperor, it seemed rather strange to her to be with sailors and perhaps have to sleep in a dock-side hotel, where you would hear nothing but native music and smell nothing but gin; and Hansen not only agreed but was highly delighted that she was not going on that trip with him or on any other. There was absolutely no trace of jealousy now and he realized what had happened to Brigitte and was only afraid that it might have been too much for her and that the Emperor of Siam might have gone to her head.'

Holk was doubtful whether to believe the story

or to look on it merely as a flight of fancy and perhaps a test of his credulity as well. If Pentz's hints of yesterday were to be believed, the last supposition was the most probable. Yet, after all, it might be true. What is impossible? And so, in order at least to protect his self-esteem, he asked half ironically: 'And where were the white elephants?'

'They must have been in their stalls', replied Frau Hansen with a mischievous laugh.

'And the pearl necklace, my dear Frau Hansen, you must let me see it.'

'Yes, I would if it were possible . . .'

'If it were possible? Why not?'

'Because after Brigitte had gone on board, all of a sudden, the necklace disappeared. She must have lost it or left it behind in the palace in her excitement.'

'In that case, I should have inquired about it at once.'

'So should I. But Brigitte is a strange girl and I heard later that when Hansen was trying to insist on asking about it, she only said: "That would be common and contrary to court etiquette".'

'Yes,' said Holk, who was now beginning to see certain things rather more clearly. 'That's quite true. And such scruples need to be respected.'

CHAPTER 12

AT the end of her story which, when it came to the lost necklace, seemed a trifle far-fetched even to the gullible Holk, Frau Hansen stood up, 'in order not to disturb the Count any more', and was allowed to leave. Not that Holk was impatient, quite the contrary, for he loved listening to that sort of gossip, and the suspicious penumbra in which everything seemed bathed served only to increase his interest. However, a glance at the bracket-clock warned him against further willing indulgence in Frau Hansen's gifts of story-telling: at eleven o'clock, barely one hour hence, he was expected at the Princess's, and beforehand he would have to write a short letter to his wife announcing his safe arrival. He had therefore to hurry—something which, on occasion, he was capable of doing—and at five minutes to eleven he climbed into the carriage which took him to the Princesses' Palace, only two minutes away.

The Princess's apartments were on the first floor. Holk, in his court-dress, which he himself found not unbecoming, went upstairs into an ante-room; and then, immediately afterwards, he was shown into a comfortable reception room, richly panelled and carpeted but, apart from the desk, sparsely furnished; it was here that the Princess received visitors or granted audiences. The flunkey said that he would announce him straightaway. Holk walked over to one of the windows that faced the door through which the Princess would enter and looked out on to the square and the street: everything looked dead—elegant and boring—and there was nothing to be seen except fallen leaves which the lively breeze was whirling about over the paving-stones. Feeling himself suddenly deserted and lonely, Holk turned back into the room and directed his gaze at the only two portraits that decorated the smooth stucco walls. One of them, over the upholstered sofa, was a likeness of the Princess's uncle, King Christian VII of ever-blessed memory, the other, over the desk, was a portrait of another close relative, also deceased, a landgrave from Thuringia. Its gilt frame was draped with dusty crepe and the dust made it look not like crepe but a spider's web. The landgrave's face was kind, courageous, and commonplace, and Holk could not help asking himself what ideas on government the deceased could possibly have contributed to further the happiness of a grateful country, since the only thing that could be deduced with some certainty from the portrait was a lively interest in that country's daughters.

Before Holk had completed his meditations on this subject, a small door at the back of the room opened and in came the Princess, who was exactly as one would have imagined from the arrangement of the room: comfortably, almost casually, dressed and, in any case, completely indifferent to elegance. Holk walked towards his mistress and kissed her hand, which was completely encased in a silk glove, and following her glance, led her to the sombre-coloured sofa, whose springs seemed somewhat weak.

'Sit down, my dear Holk. This *fauteuil* will no doubt hardly meet with your favour, but that high arm-chair over there . . .'

Holk drew up the chair and as soon as he was seated, the Princess, visibly pleased at the sight of such a handsome man, continued with great bon-homie and in a tone of long standing friendship: 'What a cheerful colour you bring with you, my dear Holk. Here I am surrounded by nothing but town-faces. Can you imagine Pentz as a gentleman-farmer or even Erichsen as a hop-grower? You're laughing and I know what you are thinking—a hop-pole, yes, he's certainly long enough for that. Town-faces, as I was saying. And so I am delighted to see your splendid Schleswig-Holstein colour, red and white like its flag. And how is the countess, your dear wife? I know that she is not so particularly fond of us but that makes us love her all the more and she can't stop us from doing that.'

Holk bowed.   *104093*

'And what do you think of all this fuss and bother here? A real cavalry charge against poor Hall. You know, he's still the cleverest and best of them all and I can even forgive him for being so attached to our little milliner, the countess, to whom, by the way, I would have allotted the appropriate coat-of-arms of a milliners' block and crinoline *couchant*, perhaps with the motto '*Per ardua ad vacua*'. I shall never be able to understand the bad taste of that nephew of mine, even if I am only his half-aunt. And although she is forty years old, I can't think the countess is old enough to rank as an archaeological specimen or, what is the same thing, as an historical antique that he has dug up, which seems to be my nephew's criterion for almost everything. But why should I be surprised? George II, whom my grandfather used often to talk about in my young days, also adhered to the motto: Fair, fat, and forty. Why not my nephew the King? Incidentally, have you seen the account of yesterday's session? A really scandalous exhibition of spite and hatred. And leading the pack, of course, as always, that odious Tompsen from Oldensworth, half a compatriot of yours, incidentally, and an unbearable bully and babbler, a mixture of pettifogging lawyer and petty Holstein patriot.'

Holk was embarrassed that the conversation was

taking a political turn from the very beginning and
something of this embarrassment must have been
reflected in his face, for the Princess continued:
'But let's forget all this miserable politics. I don't
want to cause you any embarrassment, especially as
you have only just arrived and I know that you are an
heretical Schleswig-Holsteiner, one of those who will
never be convinced. As soon as we think that we have
come to terms with you, you turn out to be further
away than ever. Don't bother to reply, there's no
need to protest your loyalty, I know that you are as
loyal as anyone can be but when it comes to the point,
the old stumbling-block is always there and that
frightful platitude, "shall remain undivided", which is
always being quoted, comes between us all the time.'

Holk smiled.

'That is really the crux of the matter. To whom
does Schleswig-Holstein belong? Your Schleswig,
Holk. Hall has had the courage to answer that question as befits a Dane, and because he wants to answer
it intelligently and not start sabre-rattling straightaway, we have this storm against him from friend and
foe alike. And that is the worst of it all. I don't find it
either surprising or frightening that your compatriot
Tompsen should attack him, but that good loyal
Danes who are of one mind with Hall, with the King
and with myself but are unfortunately hot-blooded,
that these good loyal Danes, as I was saying, should
behave like students and professors, always insisting
on the rightness of their own programme alone and
bent on bringing down the best man, the only man
who has some idea of politics and knows how to wait,
which is the first law of all politics—I find that quite
exasperating.'

As she was finishing her tirade, Baron Pentz was announced.

'Most welcome,' cried the Princess ... and at the same moment as Pentz came in through the folding doors, there appeared from the other side, by the small door through which the Princess had come, a young woman with fair hair, a good figure and complexion, though with rather irregular features, who went up to the Princess, while Pentz stopped and bowed again.

'*Soyez le bienvenu*,' said the Princess, shaking him gently by the hand. 'You have come just at the right time, Pentz, because you are putting an end to a political lecture, a task for which no one is better qualified than you. As soon as my eyes fall on you, everything is transfigured into a world of peace, and if I had just been talking about *Henri Quatre* and Ravaillac, after your arrival I should find myself talking of *Henri Quatre et la poule au pot*, which is something quite different ...'

'And most agreeable, as well, my dear Princess. I am happy to find myself installed, without effort on my part, as the bearer of such idyllic things. But ...' and his eye moved from Holk to the fair-haired girl and back ... 'even in Arcady the custom of introduction must have existed. I am not sure whether I should exercise my duty as introducer ...'

'Or resign in favour of Her Royal Highness,' laughed the Princess. 'I think, my dear Pentz, that while reason and duty are both on your side, I cannot deny myself the pleasure of personally introducing two people of whom I think so highly: Count Holk, Fräulein Ebba von Rosenberg.'

They both bowed, Holk somewhat stiffly, the

young woman easily and with self-assurance tinged with humour. The Princess, however, plainly showing little interest in this introduction, at once turned to Pentz and said: 'That having now been accomplished, etiquette, on which you have to keep your eagle eye, has been satisfied. But you will not make me believe that you have come here merely to be present at this most solemn presentation or to perform it yourself. You've something else on your mind and you are now commanded to reveal your true purpose. When one reads so many parliamentary reports, one ends by becoming a virtuoso in parliamentary expressions oneself.'

'I have come, your Highness, humbly to report that this afternoon an important military banquet is being given in Klampenborg . . .'

'What for? Or in whose honour?'

'In honour of General de Meza, who arrived here from Jutland yesterday morning.'

'De Meza. Excellent. But frankly, Pentz, what are we expected to do about it? After all, I can't preside at an officers' mess dinner and drink de Meza's health.'

'The question was whether it might not perhaps be possible. Your Highness has done more surprising things. And it is because you do them that the people are so attached to you.'

'Ah, the people. That is another matter. You know what I think of so-called popularity. The King, my nephew, is popular; but I have no desperate longing to be the ideal of every blue-jacket or even of our ladies from the market. No, Pentz, no popularity for me. But since you've mentioned Klampenborg, the sun is shining, our afternoon is free, we might perhaps drive out, not because of the banquet but in spite of it. In any case, we have been sitting at home for a whole week without any proper fresh air and my dear Rosenberg would certainly be suffering from chlorosis if her blood did not contain so much iron.'

The girl's face brightened visibly at the prospect of escaping from the monotony of the Princesses' Palace for a whole afternoon and Pentz, something of an asthmatic, was himself always ready for fresh air, in spite of the fact that the doctors all assured him that sea-breezes only aggravated his condition. He therefore eagerly acquiesced and asked at what time Her Royal Highness would like her carriage.

'Let us say half past two, but no later. It will take us an hour and a quarter and it begins to be dark at five. And when we are in Klampenborg we must naturally take a walk up to the Hermitage, if only to present my darlings to Ebba. Who these darlings are I shall not reveal for the moment. I hope that, even although his duties do not commence until tomorrow, Count Holk will join our party and make this sacrifice for an old friend.'

'And does your Highness desire any other company?'

'Only Countess Schimmelmann and Erichsen. Two carriages. I shall arrange the seating myself. *Au revoir*, my dear Holk. And if, as is your wont, you maintain an active correspondence . . .'

He smiled.

'Ah, I see that you have already written. Then it is too late for me to send my regards to the Countess. Your arm, my dear Ebba.'

And as she walked slowly towards the door, the two gentlemen-in-waiting bowed respectfully.

CHAPTER 13

PUNCTUALLY at two-thirty the carriages arrived, with their hoods down. Countess Schimmelmann took her seat next to the Princess, both ladies sitting opposite to Holk, while Fräulein von Rosenberg sat in the back of the second carriage facing Pentz and Erichsen.

Countess Schimmelmann, a woman in her forties, reminded one somewhat of Erichsen; like him, she was tall, lanky, and equally earnest; but while Erichsen's gravity verged on solemnity, that of the countess verged on peevishness. In earlier days, she had been a court beauty, as her sparkling black eyes now and then recalled, but everything else had decayed into migraine and spleen. People spoke of an unhappy love affair. The general impression was of the Spanish court in the reign of Philip II, so that you found yourself involuntarily looking for the ruff round her neck. Apart from this, the countess was kind, full of spirit, and was distinguished from others at the court, to her great advantage, by being strongly opposed to any sort of gossip or *médisance*. She would tell people the truth to their faces and if she could not do so, she kept silent. She was not loved but greatly respected, as indeed she deserved to be.

Until they had left the town, not a word was spoken in the first carriage; Holk and the countess sat upright opposite each other while the Princess reclined in the back seat. So they drove through the Bredöster and Nyöster Streets towards the Österbroer suburbs and then came down to the coast road running along the sound. Holk was delighted at the scene: immedi-

ately to the left was a row of neat villas with their
gardens still in flower, in spite of the signs of autumn,
and, to the right, the wide expanse of almost completely calm water with the Swedish coast opposite
and sailing-boats and steamers dotted here and there,
on their way to Klampenborg and Skodsborg and as
far north as Elsinore.

Holk would have examined this scene more closely
had not the activity on the causeway along which
they were driving not continually drawn his attention
away from the landscape. Vehicles of all sorts were
not only catching up with but overtaking the Princess
who, when she was out for a drive, was not fond of
hurrying. Thus there were continual meetings and
recognitions on both sides. 'That was Marstrand,'
said the Princess. 'And, if I saw aright, Worsaae
beside him. He has never been known to fail to put
in an appearance! What can he possibly want at de
Meza's banquet? De Meza is going to be fêted, not
excavated! He's still alive and not even the right size
for a barrow-grave!' The Princess seemed disposed
to embroider on this theme but was prevented by
several officers' approaching her carriage and driving
level with her on both sides. Amongst them was
Lieutenant-Colonel Tersling, our acquaintance from
Vincent's restaurant, a big handsome man with a
markedly military bearing whom the Princess greeted
with particular friendliness. He, on his part, inquired
after her health.

'I am very well, especially on a day such as this.
I hear that you and the other gentlemen are giving
a banquet for de Meza and that has tempted me out.
I want to be there.'

Tersling gave an embarrassed smile and the

Princess, enjoying his discomfiture, continued after a pause: 'Yes, to be there. But have no fear, my dear Tersling, I only want to be on the outskirts. If you toast the King or your guest of honour, I shall be in the Klampenborg Zoological Gardens with my dear countess here and Ebba Rosenberg, whom you will doubtless have already seen in the second carriage, and I shall rejoice to hear the cheers ringing out from honest Danish throats. And incidentally please give my greetings to de Meza and tell him that I am still living in the same place. I know that generals are hard to entice to court, and when they compete with Beethoven and compose symphonies, then it is quite hopeless. Meanwhile, if he hears from you that I still have pleasant memories of Idstedt, he may think it worthwhile to remember me. And now I will not keep you tied to my carriage.'

Tersling kissed the Princess's hand and drove quickly on to make up for lost time. The Princess, however, turning to Holk, continued: 'A handsome man, that Tersling; he was once a great dancer with princesses and a ladies' man *comme-il-faut*, the sharpest tongue and the sharpest blade, too. Perhaps you still remember the duel he fought with Captain Dahlberg before 1848? Dahlberg escaped with a scratch on his neck but he was killed long ago at Fridericia. Pardon, dear Schimmelmann, for mentioning all this in your presence; I've just remembered that you were the cause of the duel. To be honest, I should like to know more about it, but not today, it's a story for women's ears only.'

Holk assured her of his discretion and said that he never listened to anything unless it was addressed to him directly. But the Princess was adamant and

said: 'No, nothing about that today. We must postpone it! And as for discretion, my dear Holk, that is
a long and difficult story. I have been observing these
things for fifty-five years now, because I made my
début at the age of fifteen.'

'But surely your Royal Highness feels quite certain
of the discretion of her suite?'

'No, thank God,' retorted the Princess, 'and you
cannot imagine how seriously I say that. Discretion
à tout prix can, of course, exist but if only because it is
so unconditional, it is frightful; it ought never to
exist unconditionally. Particularly at a court, men and
women need to develop a sense of tact as to what can
and what cannot be said; but anyone who lacks this
sense and merely says nothing all the time, is not
only boring but dangerous. There is something in-
human about it because, after all, the most human
attribute is speech and we are given it in order to be
able to talk. . . . I know that where I'm concerned,
I make an inordinate use of it, but I refuse to be
ashamed; on the contrary, I'm delighted.'

In the second carriage, similar meetings and greetings were taking place; but the chief topic of conversation was Holk. Pentz wanted to hear from
Fräulein von Rosenberg what she had thought of him
at the audience that morning. Erichsen played no
part in all these questions and answers but listened
very attentively because he was very fond of this sort
of badinage, all the more because he felt himself
personally incapable of it.

'He's a Schleswig-Holsteiner,' said Ebba. 'Germans don't make good courtiers.'

Pentz laughed. 'It really is too obvious, my dear

lady, that Denmark didn't have the honour of giving birth to you. The Schleswig-Holsteiners no courtiers! You forget the Ranzaus, the Bernstorffs, the Moltkes . . .'

'They were Ministers, not courtiers.'

'But that's almost the same thing.'

'Not at all, my dear Baron. I read a good deal of history, if only in French novels, but that's sufficient for a lady at court, and I venture to state that there is all the difference in the world between a Minister and a courtier. At least, if they really deserve their name. The Germans have a certain brutal gift for ruling—forgive the adjective, because I can't bear the Germans—but it's because they know so much about ruling that they are bad courtiers. Ruling is a rough-and-ready business. Ask Erichsen if I'm not right.'

The latter solemnly shook his head and the young woman laughed as she continued: 'And all that applies more or less to the count. He might perhaps be turned into a Minister . . .'

'For Heaven's sake . . .'

'But he has absolutely nothing to recommend him as a companion for the Princess. He stands there as solemn as a high priest and has no idea when to laugh. And that's something very important. Our gracious Princess, as I think we all agree, has a number of tiny foibles, one of which is trying to play the part of an eighteenth-century *femme d'esprit*. As a result, she has a liking for out-of-date anecdotes and quotations and not only expects you to understand them but to be amused by them. But the count doesn't understand even the rudiments of the matter.'

'And you managed to discover all that from the poor count's face during an audience of barely ten minutes?'

'I'm not certain whether I can agree with your phrasing, because the important thing was that there was absolutely no expression on his face the whole time. And that is the worst thing of all. For example, the Princess spoke of King Henry IV and mentioned *la poule au pot*, which strictly speaking ought really not to be mentioned any longer. But just because the reference to the *poule au pot* was so feeble, a courtier has a double duty to smile and not to stand there like a dummy, leaving a princess in the lurch when she is looking for applause.'

A look of satisfaction spread over Erichsen's face.

'And then the Princess talked graciously about chlorosis or said that I might be suffering from it. Now, I ask you, Baron, everyone knows that *any* mention of chlorosis must always be greeted with a smile, that's a firm tradition, and when a princess is gracious enough to add something about iron in the blood, thus indicating that she has read Darwin or some other great *savant*, then the smile of amusement must be immediately followed by a smile of admiration, and when absolutely nothing like this happens and a gentleman-in-waiting just stands there like an oaf for all the world as if someone had merely said 'It's ten o'clock', then I'm afraid that I find myself compelled to deny that gentleman-in-waiting any claim to the profession of courtier.'

It was nearly four o'clock when they arrived at Klampenborg. Holk helped the Princess to alight, and having decided to take coffee at the Hermitage, the party moved off towards the adjacent Zoological Gardens, at the north end of which lay the Hermitage. Their way led them first past a large hotel, in front of which was erected a marquee a good hundred feet long and open on one side; it stood on a stretch of lawn between the path and the beach, with the open side facing the path up which the Princess now proceeded. The banquet itself had not yet begun but numerous officers of almost every unit of the Copenhagen garrison were already assembled; everywhere there could be seen the brilliant uniforms of the Horse Guards and the Hussars, and even more colourful than the uniforms were the flags and pennants fluttering from the top of the marquee. When the Princess was still some hundred yards away, she turned sharply left down a gravel side-path, since she did not wish to disturb the festivities but she had already been recognized and de Meza, who had been informed of her presence in Klampenborg, hurried across the lawn and greeted her respectfully.

'My dear General,' she said, 'this was not at all my intention. It is just striking four and I can see the soup-column already on the march from the hotel. And I could not bear to be responsible for cold soup, least of all on an October day with a fresh breeze. General de Meza only likes such weather, I believe, when he is on campaign and lying in bivouac amongst his men.'

She said all this with a certain princely graciousness and the General, who was far from insensible to it, left her with renewed expressions of respect. From the tent, various toasts could already be heard and the band struck up the national song: 'King Christian stood beside the lofty mast', and then went on to the 'Valiant Soldier Lad'.

Together with her suite, the Princess had now reached the Zoological Gardens, the southern tip of which adjoined the causeway just beyond Klampenborg. Here she gave Erichsen her arm; then followed Countess Schimmelmann with Pentz and, further behind, Holk with Ebba, the former obviously perplexed as to how to start the conversation. It had not escaped his notice that during the audience with the Princess that morning, Ebba had regarded him with a slight air of mockery and superiority and the drive that afternoon had not yet given them the opportunity of speaking to each other. Finally he ventured: 'We are going to have a wonderful sunset. And there could be no better place from which to see it than here. What a magnificent plain! It is seven years ago since I was last in Klampenborg and I have never been to the Hermitage.'

'Did the name scare you?'

'No, because I am myself by inclination and habit something of a hermit and, but for the Princess who now and again recalls me to the world, I might almost call myself the hermit of Holkenäs: sky and sea and a lovely castle on a dune.'

'On a dune,' repeated the girl. 'And a lovely castle. How enviable and how romantic. It sounds almost like something out of a ballad, the *König von Thule*, for example. It's true that, if I remember rightly, the king of Thule wasn't married.'

'I am not so sure,' replied Holk, now put completely at his ease by the young woman's tone. 'I am not so sure. Was he really unmarried? It is almost a subject for a thesis. If I remember rightly, he bequeathed everything to his heirs, which does seem to suggest some sort of family. Of course, it may have been a collateral branch. In spite of that, I should like to assume that he was married and had a wise wife who perhaps, or indeed probably, smiled at her old husband and allowed him to enjoy his youthful enthusiasm with the goblet.'

'Now that really *is* interesting,' cried the girl, her eyes sparkling mischievously. 'Really remarkable. Till now that ballad has always seemed to me quite unambiguous: the king dead, the goblet emptied and sunk, and the realm (always the least important thing in a ballad, of course) split up and given away amongst everybody. But if we can assume the existence of a queen—and on second thoughts, I quite agree with you—then when the old man dies, everything is really only just beginning and the *König von Thule* is unfinished, to say the least, and needs a sequel. And why not? In the end I expect a page can be found who up till then had been consumed by a hopeless passion and now gets his colour back—or "iron in the blood", to quote our gracious Princess.'

'Ah, my dear Fräulein von Rosenberg,' said Holk, 'you're poking fun at the Romantics and forgetting that your own name is connected with an extremely romantic episode which certainly deserved a ballad.'

'My name?' she laughed. 'A romantic episode? Do you mean Ebba? Well, that might well be so, I suppose. After all, most ballads have something to do with Ebba, more or less. As you know, Ebba means Eva, and it is notorious that there's nothing romantic without the apple. But you're shaking your head, so you must mean not Ebba but Rosenberg.'

'Certainly, my dear young lady, I mean Rosenberg. Genealogy happens to be a hobby of mine and my great-uncle's second wife was a Rosenberg so that I know something about the traditions of your family. All the Rosenbergs—at least all the Rosenberg-Gruszczinskys, because the Lipinskys are rather different—descend from a brother of the Archbishop of Prague who was dragged from the pulpit on the so-called Amber Coast and murdered by heathen Prussians. This pulpit still exists as a family shrine, even although it is all decrepit and worm-eaten.'

'And I am afraid that I have never even heard of it,' said Fräulein von Rosenberg, seemingly, or perhaps really, in earnest for a moment.

'From which I should deduce that you probably belong to the Lipinsky and not to the Gruszczinsky branch of the family.'

'To my great regret, not even that. True, if I'm allowed to put Lipeson instead of Lipinsky, a boldness which that illustrious family will, I trust, forgive, then perhaps I might claim a link between me and that family by using that form of the name. You see, I'm a Rosenberg-Meyer or more correctly a Meyer-Rosenberg, granddaughter of the Meyer-Rosenberg who was well known in Swedish history as King Gustav III's personal pet Jew.'

Holk could not repress a slight movement of shocked surprise but the young woman continued in an affectedly casual tone: 'Granddaughter of Meyer-Rosenberg whom King Gustav later ennobled under the title of Baron Rosenberg, Baron Rosenberg of Filehne, a place on the Prusso-Polish border, where our family had lived for several centuries. And since you're interested in genealogical curiosities, let me briefly add that the act of nobility came not one moment too soon, because three days later the chivalrous and, as far as our family is concerned, unforgettable, king was murdered by Lieutenant Anckarström. In fact, an event just as suited for a ballad as the murdered archbishop but I suppose rather loosely connected with my family. But you mustn't give me up just for that reason. The grass has grown over all that and my father married a Wrangel, in Paris at that, where I was born exactly on the same day the July Revolution broke out. Some people say that they can see cause and effect. In any case, it enables you to calculate how old I am.'

Holk was an out-and-out aristocrat who never failed to take for granted the closest connexion between the continuance of his family and the continuance of the Divine order, and normally refrained from talking about such matters only because he considered them too sacred. In this sphere he would, indeed, have been glad to reintroduce the most medieval practices, and the more searching the probe into his and his family's ancestry, the better it would have pleased him, since his name would have emerged with all the greater lustre. His easy and agreeable manners, as agreeable to his middle-class friends as to his equals, sprang from this feeling of complete assurance as to this most important matter of origins. But the more confident he was about his own family tree, the greater his doubts about any other, not excluding certain ducal houses, and as a result, you could speak with him very freely about such matters—as long as his own family was not in question. This is what now happened: quickly recovering from his first shock on hearing about the first Meyer-Rosenberg and particularly the rather strange epithet that had been used to describe him, he now found it highly piquant to see such an obviously intelligent person treating with levity a question which, in the majority of cases, from his extremely strict viewpoint, could hardly be taken lightly enough.

CHAPTER 14

THEIR path ran along the eastern edge of the Zoological Gardens, mainly beneath high plane-trees whose branches, many still bearing their yellow foliage, hung down, obscuring the view, so that it was only after coming out of the avenue that they saw the Hermitage standing in the middle of a sunny forest glade. The two leading couples were familiar with the view, but Holk and Fräulein von Rosenberg who were seeing it for the first time, stopped in their tracks, almost taken aback by the entrancing sight of the solitary castle which they could perceive, still some distance away, towering up to the clear autumn sky. No smoke was rising from its chimneys and the sun shone brightly over the broad meadows, still green, while in the steel-blue sky above hovered hundreds of gulls, resting on their way from the sound towards Lake Fure.

'Your own castle can hardly be more solitary than this,' said Ebba as they walked along a narrow path which led diagonally across the glade towards the Hermitage.

'No, neither more solitary nor more beautiful. But

lovely though this is, I still shouldn't want to change. I find this stillness oppresses me. In Holkenäs there's always a slight swell and a breeze comes up from the sea and blows in the tops of the trees in my park. But here even the blades of grass aren't moving and every word you utter sounds as if the whole world could overhear it.'

'A good thing that no harm could come from it,' laughed the girl, 'because I cannot imagine a conversation more suitable to be overheard.'

Holk, rather nettled by this remark, was about to say so, when, before he could answer, they reached the broad terrace steps leading to the castle. At the foot of the steps stood an old gamekeeper who was at the same time the caretaker and who respectfully doffed his cap as the Princess approached and ordered coffee to be served upstairs in the large central gallery. She said this in a loud voice for all to hear, but she then drew the servant to one side for a moment to make further arrangements with him. 'Not later than five o'clock', she said in conclusion. 'Evening comes before one realizes it and we need a good light.'

The old man bowed, the Princess walked on towards the castle and, leaning on the countess's arm, climbed to the top floor. Here in the central gallery, high arm-chairs had already been placed round a long oak table and the balcony windows facing east and west had been opened, so that the whole magnificent landscape could be admired as if through two vast picture frames. The flat meadows surrounding the castle on all sides seemed to have disappeared, for they were too close to be seen, but the distant prospect was clear and bright and whilst,

on the left, the tree-tops of a broad stretch of woodland twinkled in the rays of the declining sun, on the
right could be seen the blue, shimmering surface of
the sea. Holk and Ebba would have liked to have remained standing in order to enjoy the view more fully
from both windows but this the Princess refused to
allow. She knew all about landscape, she said, and
could assure them that the view was best exactly as
it was. What is more, coffee (and the caretaker's wife
appeared at this moment with a tray set with an
exquisite Meissen coffee service), coffee must not
be neglected either, and as far as the magnificent
meadows were concerned, which in any case were not
visible for the moment, they would make their
appearance later on. All in its own good time. 'And
now, my dear Schimmelmann, please do the honours.
Frankly, I am longing for some refreshment. The
distance may not be great but it was quite far enough
for me.'

The Princess was in the best of humours, as was
shown, amongst other things, by her talkativeness
which was even greater than usual. She joked about
that too, and asked Pentz, who seemed very silent
today, to *indemnify* her.

'Indemnify,' she continued, 'even that word is one
of those everlasting parliamentary expressions. But
parliamentary expression or not, I really have a right
to indemnification, to remission of sentence, in-
asmuch as there is no place, not even excluding my
dear Fredericksborg, where I feel that I can chat so
freely as here. There were times when I came here
almost every day and enjoyed all this magnificent
sea and forest for hours. To be sure, if I were to say
that this pleasure was what is commonly known as

happiness, I should be incorrect. All that I have ever known here is peace, which is not as much as happiness, yet in some ways more. Peace is the best thing.'

Holk suddenly pricked up his ears. It seemed to him that he had heard those very words only a short while before. But where? And after a moment of searching, all at once he remembered the evening at Holkenäs and Elizabeth Petersen's clear voice and once again he seemed to hear the song. It was not a week ago yet already it seemed far, far away.

The Princess must have noticed that Holk's attention had wandered and so, leaving her generalities, she continued: 'You will hardly guess, my dear Holk, what coast-line that is which we can see through the window.'

'I thought that it was Sweden.'

'No, not really. It is Hven, the little island on which our famous Tycho de Brahe built his observatory, his "star-castle" as they called it. Yes, I always think of the Brahes with much love and affection, for personal reasons. It must be forty-five years ago since Ebba Brahe, the court beauty of the day, was my lady-in-waiting and my friend as well, which meant much more to me. Because we need friends always and at all times' (here the Princess stretched out her hand to Countess Schimmelmann) 'and especially when we are young and in the first year of our marriage. Pentz is smiling, of course. He doesn't know what the first year of a marriage is like.'

The Baron bowed and seemed about to express not only his agreement but a certain humorous satisfaction at this statement, but the Princess forestalled him and said: 'But I wanted to talk about Ebba Brahe. There is a sort of blessing attached to certain names and I've always been lucky with my Ebbas. I can see it as if it were yesterday, the day I pointed over to Hven from this very spot and said to Ebba Brahe: "Now Ebba, would you not like to change? Don't you long to be over there, in the castle of your ancestors?" But she refused to listen to me, and I can still remember her saying in her enchanting voice: "The view from the Hermitage to Hven is much lovelier for me than the view from Hven to the Hermitage." And then she began to joke and say that she was completely earthy, far too earthy to be enthusiastic about the "star-castle". Amongst all the stars, she said, it was only the earth that interested her, and the others were merely there to illuminate it by night. Oh, she was charming and lovable, the darling of everybody, and I might almost say that she was more of an Ebba than a Brahe, whereas our Ebba . . .'

The Princess stopped suddenly.

'Is more of a Rosenberg than an Ebba,' interposed the young woman, bowing with the greatest aplomb to the Princess.

Hearty laughter in which even Erichsen and Countess Schimmelmann, the two most passive pillars of the company, felt compelled to join, greeted this charming act of self-depreciation, for everybody knew the girl's family tree only too well and quite understood the implication of her words, not least the Princess who was about to make some particularly friendly remark to Ebba when the old gamekeeper appeared in the doorway, thus giving the Princess the prearranged signal. They all stood up and went out on to the overhanging balcony from which they had a superb prospect of the great mass of woodland which filled the whole horizon to the west. The intervening meadow-land was also extensive but in a few places the forest encroached on it and from these projecting spinnies there now appeared small herds of deer, which then came out into the plain and, playfully, neither quickly nor slowly, trotted towards the Hermitage. Ebba was enraptured but before she could speak she saw that in the background the whole broad stretch of woodland was beginning to come to life and just as the isolated herds had come out of the spinnies, scores and scores of them now appeared out of the more distant depths of the forest and, anxious not to miss the impending parade, broke into a lively trot, at first all confused and jumbled together until, as they approached, they formed themselves into orderly groups and moved past the Hermitage in squadrons. Finally, after the last of them had passed, they once more scattered over the meadow and now for the first time they could be seen as a whole. All sizes and colours were represented and although Ebba admired the black stags, still more did she admire the white hinds, which were relatively even more numerous. But Ebba could never remain serious for long and, quoting various lines from Danish and German folk-songs, she declared that fallow deer had always been the most popular characters with the exception of white hinds, which were even more important. Pentz, for his part, refused to accept this view and strongly asserted that the Princess and the Page took precedence and always would, to which the Princess assented with a touch of melancholy 'I accept what Pentz says and you mustn't contradict him. We poor princesses have very little left in any case and we have almost been pushed out of the world of reality already, so that if we lose our place in ballads and fairy-tales as well, I hardly know where we shall be able to go.' They were all silent, realizing only too well the truth of what she had said and it was left to Ebba to kiss her benefactress's hand and say: 'Dear Princess, there is, thank Heaven, still plenty left to do: you will always be a refuge for others and make them happy and able to laugh at prejudice.' It was plain that these words comforted the Princess, perhaps because she sensed that, although they came from Ebba, they were more than mere words; but in spite of this she shook her head and said: 'Dear Ebba, all that will soon be a fairy-tale as well.'

While they had been talking, the carriages, which they had been intending to go to meet, had come up to the terrace steps and the Princess, realizing that dusk was falling, bringing with it the cool of evening, stated that she would forgo her walk and start the return journey straightaway. 'But we shall arrange ourselves differently and I hereby release the gentlemen from accompanying me.'

This arrangement was to everyone's taste. The Princess took her seat with Countess Schimmelmann beside her and Ebba opposite; Pentz, Holk and Erichsen followed in the second carriage. When they passed through Klampenborg, the front of the officers' marquee was closed and only a narrow strip of light was shining out through a small crack on to the dark lawn in front. A few words from a speech were carried on the wind as they passed and then this, too, ceased and only cheers and shouts of approval could still be heard in the evening air.

CHAPTER 15

THE return journey was made without any untoward incident but not without a certain *médisance*, to which Ebba was strongly addicted. The story of the Rosenbergs and the various branches of the family was naturally a heaven-sent opportunity. 'Poor count,' she said. 'It certainly is true that he studies everything very thoroughly. Naturally enough, of course, because he's a German, and especially in genealogical matters you always need to keep probing and searching. I'm sure he never fails to seize on every name and if I had been unlucky enough to be baptized Cordelia, I wager anything that he would have asked me all about old Lear straight away.' The Princess gave Ebba an affectionate tap on her hand, more to encourage her than otherwise, and she went on: 'He's rather like a museum catalogue with historical commentary. I can still see his face as Your Highness was talking of Tycho de Brahe and pointing over to Hven island. He was completely absorbed and his soul was obviously yearning for a talk on cosmology. That would have been just the subject for him, all the way back to Ptolemy. Thank Heaven something prevented him because quite frankly as far as I'm concerned astronomy is even more boring than genealogy.'

The following day was spent in similar gossip, though this did not prevent Holk from receiving the friendliest treatment from the ladies, so friendly as not only to flatter him but to put him in the best possible humour. It was in this mood that he returned to his comfortable lodgings and while eating his breakfast the following day, he once more realized all the excitement and stimulation that he derived from his life at court. How dull, in comparison, seemed the days he spent at home, and when he recalled that in ten minutes time he would have to sit down at his desk and report all his impressions to Holkenäs, he felt appalled to think how difficult it would be to strike the right note. And yet the tone was far more important than the contents, for Christine knew how to read between the lines.

He was still reflecting when there was a knock on the door and Frau Hansen came in, not the mother this time but Brigitte the daughter. He had scarcely caught a glimpse of her since the first evening but he had not forgotten how she looked, even when he was talking with Ebba. Brigitte's appearance at this moment portrayed what might be termed a subdued grandeur; grand, because she was well aware of the power of her beauty; subdued, because she realized her modest social position, at least as long as the count was a lodger in her house. With a brief 'Good-morning', she walked, upright and almost statuesque, straight to the table and began to collect up the breakfast things, while in her left hand she held a large tray in front of her bosom. Holk had meanwhile risen from his seat in the window to give her a friendly handshake.

'Welcome, dear Frau Hansen, and if you have the time to spare . . .'

He waved a polite hand towards a chair, at the same time returning to the window-seat. However, the young woman remained standing, still holding the japanned tray in front of her like a shield, and looked calmly and without the slightest trace of embarrassment at the count, evidently expecting him to add something. Holk could not fail to notice her studied demeanour and especially her way of dressing. She was wearing the same house-dress that she had worn the first evening, loose and comfortable, without cuffs or collar, because these would have detracted from the effect of the wearer. Her neck and shoulders were particularly lovely and had, as it were, a complexion all their own. This same calculated effect showed in every detail. Her full half-length house-coat with a loose belt of the same material, although seemingly without shape or cut, merely served to reveal her own shape more plainly. She looked exactly like the traditional picture of a beautiful Dutch girl and involuntarily Holk found himself glancing at her ears to see if she was wearing the appropriate flat gold ear-rings. As she continued to meet his glance unwaveringly, he continued: 'I notice you prefer to remain standing so that you can be seen full-length and I see that you know exactly what you are doing, my charming Frau Brigitte. Really, if, at the time of your trip from Shanghai to Bangkok which your mother was telling me about yesterday, I had been the Emperor of Siam, I should have made quite other arrangements in the matter of the throne in front of the palace and instead of sitting, which is never so attractive, I should have made you stand beside the throne and just rest your arm on its ivory back. Then we should have seen which of the two was whiter, the ivory or the arm of the beautiful Frau Hansen.'

'Oh,' said Brigitte with well-simulated embarrassment, 'Mother is always talking about that as if it was something special but it was really only a game.'

'Yes, a game, Frau Brigitte, because it was in Siam. But we are not there all the time and in good old Copenhagen there's one thing that we all have as well as in Siam and that is, an eye for beauty. And the one who has it most and, in his exalted position, no doubt the most effectively. . . . But we need mention no names, dear Frau Hansen, and I only want to express my admiration for your dear husband about whom I have heard so many admirable things . . .'

'About my husband? Well yes, he knows his Brigitte,' she said, modestly lowering her gaze.

'He knows you, my dear Frau Hansen, and he knows the complete and utter trust he can have in you. And I should like to say that I know it, too. Because if on the one hand, beauty is a danger, on the other it is a shield and protection as well', and as he spoke he let his eye rest on the tray. 'One look at your pure white brow is enough to tell me that you are not subject to the weaknesses of your sex. . . .'

Frau Brigitte was hesitating how to take such flowery language but suddenly noticing that Holk had a gentle twinkle in his eye, she realized that Pentz or Erichsen or both must have been talking and so, dropping her pretence of dignity, she answered his smile with an understanding smile of her own, at the same time leaning her elbow on the high mantelpiece so that, as on the first evening, her wide sleeve fell back . . .

This would certainly have been a suitable time to give a more intimate turn to the conversation but Holk preferred for the moment to play the part of moral tutor, even if jokingly and ironically: 'Yes, dear Frau Hansen, let me repeat, not subject to the weaknesses of your sex. There is no doubt of it. And yet I may perhaps be allowed to raise a warning voice. As I ventured to hint a moment ago, it is always dangerous to live in a town where kings have such an eye for beauty. One can perhaps resist the *love* of the powerful ones of the earth—but not their power. And as for Countess Danner, who to be sure is still to be reckoned with at the moment, surely she cannot go on living for ever . . .'

'Oh yes, she can.'

'Well then, perhaps the affection of her royal admirer might wane . . .'

'Not that either, Count Holk. The Countess has a special charm and you hear all sorts of things about it.'

'Can't you tell me what it is?'

'No, my mother is always saying: "Listen Brigitte, you're always giving everything away", but this question of Countess Danner's charm is really too much.'

'Well then, I shall have to ask Baron Pentz.'

'Yes, he can tell you, he knows all about it. Some people say that she has been given the apple of beauty, I mean Countess Danner; but that is not her greatest charm, at the best it's just a minor one . . .'

'I agree with you entirely. And in general, frankly speaking, I can't understand why it should always be an apple. It's always seemed to me quite incomprehensible. Now if it were cherries I can imagine what it might be, but an apple . . .'

'I'm really not sure, Count Holk,' replied Brigitte, smoothing down her jacket to give full value to her figure. 'I'm really not sure whether you are quite

right about that. . . .' And having reached this slippery
slope, she seemed quite prepared to pursue the topic,
but before she could do so, she heard a voice calling
from the stairs: 'Brigitte!'

'That's Mother,' she said with annoyance and put
the breakfast things on the tray. Then with a dignified
bow, as if they had been discussing important affairs
of church or state, she left the room.

When the door had closed behind Brigitte, Holk
walked up and down the room, a prey to very mixed
feelings. He was by no means insensitive to the beauty
or the flirtatiousness of this attractive young woman,
both of which seemed calculated to create all sorts
of entanglements; but the danger was diminished by
the very excess of her calculation. Many conflicting
feelings struggled within him until finally his better
nature won the day and enabled him to view the
events of the last few days with a certain detached
humour. By so doing, he at last achieved the mood
required for his letter to Holkenäs, to follow on the
few lines he had already written announcing his safe
arrival. For a brief moment he once more recoiled at
the amount of news that he would have to retail, for
a distaste for letter-writing was another of his cardinal
weaknesses; but finally he sat down at the roll-top
desk, straightened the sheet of paper and began:

> Copenhagen, October 3rd, 1859.
> 4, Dronningens-Tvergade.

My dear Christine,

You will by now have received the note in which
I informed you of my safe arrival. It is now time
for me to give a further sign of life and, as I can

fortunately add at once, well-being. Let me begin
with the most immediate: my lodging at Frau Hansen's. It is exactly as it was before, only more elegant,
so that it is plain that their circumstances have improved. This is perhaps due to the fact that she now
has her daughter living with her, also called Frau
Hansen, the wife of a sea-captain who used to sail with
her husband on his voyages to China. No doubt this
brings more money into the household. The young
Frau Hansen is a fine-looking woman, so beautiful
that when on one occasion she was presented to the
Emperor of Siam, she was given an official court-
reception. She has a Junoesque calm, auburn hair
(not a great deal of it but very nicely arranged), and
of course the complexion that goes with auburn hair.
I should call her a Rubens, if Rubens were not often
too coarse. But let us not bother with Frau Hansen
now. You will no doubt be laughing—as you have
every right to—at the interest that my comparison
with Rubens might suggest. And better than Rubens
at that! The very first evening I went to Vincent's
restaurant in Kongens-Nytorv; Pentz and Erichsen
took me there. Saw a large number of acquaintances,
and de Meza, who had come over from Jutland—but
spoke to no one, because of the big political hubbub
that is taking place at the moment. Hall is to be
dismissed and Rottwig put in his place. Of course,
only a pure caretaker government, even if it suc-
ceeds at all, which is doubtful. Read the reports in
Dagbladet, they are more detailed and less biased
than those in the *Flyveposten*. The following morning, I presented myself at the Princess's. Her treatment of me was exactly as before: she knows that I
don't share her political views but she forgives me

for preferring the old Denmark to the new. She is sure of my loyalty and complete devotion to her person. For this reason she can afford to overlook the rest, at least as long as the King is still alive and there can be no question of a serious political crisis. So we are in the agreeable position of being able to talk on an entirely amicable footing.

In the Princess's *milieu* scarcely anything has changed, in fact not enough. Everything is comfortable and cosy but at the same time grey and dusty; the Princess herself has no eye for such things and Pentz, who could perhaps bring about some change, thinks it wiser to let things go quietly on as they are. Countess Schimmelmann is dignified and benevolent but rather depressing. In place of Countess Frjis who has been the Princess's favourite for the last ten years, a Fräulein von Rosenberg has appeared. The Rosenbergs come from the little West Prussian town of Filehne and were only made barons under Gustav III. They bear no relationship either to the Bohemian or Silesian Rosenbergs. Fräulein Rosenberg herself is very intelligent and witty and has a good deal of influence over the Princess, in so far as anyone has. She has undoubtedly—and for this alone she must be thanked—she has undoubtedly helped to reduce the boredom of the Princess's little court, which was previously its chief characteristic. Yesterday when I was on duty, I was able to notice the change and even more so the day before when we drove out in a small party to Klampenborg and the Hermitage. It was a wonderful day and when, at sunset, two thousand deer paraded in front of us in whole squadrons—a sight of which I had often heard but never seen—it was so exciting and enthralling that I wished that you and the children could have been there to witness it. And by the way, I'm anxiously waiting to hear from you. What have you decided about the schools? I was delighted to be able to give you a free hand and I have every confidence in your judgement but I do hope that you will not do anything too hasty. Sending children away from home certainly has obvious advantages but the family and the home is still the best thing of all. And if it's your hand that is running the household, then what I have just written is all the truer. Give my regards to Julie and Alfred when he comes over from Arniewieck, which I hope he is doing frequently. When Asta goes down to the Petersens, ask her to remember me to him and give him and his granddaughter my kindest regards. See that Strehlke doesn't harass poor Axel too much with algebra and mathematics but tries to form his character. It's a pity that he hasn't any himself, nice enough fellow though he is. But after all, who has got character? Not everyone is as lucky as you; you possess what most of us lack. But if I'm not mistaken, even you are feeling a slight desire to have somewhat less of your most outstanding quality. . . . Am I wrong? Send news of yourself and the children—good news if possible.

> Your
> Helmut.

He put down his pen and re-read what he had written, not without satisfaction at certain passages. But when towards the end he read the words: 'the home is still the best thing of all . . .' and then: 'if it's your hand that is running the household . . .', he felt a certain emotion whose nature and cause he would have found it difficult to define. Had he been able to do so, he might have realized that it was his guardian angel warning him.

CHAPTER 16

HOLK posted the letter himself and then proceeded towards Pentz's, having been invited to lunch at his flat. None of the Ministers was there, not even Hall, although he had accepted, but there were members of Parliament and of the armed forces: General Bülow, Colonel du Plat, Lieutenant-Colonel Tersling, Captain Lundbye of the navy, and Worsaae of course, who was bound to be there as an almost official *esprit fort* and *raconteur*. Tersling was in good form and Worsaae too, as was seen in the mutual banter they exchanged; but entertaining though the pair were, Holk found himself only moderately amused, partly because, not being a Copenhagener, many of the points escaped him and partly because there were questions on his mind which he found no opportunity of asking because of the incessant badinage of the two competing humorists, for Pentz was all ears and heard nothing but the chaff. Like all good lunches, it lasted until evening. When it was over, several of the younger men went off to Tivoli to see the last act of an operetta; but Holk, unaccustomed to metropolitan life and always anxious, indeed almost pedantically anxious, about his health, accompanied Bülow and du Plat to the War Ministry and then returned to his lodgings. The elder Frau

Hansen welcomed him as politely and attentively as ever, asked after his health and brought him tea. She was much less talkative today and what she was saying was all in the sentimental mode: her daughter was not very well and when she considered that the poor young woman was still only a girl and her husband away seven months already and not likely to be back for some time yet, yes, when she considered all that and Brigitte might fall seriously ill and even perhaps 'pass on', then really she would just as soon die herself straight away. 'What's the point of it all? When you are fifty and a widow'—she dried a tear— 'yes, Count Holk, what is there left in life? The sooner it comes to an end the better. The worst thing is not poverty but loneliness, nothing but loneliness and nobody to love you. . . .' Holk, amused by this pathos, naturally agreed with everything she said. 'Yes, my dear Frau Hansen, of course, it's just as you say. But you mustn't take it too hard. There's always a little love to be found somewhere.'

She glanced sideways at him and was pleased to find him so understanding.

The following day, Holk was again on duty, something which was not, in fact, very arduous at the Princess's court. Almost a septuagenarian, she always went late to bed and rose even later in the morning, never appearing in public before noon. Until then, the gentlemen-in-waiting on duty had nothing to do except wait in the ante-chamber, reading newspapers or even writing letters, and when, long before the appearance of the Princess, the flunkey brought in a generous cold collation, Pentz would move over to the window-corner, half-filled by a horseshoe-shaped divan, where Erichsen or Holk joined him. So it was today, and after a sip of sherry, Pentz having expressed his appreciation of the sardines, Holk said: 'Yes, really excellent. But today, my dear Pentz, I should like to hear from you about something other than culinary matters. I had intended asking you a few questions yesterday but those two fighting cocks took all your attention. Worsaae really was very amusing, wasn't he? And then I said to myself that so remarkable a host as yourself is a host and nothing more and he has no time for private conversation in a discreet corner.'

'Very kind of you, my dear Holk. I really did neglect you yesterday and instead of blaming me, you are singing the praises of my hospitality. And incidentally, I must confess to you that if I lost the chance yesterday of a private conversation with you and what is more, if I heard you correctly, of a private conversation in a discreet corner, then I am prepared to condemn all those hospitable virtues with which you credit me. In a discreet corner—now there I should expect to hear something quite out of the ordinary.'

'Yes, I'm afraid that I feel rather doubtful about it myself. In any case, at first sight it seems nothing at all extraordinary. It concerns a topic that we talked about on our very first evening, but when I recall how everything we said on the subject was veiled in mystery, it no longer seems to be quite so commonplace and trivial. In a word, I'm not quite sure what it's all about myself exactly, except that I feel curious. So tell me, what is all this about those two women, the mother and daughter?'

Since Pentz either failed or pretended to fail to

understand, Holk went on: 'I mean, of course, the two Hansen women. I suppose that, quite apart from what you have told me yourself, I ought to be as well informed as you, for both women come from Schleswig, from Husum, I think, and then later on Glücksburg, and I was living in the mother's house last time I was on duty here. I must have been very unobservant or else the daughter who is there now has put a different complexion on the household. The fact remains that I'm still uncertain what they are up to. Sometimes I feel quite sure that it's all part of a carefully thought-out game but then I become conscious of all kinds of superior airs and graces and although I know very well that people can put on grand airs, all the same it makes me doubtful again. For example, there's this wonderful story of the Emperor of Siam with all sorts of homage and presents that seem to have come straight out of a fairy-tale and there's even a magnificent pearl necklace. Now, is that the truth or a lie? Perhaps it's a sort of megalomania. The daughter is certainly very good-looking and anyone who has ever been fêted in such a remarkable way because of her beauty, which is unquestionable, and then has to sit quietly at home brooding and waiting, would, I suppose, through her loneliness be quite capable of exaggerating her success and so we have the Emperor of Siam with a pearl necklace and elephants without knowing exactly how they came to be there.'

Pentz was smiling to himself but continued to say nothing, as he realized that Holk had not yet finished speaking. The latter went on: 'So everything may be just an hallucination, the creation of too vivid an imagination. But when I think of all the giggling and the way her eyes suddenly light up, both of which things happen on occasion, and especially when I remember the remarks you made to me the very first evening, remarks containing something about "security authorities", then I admit quite frankly that I have rather an uncanny feeling. And not only uncanny but in fact, real fear and real anxiety. After all what does "security authorities" mean exactly? It means the police and their most skilful and industrious members in addition form part of political security organizations. And the thought of that makes my blood run quite cold! If there really is any connexion between a security officer and the daughter or even between a chief of police and the mother—that sort of thing is not unknown and police-chiefs are quite incalculable in their tastes—then in this Hansen *ménage*, I'm little better off than in a den of thieves. The fact that there is gilt and Turkish carpets and that both mother and daughter brew a tea that might have come straight from heaven and not only from Siam, all that isn't going to be any consolation for me in the long run. It seemed to me, too, that when the Princess heard the name of Frau Hansen she looked rather as if she were not very edified. In a word, what is all this about? And now, out with it!'

Pentz touched Holk's sherry glass with his own and gave a hearty laugh: 'I shall tell you something, Holk. You are head over heels in love with this young woman and because you are afraid of her or, what amounts to the same thing, because you lack confidence in yourself, you want me to produce some frightful story that you can pull out of your pocket as a sort of insurance policy and use as a screen between yourself and the beautiful Frau Hansen. But with the best will in the world, I'm afraid that I can't provide this cautionary tale. And just think, how would I have dared, when I recommended you to go to Frau Hansen's for the first time two years ago, how would I have dared to send you, Count Holk, Gentleman-in-Waiting, to a *chambre garnie* which, with a pungency only equalled by your *naïveté*, you have just referred to as a den of thieves . . .'

'No offence, Pentz. The more so as it was your hints that were really responsible for my suspicions. Why did you mention security authorities?'

'Because it's the truth. Why shouldn't I mention security authorities? Why shouldn't a member of that body find Frau Brigitte just as pretty as you do? He may be a cousin of hers or even of the elder one—whom, by the way, I trust even less than the young one.'

Holk nodded agreement.

'But in any case, you needn't rack your brains too much over this and much else besides. Copenhagen is like that and always has been. Three thousand years ago, we had the Dyveke[1] business, mother and daughter, and it doesn't make much difference whether it is Hansen or Dyveke. By the way, you know that Dyveke was not a name but a descriptive adjective, don't you? And rather apt, too: little dove, the little dove from Amsterdam—can you imagine anything more innocent?'

Holk could only agree; but Pentz who was not

---

[1] Dyveke was the Dutch mistress, of humble origins, of the sixteenth-century Danish king Christian II, on whom she and her mother exerted political influence.

only a living reference library for the *chronique scandaleuse* of the capital but especially for the love-stories of kings ancient and modern, was not reluctant to embroider on a theme in which he had such expertise. 'There's something quite peculiar about the Dyveke story. You know that she is supposed to have been poisoned by red cherries. But whatever it was, the whole thing was more or less forgotten and no one was worrying about Dyveke and was more interested in models nearer home when, all of a sudden, our dear little milliner Rasmussen was converted into a countess. And will you believe it, from that day on, that old story has taken on a new lease of life and there is not a girl in Denmark with a pair of rosy cheeks, or even who's as pretty as that Frau Brigitte of the ever-drooping eyelids, who does not dream of becoming a Dyveke and having a title and a villa by the sea, and they place their pretty hands in their laps and preen themselves and . . . wait. And they all think that if the King himself doesn't come along, our ever-gracious sailor-king Frederick VII— because they can see that the Danner knows how to hold on to him and must have some charm that the rest of mankind hasn't yet discovered—if, as I was saying, the King doesn't come along, then someone else will, be it Holk or Pentz—you must excuse me for coupling my name so unceremoniously with yours. No, Holk, not a den of thieves. That beautiful *capitana*, whose husband, incidentally, I am *not* inclined to envy—and, by the by, he's rumoured to be rather partial to rum—this *capitana* is no worse than any of the others, only rather more dangerous because she's more beautiful, with her auburn hair and her house-coat that won't button up. . . . I hope that I don't need to appeal to your sense of chivalry, my dear Holk, to ensure that this poor young . . .'

'You will have your little joke, Pentz. But you are quite, quite wrong and you're forgetting, too, that I'm forty-five years old.'

'And I am sixty-five, my dear Holk. And if I calculate according to that, then it may well be a bad thing for you or alternatively for the lovely Brigitte . . .'

He was clearly keen to continue in this strain, but at that moment a footman came out of the Princess's apartments to announce that Her Royal Highness desired to speak with the gentlemen.

Pentz and Holk went in. The Princess held a newspaper in her hand and was obviously not only agitated but in a bad temper. She threw the paper to one side and instead of her customary gracious greeting, there came only the question: 'Have you read what it says, gentlemen?'

Holk was unperturbed for, being half an outsider, he had no special duty to read the newspapers; but Pentz was embarrassed, the more so as in recent times he had quite frequently been caught out in such sins of omission. This visible embarrassment, however, immediately restored the Princess's good humour. 'Now, my dear Pentz, you mustn't be too scared and let me restore your peace of mind at once by saying that over the years—and that is the view we must take—a man like you, let us say a man of game-and-truffle pie, is greatly to be preferred to a man of politics or newspaper gossip or even newspaper scandal. Because that is what we have here. It is true that the ostensible reason is a business house in Kokkegarde but we don't need a great deal of insight or knowledge to guess the real persons who have staged this scandal.'

The expression of embarrassment vanished from Pentz's face, to be replaced by one of curiosity. 'I presume that it's something improper about the countess . . .'

'Oh no,' laughed the Princess. 'In the first place, there is nothing at all improper about the countess and if you were a paragon of a gentleman-in-waiting, which thank the Lord you are not, you would pay more attention to my frequently expressed views on the countess. But that is just like you, Baron, and the prospect of your mid-morning breakfast, if you haven't had it already, has made you forget that a lampoon on the Danner would have put me into a good and not a bad humour. Yes, my dear Pentz, you were on the wrong track there, or perhaps you gave yourself away and if we lived in other days, I should present myself before the King and without more ado urge him to institute a Struensee[1] suit against you for unlawful relations with the milliner countess. Just think if your head were to be chopped off! But I shall not threaten you too much and shall merely condemn you to read the article in question; Ebba has underlined it all in red, she likes doing that; and then you may ask yourself how far we have already gone with gutter government in Denmark. Yes, gutter government—unfortunately; mind you, we ought to be careful about admitting it in front of Holk, because it is all grist to his Schleswig-Holstein mill. But what's the use? There is the article and if he does not read it here, he will read it in his lodgings,

---

[1] Struensee, lover of the wife of the eighteenth-century Danish king Christian VII, was impeached for treason on this count and executed.

or the wife of Captain Hansen will read it to him.
People who might well lay claim to an article themselves, or something similar, are always the first to
be interested in *sensation*.'

Holk was rather perturbed by this remark, because
it revealed once more the dubious reputation of the
Hansens. However, it was no time to pursue such
matters for Pentz had already taken hold of the paper
and, with pince-nez in action, began to read: 'For
sale: Notes of hand of Prince Ferdinand, the heir-
presumptive!'

'Well, Pentz, you have stopped reading already
and are looking for your handkerchief, presumably
to clean your glasses and reassure yourself that you
have read aright. But you have read aright. Now
go on.'

'Various notes of hand of His Royal Highness
Prince Ferdinand are for sale; they are all signed:
'On my royal honour' and endorsed by his Privy
Purse Chamberlain Plöther. The price will be what
any amateurs or collectors of curiosities may consider
appropriate for such rare and important documents,
but in no case less than fifty per cent. of their face
value. Please apply to the business-house at 143 Kokkegarde.'

Pentz laid the paper down; the article was at an
end.

'Now, gentlemen, what do you think of such a
thing? Personally I must say that, in sixty years
experience, I have never known anything like it.
You refuse to say anything and Holk is presumably
thinking: "As you make your bed, so you must lie
in it", and that anyone who signs I.O.U.s and, above
all, if he adds "on my royal honour", ought to redeem

them and if he fails to do so, he must, as has happened here, expect to be pilloried from 143 Kokkegarde. Presumably Holk thinks that, and he's right, quite right. I have no personal feelings about the Prince and the more he ruins himself, the more it benefits the person who is destined to be the real heir to this country, in place of this so-called heir-presumptive. But I cannot selfishly sit back and enjoy seeing the furtherance of my political schemes, when so much else, of greater importance after all, is at stake at the same time. A bird doesn't foul its own nest and there is a solidarity of interests which monarchy has to recognize, if monarchy is to continue to exist. I might blame *Dagbladet* and I admit that my first feeling of irritation was directed against them. But what is a newspaper? Nothing. I blame the King who has lost his sense of solidarity. He thinks of nothing else but his Danner and of digging up giant stone beds, two very different things in themselves, although posterity may perhaps link them in some strange way. Above all, he thinks: "*Après nous le déluge*." And that is most unfortunate. I hate preaching as much as I hate virtuous platitudes but, on the other hand, it must always be remembered that loose principles are fatal—principles are much more important than facts. It is to you, Pentz, that I am saying all this. With Holk it's different, he's a German and if he perhaps finds himself weakening (Ebba has been telling me all sorts of wonderful things about Frau Brigitte Hansen), then he only needs to think of his wife Christine at home; and I must be very much mistaken in her if her power doesn't extend from Holkenäs as far as Copenhagen. And now, gentlemen, au revoir.'

CHAPTER 17

HOLK had no time to reflect on what he had just heard, for it was a day full of visits and, in general, rather busy. At noon, there appeared two *petites-nièces* of the Princess, both as pretty as pictures and still only children, who came to fetch their great-aunt to visit an historical exhibition which Professor Marstrand and Professor Melbye had opened on 1 October in some of the side-galleries of the Museum. The whole town was talking about this exhibition and, as usual, politics took second place, although they were days when not only the government but even the monarchy itself seemed threatened. But of what importance was that, compared with the desire of the inhabitants of all big towns, and especially of Copenhagen, to find amusement—an amusement that, on this occasion, could masquerade behind a grand name—patriotism. What was on show was something unprecedented—a Danish national exhibition for which both town and country had been scoured to find historical portraits. It began with knee-length portraits of Christian II and his wife Isabella and concluded with three full-size portraits of Frederick VII, the present reigning monarch. Some distance away hung the portrait of Countess Danner. In between, endless battles on land and sea, fights against Lübeck, the assault on Wisby, the bombardment of Copenhagen, with red-coated generals everywhere but, even more, all the naval heroes over at least three centuries and, inevitably, Thorwaldsen and Öhlenschlager and ugly old Grundtvig. The Princess showed only a lukewarm interest because, as most of the pictures came from the royal palaces scattered all over Zealand, they had long been familiar to her. The young greatnieces, however, were extremely enthusiastic, asking a thousand questions and for a moment creating the impression that they were filled with admiration for all the old admirals, of whom one of the most famous had a black patch over one eye. But in the course of the visit, it became obvious to everyone, including the Princess and her suite, that their interest in admirals was mere pretence and make-believe and that the young princesses lingered with real reverence only in front of the likenesses of those persons, men or women, whose names were connected with some romantic or mysterious love-story or other.

'Strange,' said Pentz to Ebba, pointing to the elder of the two princesses who seemed barely able to tear herself away from the Struensee portrait.

'Not at all,' laughed Ebba. 'Not strange at all. Or do you expect young princesses to show an interest in old Grundtvig or perhaps in Bishop Monrad? The episcopal doesn't carry much weight when you are only fourteen years old.'

'But Struensee does?'

'*Sans doute.*'

In the afternoon, the Princess made an excursion into the surrounding countryside, a very rare thing for her to do, and in the evening, something even rarer, she put in an appearance in her box at the theatre, with Countess Schimmelmann and Ebba sitting behind her and Pentz and Holk behind them.

Shakespeare's *Henry IV part II* was being given

and in the long interval after the third act, tea was served and, as usual, the play and players were subjected to lively criticism, for the Princess still followed the literary customs of the preceding century. She was amused not only to see that no sort of uniform judgement emerged but that everyone had his or her favourite or *bête noire*, not only among the actors but also among Shakespeare's characters. The Princess herself, determined as ever to have an original judgement, was greatly in favour of the three justices of the peace and declared that, even as a young girl, her preference had always been for them; a perfect representation of philistinism had always delighted her, not only on the stage, for magistrates such as these were also to be found in politics and even Ministries—indeed, she could not even entirely exclude her friend Hall—but especially in every synod, you would find at least half a dozen characters like Shallow and Silence. Nobody had a good word to say for Falstaff, perhaps because he was not very well acted, whereas Holk was enthusiastic about Ensign Pistol and Pentz for Mistress Tearsheet, although instead of using her full name, he insisted on calling her Doll. The Princess allowed him to persevere in what she referred to as his error of taste and indeed she even expressed sympathy for his view, since it was at least sincere and consistent; most of all, however, it was the wisest thing for him to say because any other opinion on his part would, she said, only have aroused her suspicions. Ebba endeavoured to emulate the Princess's joking manner but failed completely, finally being almost overcome by nervous twitching and trembling. Holk, who noticed this, tried, without great success, to turn the

conversation and was heartily glad when the play
started again. They did not, however, stay long,
barely until the end of the next act, and then the
Princess's carriage was ordered and Pentz and Holk,
having been graciously released by the Princess, they
strolled by a roundabout route to Vincent's restaurant, where they intended to finish the evening with
an hour's gossip over a glass or two of Swedish punch.

On the way, Holk said: 'Tell me, Pentz, what was
the matter with our friend Ebba? She was almost in
hysterics. It was painful to watch and even more
extraordinary.'

'Painful, yes. Extraordinary, no.'

'Why not?'

Pentz laughed. 'My dear Holk, I can see that you
don't know anything about women.'

'Well, I can't prove the contrary, because I detest
boasting and particularly boasting about women.
But as far as Ebba is concerned, I thought I understood her and I still think so. I think that she's an
emancipated and impertinent young woman and
I maintain quite seriously that anyone who plays
with religious and moral questions in the way she
does is, so to speak, in duty bound to enjoy Falstaff's
Doll Tearsheet without reservations or at least not to
take offence at her.'

'Yes, that's what you think, Holk. And that is
precisely why I accused you a moment ago of knowing nothing about women. If you did, you would
know that it is those who have an iron in the fire
who are most offended when they see an outspoken
caricature of themselves—it may even be quite an
inoffensive one. They have become accustomed to
their own idea of themselves, even if they may

occasionally have doubts as to the special justification of their morality; but if, beside this image of themselves, a second one appears, exaggerating their own doubts still further, then their complacency completely evaporates. In other words, they are quite prepared to accept the small amount of old Eve which such dubious characters represent, but not one atom more. No exaggeration whatever can be allowed at any price, and so, if they do happen to meet it, they just collapse and burst into tears.'

Holk stopped and said: 'Is that really so? Aren't you asserting more than you can prove? For one thing, I cannot imagine that, apart from any other scruples, the Princess would have chosen to introduce into her court any undesirable woman, in view of her opinion of Countess Danner, whose conduct she's always criticizing.'

'And yet it is so. I refuse to withdraw anything. Ebba is clearly ambitious for her future and there's only one thing more certain—she has a past.'

'Can you tell me about it?'

'Yes. I happen to be the sort of person who fortunately stops at nothing, least of all where Ebba is concerned. Anyone who is as outspoken about other people, has forfeited the right to any consideration herself and anyone who so completely disregards discretion—the things I've heard from the mouth of that little hussy!—can certainly not appeal for discretion for herself.'

'And what was it?' interrupted Holk, more and more intrigued.

'Well, in one way, nothing or at least, nothing much. Quite an ordinary sort of affair. She was lady-in-waiting to Queen Josephine, over in Stockholm.

As you know, the Leuchtenbergs are all very friendly. Now, it must be about a year ago, or rather longer, people began to wonder at the affectionate attentions that the Queen's youngest son . . .'

'The Duke of Jämtland?'

'Yes . . . that, quite suddenly, the Queen's youngest son was starting to show his mother. Not that people were left wondering very long. You know those little boats that ply between the Islands of Love in Lake Mälar? Well, since a gondolier from Stockholm can be just as easily bribed as one from Venice, the motives of the prince's affection soon came to light; they were simply: Fräulein Ebba. Naturally, there was a scene. In spite of all that, the Queen, who was just as besotted with the girl as our Princess, wouldn't hear of dismissing or disgracing her and only gave in, most unwillingly, to pressure from the court. It was the King who opposed her most of all and who saw quite plainly in all this . . .'

'So that is why she is so passionately anti-Bernadotte,' interrupted Holk, suddenly remembering some remarks that Ebba had made on the way to the Hermitage, 'and hence her burning enthusiasm for the house of Vasa.'

'The house of Vasa,' laughed Pentz. 'Yes, that's her favourite expression now. And yet, believe me, there have been times when our Ebba would have given the whole of the house of Vasa, including the great Gustavus Adolphus himself, for the ring-finger of the youngest Bernadotte. It may perhaps still be so and the bridges to Sweden may not yet be completely cut, because until quite recently at least, some correspondence was still continuing. It's only this autumn that things seem to have quietened down and, as far as I know, there are no letters arriving now. Presumably there is something else in train. Ebba has always had several irons in the fire.'

'Does the Princess know anything?'

'As far as her past in Sweden is concerned, certainly she knows everything and perhaps more than everything, because it's not a bad thing to invent one or two extra details. It adds to the flavour. Love-stories must never be left unfinished and when harsh reality has cut the thread before its time, then it must be spun out artificially. Every novel-reader expects that and so does our Princess.'

Here their gossip came to an end as they had arrived at Vincent's, and when, an hour later, they left the restaurant again, they were not alone and so the subject was not renewed.

When Holk came into the entrance-hall, the widow showed herself somewhat monosyllabic, merely handing him a telegram which had arrived in the course of the afternoon. It was brief. With a concision that any business man would have envied, Christine made known three things: her thanks for his note, her satisfaction that he was well, and a promise of a longer letter to follow. Holk quickly perused the telegram in the hall, wished Frau Hansen good night and saying that she need not accompany him, immediately went upstairs to his room, where the lamp was already lit. It could not be said that he was particularly preoccupied by Christine's words, because he was thinking more of Pentz than of the telegram and was looking forward more to further information about Ebba than to the promised letter. Before going to sleep, however, even these thoughts left him because it suddenly seemed to him that he could quite clearly hear giggling and, in between, a more penetrating sound like the tinkling of glasses. Was it in the house next door or directly underneath him? He found himself resenting it, the more so as he could not conceal from himself a slight feeling of jealousy, jealousy of the 'security authority'. But as soon as he had uttered the word, it provided its own remedy, and when he had repeated it once or twice, his good humour returned and sleep came to him at once.

Next morning it was the younger Frau Hansen who appeared with the breakfast and as Holk studied her, he was almost ashamed of his thoughts while going to sleep the night before. Brigitte looked as bright as a spring morning, her eye and complexion were clear and her calm, womanly beauty had almost an air of innocence. She was as reticent as usual and only as she was about to go did she turn to him and say: 'I hope the Count was not disturbed. Mother and I couldn't shut an eye before midnight, they are such strange people next door, never still until late at night and you can hear every word through the wall. And if only that was all . . .' The count assured her that he had heard nothing and when Brigitte had gone, he had once more fallen under her spell. 'I don't trust her any more than her mother and all I really know about her is that she is very beautiful. But after all, that conversation that I had with her yesterday or the day before, what did it amount to, in fact? You can have a conversation like that with any young woman, or at least with very many. In fact, she said nothing that anyone else might not have said; looks are always uncertain and what's more, it seems to me that what Pentz was saying was all stuff and nonsense. Now what he said about Ebba was quite different.'

An hour later the postman brought the promised letter. Holk was glad because he did sincerely want to escape for a while from all the disturbing thoughts that these women, including Ebba, had aroused in him, and nothing was better calculated to do this than a letter from Christine. It came from an honest heart and he breathed more freely as he opened the envelope and took out the letter. But he was in for a disappointment, for the letter was so matter-of-fact that all it did was to make him feel uncomfortable.

'Dear Helmut,' the letter ran, 'I had intended to write you a longer letter but Alfred, whom you appointed your alter ego during your absence, has just come over from Arnewieck and so I have to make a report to your representative. Schwarzkoppen has, of course, come over with him, which is also very agreeable but takes time, too, and so I must be brief and put off any further information until later. Your hunger for news will, I know, not in any case be very great, as you always let yourself be completely absorbed by your immediate surroundings. And when your immediate surroundings are as beautiful as the captain's wife and as piquant as Fräulein von Rosenberg whose only fault seems to be that, unfortunately, she did not quite come up to your genealogical expectations, then you are unlikely to be anxious to have news from our dull old Holkenäs, where it is an event if the black hen has seven chicks. The subject that we discussed before you left, I hope to be able to settle finally with Schwarzkoppen's help. I shall not bother you with details until a definite decision has been taken, as you authorized me to. We are all well. Old Petersen had a bad fainting attack the day before yesterday and we thought it was the end; but he has since completely recovered and came to see me this morning more cheerful and spry than ever. He wants to start excavating behind the farmyard, between the small pond and the old paddock where all the crows' nests are, and he feels certain of finding something, urns or stone tombs or both. I have given him permission on my own authority and your regent Alfred, as well as you, will, I think, approve. My dear Julie has had a nasty cough but Vichy water and whey have, as usual, worked wonders. Axel is fresh and lively, which no doubt comes from the fact that Strehlke is more interested in shooting than grammar. For the moment, I am taking no steps but it must not be allowed to continue. Asta spends half of every day with Elizabeth. They are very fond of each other, which makes me very happy indeed, for childhood friendships are the most beautiful thing in life. I thank Heaven that in *this* you agree with me.

As ever,
Your Christine.'

Holk put the letter down. 'What on earth is all that about? I expected affection and find nothing but sneers. The fact that they are veiled only makes matters worse. "Your regent Alfred" and earlier on "as beautiful as the captain's wife and as piquant as Fräulein von Rosenberg" would have been quite enough but that final remark about childhood

friendships being the most beautiful thing in life—
that really is going too far. It all has the taste of bitter
honey. And then all these questions of schools and
education. Perhaps that's the explanation, and she is
adopting this sarcastic tone merely to intimidate me
and have a freer hand. But it really wasn't necessary
to use those means. She's free to dictate what is to
happen. Best of all, I should have liked to have kept
the children at home because, once they have gone,
I shall be left alone with a wife who possesses all the
virtues which I find depressing. She knows that as
well as I do, and meanwhile I think she is rather
afraid herself of all her virtues. But if the children
are to go anyway, it makes not an atom of difference
to me whether they go to Gnadau or Gnadenberg or
even Gnadenfrei. I have no doubt that there will
always be religion about somewhere. It may not be
too bad, for Asta at any rate. And Axel? Well, as far
as I'm concerned, for him, too. He's a Holk and if he
finds himself completely *herrnhuterised* for the
moment and becomes a missionary and perhaps has
three years among the Eskimos in Greenland, he'll
recover from it later on, I've no doubt.'

CHAPTER 18

THE weather had broken and there followed a
number of rainy days. The Princess kept mainly
to her private apartments and, except for fleeting
encounters, she saw Holk only in the evenings
when, after a game of whist, they had tea together.
Nothing was changed in their relationships, at least

for Holk and Ebba. Every day she became more and more impertinent and mischievous and when she realized that Pentz must have gossiped over her affair in Stockholm, she made allusions to it herself and talked of love affairs and especially court love affairs as if they were not only respectable but almost compulsory. 'There are all sorts of ways of living,' she said. 'One can be Countess Schimmelmann and one can be Ebba von Rosenberg; each way has its own justification but one must not try to follow both at once.' Holk, somewhat taken aback, looked at her half amused, half shocked, but Ebba continued: 'There are so many standards by which to judge human beings and one of the very best and surest is their attitude to love affairs. There are people who get goose-flesh at once when they hear of a *rendez-vous* or a *billet doux* but personally I don't feel like that at all. What would life be without love affairs? Dull, bleak, and boring. But when someone can see, with love and understanding, how, from the briefest encounter, from the most fleeting glance, something is created that is stronger than death itself—oh, there's only one thing better than observing it and that is experiencing it! I'm sorry for anyone who can't understand that or, while understanding it, won't accept it freely and with joy. Anyone with the courage of his convictions will always find someone to sympathize and, after all, it's sufficient if there is just one such person.' Not an evening passed without similar remarks which Holk for a time strove to resist, with less and less success. Every day, he saw more clearly how right and how acute Pentz had been when he had spoken of the power of so-called piquant relationships, relationships which women seem better able to foster than to restrain. Yes, Pentz was right and with a strange feeling of mingled delight, irritation, and anxiety, he realized more and more plainly that Ebba was playing with him. The Princess, however, noticed this too and decided to have a word with Ebba about it.

'Ebba,' she said, 'Holk has been with us a fortnight now and I should very much like to know what you think of him. I have confidence in your excellent judgement . . .'

'Political?'

'Ah, you minx, you know that I'm quite indifferent to his politics, otherwise he wouldn't be in my service at all. I mean his character and I might almost add, his heart.'

'I think he has a kind heart and a weak one.'

The Princess laughed. 'Certainly, he has that. But that doesn't help us very much. So tell me something about his character. Character is more important than heart. Someone may have, at one and the same time, a weak heart and a strong character because he has principles. And then his strong character can save him.'

'In that case Holk is lost,' laughed Ebba, 'for I think that his character is much weaker than his heart. It's his character that is his basic weakness. And the worst of it is that he doesn't even know it. Because he looks like a man, he considers himself one. But he's only a good-looking man, which usually means not a man at all. All in all, he hasn't had the proper training to develop his very modest talents in the line that would have suited him. He ought to have been a collector or an antiquarian or the director of a home for fallen girls or just a fruit-grower.'

'Now, now,' said the Princess, 'that's a great deal all at once. But do go on.'

'He's confused and half-hearted and it is this half-heartedness that will cause his downfall. He pretends to be a Schleswig-Holsteiner and yet he serves as gentleman-in-waiting to an obviously Danish princess; he's a living work of reference on genealogies who can reel off all the Rosenbergs, except the Filehne branch, and yet he sets himself up as an enlightened liberal. I haven't known him long enough to have caught him out in all his contradictions but I am quite certain that they exist in every sphere. For example, I've no doubt for a moment that he goes to his little village church every Sunday and comes out of his nap just when the Creed is being read, but I doubt whether he knows what there is in it and if he does, I doubt if he believes in it; yet in spite of that, or perhaps even because of that, he springs to his feet at once.'

'Ebba, you're going too far.'

'Indeed I'm not. Let me only mention a much more important example of his half-heartedness. As far as his morals are concerned, he is what one might describe as almost virtuous and yet he has a yearning to be a man of the world. And that sort of half-heartedness is the worst of all, worse than half-heartedness in so-called important questions, which are often not important at all.'

'That is very true, but here, Ebba, I have you just where I want you—and where I intend to keep you! You say that he has a yearning to be a man of the world. Unfortunately, you are exactly right there: I can see it more and more every day. But because he has this weakness, we must throw him a rope, a

golden rope, not so that he can move up to the attack
but so that he may beat a retreat. You must stop
flitting about in front of him like a will-o'-the-wisp
as you keep doing at the moment. He has already
been dazzled enough. As long as he is here, you must
hide your light under a bushel. I know very well that
that is asking a great deal of you, because if one has
a light, one likes to see it shining; but you must make
this sacrifice for me and if you find it difficult, then
to console yourself you must keep in mind that he
will not be here for ever. In the New Year he will be
leaving us and for better or worse we shall be having
our old trio again, and then you may do what you like,
marry Pentz or run away with Erichsen or even with
Bille, whose measles must come to an end sooner or
later. Whatever you do, I approve of, in advance. Perhaps you could oust the countess, not Holk's but Countess Danner; perhaps that would be the best thing.'

Ebba shook her head. 'That's not allowed, ousting
the Danner would mean that I could no longer be my
Princess's grateful and devoted servant.'

'My dear Ebba, you mustn't talk like that, you
don't deceive me in the least. I receive as much
gratitude from you as you choose to give me. Nor
do I do anything for the sake of gratitude. That is the
most ungrateful and unwise thing there is, to expect
gratitude. But do think over the question of Holk.'

'My apologies, Your Highness—but what am I to
think over? Ever since I have been able to reason,
I've always said to myself: "a girl must look after herself" and I'm right, you must be able to. And if
someone can't do it, it merely means that she doesn't
want to. All right, then, we must look after ourselves.
But what is a girl to do against a fully grown count of

forty-five who may become a grandfather any day? If anyone ought to be able to look after himself, it's the count, who has, I believe, been married for sixteen years and has an excellent and capable wife who is beautiful as well, as Pentz was telling me only the other day.'

'It's for the sake of his wife that I am urging you . . .'

'Well, if your most gracious Highness orders me, I shall endeavour to obey. But are you speaking to the right person? Surely not. It should be Holk. It's he who owes it to his wife to be faithful, not I, and if he is not faithful, it's his responsibility, not mine. Am I my brother's keeper?'

'Ah, I know that you're quite right,' said the Princess, running her hand over Ebba's wavy fair hair. But however that may be, you must realize that we are under constant observation, just as surely as we are in a position to observe so many things ourselves, and I shouldn't like it if we were to expose ourselves to the King and his countess.'

On the day following this conversation, Holk, being off-duty, intended to deal with his correspondence. On his desk lay all the letters he had received during the last fortnight, including some from his wife. He quickly perused them, which did not take long since there were only a few, and then, finally, he read a telegram in which she excused herself for not having written for four days. That was all and if their extent was slight, their contents were even slighter. This annoyed him, because he was careful to avoid asking himself who was really to blame. He merely said to himself—and here he was justified—

that, earlier, things had been very different. Earlier, indeed even during his last absence in Copenhagen, the letters they had exchanged had all the time been real love letters, full of the affection that they had felt for each other in their younger years. But this time all tenderness was absent, the tone was chilly, and if his wife tried to make a joke there always seemed to be something caustic or sarcastic in it which cancelled all its charm. Yes, that was unfortunately how things were and yet a letter had to be written. But how? He was still brooding over this problem when Frau Hansen entered and handed him the letters which the postman had just bought. Two of them bore the Copenhagen postmark but the third, in Christine's handwriting, was in an envelope of a different shape from the usual and instead of the Glücksburg postmark bore that of Hamburg. For a moment Holk was surprised and then, even before opening the envelope, he realized what had happened: 'Of course, Christine is on her tour of the boarding-schools.' So it proved to be and this is what he read:

> Hamburg, Streit's Hotel,
> October 14th, 1859.

Dear Helmut,

You will by now have received my telegram of excuse for not having written for several days. Now you will see from the postmark the reason for my silence. I was preparing for my journey which took all my energy, in spite of help from dear Julie and in spite of reducing everything to the minimum. We went to Schleswig by carriage and thence by train and since yesterday morning we have been installed here in Streit's hotel, which holds such pleasant memories for us both. That is, assuming that such memories still mean anything to you! I have taken rooms on the second floor with a view of the Alster, with its villas and its bridges, and as dusk was falling I leaned out of the window and, as before, lost myself in all the loveliness of the scene. Only Asta was with me, as Axel has gone into the town. He wanted to go with Strehlke (who has come with us this far) first to the Lancers' cavalry stud and then on to Rainville's riding school. From there to Ottensen to see Meta Klopstock's tomb. I was very willing to agree because I know that such experiences remain in the memory and give one depth. And this would seem the appropriate moment to let you know my decisions regarding the children, after taking further careful advice. Alfred has agreed as well, even though he queried the importance of the whole matter. Asta, of course, will go to Gnadenfrei; even you must have realized that it could not be anywhere else. I spent some very happy years there, I must not say the happiest years of my life, because do you know which they were—and I want my child to enjoy the same enviable opportunity as I had and an equally balanced harmonious adolescence. As for Axel, on Schwarz-koppen's advice, I have decided on the *Pädagogium* at Bunzlau. It has the best of reputations and while not inferior to the Thuringian schools in the strictness of its principles, it is less strict where principles are *not* involved. Strehlke, who at first wanted to go to Malchin, will now be going as curate to his brother. I have made him promise to be our guest during the summer holidays, to look after Axel. He is a good man and would have been quite outstanding if, before finishing his studies in Berlin, he had spent the previous years in Halle instead of Jena. The influence of Jena can never be completely eradicated later on. I do not know if there is anything I need add with regard to the children. This one thing perhaps: I was surprised and hurt to detect a certain rejoicing on their part when it was finally decided that they should leave home. The taste for novelty natural to all young people seemed to me not to be the cause in this case or at least, not the sole cause. But if it was not, then what is it? Have we ever been found wanting in our love towards them? Or did they long to escape from the disagreements that they witnessed all too frequently? Oh, dear Helmut, I would gladly have avoided such disagreements but I didn't succeed in doing so and as a result I chose what I thought was the lesser evil. In doing this, I may have sacrificed a good deal but I was only doing what my conscience dictated and I am sure you are prepared to accept that admission. My trip will not keep me away for more than five or six days and I hope to be back in Holkenäs by about the 20th. Meanwhile Julie is in charge. Please send my most respectful homage to the Princess, who was so kind as to remember me, and my regards to Pentz and Fräulein von Rosenberg, although I must confess that I cannot feel much sympathy for her. I do not like those free-thinking ways! I am looking forward eagerly to the New Year when I hope to see you once again, perhaps even on New Year's Eve. Do try to arrange that your present stay in Copenhagen may be your last visit to the capital, at any rate in your present post. Why be a lackey when one can be free?

With love,

Your Christine.

After he had read the letter, Holk felt somewhat sentimental. It contained so much affection that it revived memories of past happiness. She was still the best of them all. What was the beautiful Brigitte by comparison? Yes, and what was Ebba, even, by comparison? Ebba was like a rocket that you followed with an 'Aaah . . .!' of astonishment as long as it continued to shoot upwards but when it was all over, it was nothing but a firework after all, something completely artificial. Christine, on the other hand, was like the simple, clear light of day. Immersed in this feeling, he quickly read through the letter again, only to find that his pleasure had quite evaporated, all the pleasant impressions had gone, leaving only one, or predominantly one, thing behind: the tone of self-righteousness. And once more his thoughts took their familiar turn: 'Oh, these virtuous women! Always sublime, always serving the Truth; and I suppose they even think so themselves. But without wishing to deceive anyone, they deceive themselves. Only one thing is quite certain: their excellence is appalling.'

CHAPTER 19

FOUR weeks had meanwhile passed and it was approaching the middle of October. Holk had by now completely adapted himself to life in Copenhagen, enjoyed all the scandals of the town, big and little, and remembered, not without alarm, that in another six weeks his monotonous life in Holkenäs would be starting again. The letters arriving from home were not calculated to allay his misgivings; since Christine's return from her journey she had been, it was true, writing more regularly and even avoiding irritating comments, but the prosy, matter-of-fact tone was still there and, above all, the dogmatism that had now become ingrained. And it was just this tone, with its assumption of utter in-fallibility, that continually aroused Holk's ire. Christine was always so certain of everything: but what, in fact, could be considered entirely beyond question? Nothing, absolutely nothing, and every conversation with the Princess or with Ebba only served to confirm him in that opinion. Everything was provisional, everything a mere majority decision of the moment: morals, dogma, taste, everything was uncertain and it was only for Christine that every question had been settled once and for all, only Christine knew, with absolute conviction, that the doctrine of predestination was false and must be rejected, while the Calvinist form of the Eucharist was an affront; and with equal certainty, she knew which books were to be read or not read, which people and principles were to be followed or not followed and, above all else, she knew how all problems of education were to be solved. God, how clever the woman was! And if she occasionally confessed to not knowing something, then she always accompanied this admission with a look that said only too plainly: 'such things are not really worth knowing'. Holk would give himself up to these reflections while looking out of his window in the morning over Dronningens-Tvergade, which, quiet though it was, was always lively compared with the deserted road leading from Holkenäs to Holkby village. And while

he was thus meditating and brooding, there would
come a knock on the door and old Frau Hansen or
even the beautiful Brigitte would come in to clear
away the breakfast and if it was the talkative widow,
he was all ears for what she was saying and if it was
the taciturn Brigitte, then he was all eyes for what
he saw. There was something in this relationship
which, in spite of the fact that neither woman and
especially Brigitte, was particularly interesting, continually stimulated Holk, even although he had long
since solved the Hansen problem and there was no
longer any question of mystery. The Emperor of
Siam was becoming a more and more shadowy figure,
the 'security authority', on the other hand, less and
less so. Everything was exactly as Pentz had related,
although appearances were preserved, as well as those
small attentions which the two women both cleverly
adapted to Holk's taste, and so it came about that
Holk looked forward to these meetings with pleasur-
able anticipation, especially since he felt that they
had ceased to hold any further danger for him. Was
he aware of the real reason why all danger had
ceased? He may not have realized it himself but
others saw only too clearly that the reason was
Ebba.

Politically, meanwhile, everything continued
quietly on its course. No new campaign was planned
until the beginning of December and the Princess
opined that this time, if only for reasons of ex-
pediency, they should give way before the attack:
the moment Hall had gone, the country would realize
the sort of man they were losing. The Princess's
court naturally adopted the same view and Holk was
on the point of writing to Christine in this sense and

explaining Hall's statesmanlike intentions to her, when Pentz came in.

'Well, Pentz, what gives me the honour so early in the day?'

'Great news.'

'Louis Napoleon's dead?'

'More important than that.'

'Tivoli must have been burnt down or the Nielsen woman has caught a cold?'

'Something between the two: tomorrow we are going to Fredericksborg.'

'We? Who are "we"?'

'The Princess and all her suite.'

'So soon?'

'Yes. The Princess never does anything by halves and once she has decided to do something, then, if possible, it's no sooner said than done. I confess that I would rather have stayed here. You don't know Fredericksborg yet because, as a Danish gentleman-in-waiting, you have shown persistent negligence in your duty of learning all about Danish castles. And since you don't yet know Fredericksborg, you will be able to bear it for three days at least or if you want to study various sorts of gewgaws from bewigged portraits to Runic inscriptions, you might even manage to hold out for three weeks. There is a good deal of that sort of thing to be seen there: an ivory comb belonging to Thyra Danebod, a head of hair dressed *à la chinoise* belonging to Gorm the Old, and a peculiarly shaped molar in respect of which scholars are undecided as to whether it comes from Harold Bluetooth or a boar of the alluvial age. Personally, I favour the first theory. After all, what's a boar? It's really nothing at all, if only because the

only thing of importance is what is in the historical
commentary in the catalogue and while there is
usually very little one can find to say about a boar,
there's a great deal to say about an almost legendary
Viking. I believe I'm right in assuming your interest
in such things and as a genealogist, you will no doubt
be able to establish the consanguinity of Harold
Bluetooth and Ragnor Lodbrok or perhaps even
with Rolf Krake.[1] So, as far as you are concerned,
Holk, everything is provided but as for me, I am
rather for Lucile Grahn and Vincent's and if there is
nothing else, even for an ordinary everyday Harlequin
pantomime.'

'I can well believe it,' laughed Holk.

'Yes, you may laugh, Holk, but we shall see. A
moment ago, I was saying three weeks; well, three
weeks may be all right, but six, or more exactly
seven—because the Princess makes no concessions
and will have no confidence in the New Year unless
she has buried the old one in Fredericksborg—as I
was saying, seven weeks will presumably be too long
even for you, in spite of the fact that Pastor Schleppegrell is a character and his brother-in-law, Doctor
Bie, a buffoon. Don't misunderstand me, incidentally,
I'm not underrating the value, in certain circumstances, of characters or, even more, of buffoons;
but for seven weeks that is really not quite enough.
And if it is not snowing, it's raining and when it is
doing neither, there's a storm. I've often heard
weather-vanes squeaking and gutters and lightning-
conductors rattling but squeaks and rattles such as are
heard at Fredericksborg cannot be found anywhere

---

[1] Thyra, her husband Gorm and their son Harold Bluetooth date
from the tenth century, Rolf Krake from the sixth.

else in the world. And if you are lucky, you may see a ghost as well and if it is not a dead princess, it will be a live lady-in-waiting or a lady from the court with piercing pale-blue eyes.'

'Ah, Pentz, you can't say a word without doing that poor girl some injustice, because the lady with the pale-blue eyes must certainly be Ebba Rosenberg. If you weren't sixty-five and if I didn't know that you worship at the feet of other gods, I should really believe that you were in love with Ebba.'

'I leave that to others.'

'To Erichsen?'

'Yes, of course, to Erichsen.' And he gave a guffaw.

The following day, at noon exactly, two carriages halted in front of the Princess's palace; her servants had left with the luggage an hour earlier by the train for Elsinore. The Princess and her suite took the same seats in the two carriages as on the return journey from the Hermitage; in the first carriage sat the Princess with Countess Schimmelmann and Ebba; in the second, the three men. It was a sunless day and massive grey clouds were moving across the sky. But the tone that these clouds gave to the landscape only emphasized its charm and as the carriages drove along the edge of Lake Fure, Ebba stood up in her seat and could hardly contain her delight at the sight of the gently rippling steel-grey surface which the gulls were almost brushing with their wings as they swooped low over it. All along the edge of the lake were thick banks of rushes extending far out into the water and now and again there were a few weeping willows with their leafless branches overhanging the water. On the other side of the lake ran a dark ridge of woodland, from which a high church tower emerged. Everything was completely still and the silence was only broken by an occasional shot in the wood or the rumble of a passing train half a mile away.

Ebba, too, was making this journey for the first time. 'I don't know the south,' she said, 'but it can't be more beautiful than this. Everything seems so mysterious, as if every inch of earth held some story or secret. I feel as if sacrifices used to be made here, or perhaps still are; even those weird-shaped clouds overhead seem to know all the secrets of the earth.'

The Princess laughed: 'What a romantic young woman I have brought with me! Who would have thought it: my dear Ebba suffering from an attack of Ossian![1] Or if I may venture a play on words, Ebba in pursuit of the Edda.'[2]

Ebba smiled, for even she felt rather strange in her romantic role; but the Princess continued: 'And all because of Lake Fure, which is only a lake like hundreds of others. Wait until we reach our destination in Fredericksborg, with Lake Esrom on the right and Lake Arre on the left, the great Lake Arre which joins up with the Kattegat and the North Sea. And it never freezes over except in the narrows and bays. But why am I talking about the lakes, the main thing is the castle itself, my dear old Fredericksborg with its gables and towers and hundreds of marvellous carvings on every keystone and capital. And where other castles just have ordinary drain-pipes, at Fredericksborg the gutter projects ten feet and at

[1] A Celtic bard, an alleged translation of whose works by Macpherson was extremely popular in the eighteenth century.

[2] A collection of Norse sagas, one of whose authors was Sturleson (see p. 228).

each end there's a crouching basilisk with its mouth
wide open and three iron bars across it and the water
gushes out between them down into the courtyard.
And then, when the weather changes and the full
moon is shining white and bright over everything
and all is silent and uncanny and this devilish sort of
menagerie stares at you from every corner and pro-
jection as if they were only biding their time, then
you can't repress a shudder. But it is that shudder
that makes me love the castle so much.'

'I thought that Fredericksborg was one of the
"good" castles, without any ghosts, because there
had never been any murders or stabbings or even
anything guilty or evil about it at all.'

'No, there I'm afraid that you are expecting more
than my lovely Fredericksborg can offer. No blood
or murder, that may be true; but guilt and evil!
My dear Ebba, what house a hundred years old can
possibly be without guilt or evil? At the moment, it
is true that I can't recall any episodes involving shud-
dering and moaning but I'm sure that there has been
plenty of guilt and sin.'

'I'm almost tempted to venture to contradict Your
Highness,' said Countess Schimmelmann. 'I think
Ebba is right when she talks of a "good" castle. Our
dear Fredericksborg is, after all, really a museum
and a museum, to my mind, is the most innocent
thing . . .'

'. . . that exists,' laughed the Princess. 'Yes, people
say so and, as a rule, I suppose it is so. But there are
exceptions. Altars and sacristies and tombs and
naturally even museums—all such things can be
desecrated and they have all known what it is to
suffer sacrilege. And then there is always the question

of what is kept and exhibited in a museum. There are often strange and wonderful things which I would hardly call innocent or, at least, they are quite sad and gloomy. As a young girl, I was once in London and there I saw the axe with which Anne Boleyn was beheaded. That was in a museum too, in the Tower of London, it's true, but that doesn't really make any difference, a museum is a museum. But anyway, we must not spoil our loveliest castle for Ebba, our loveliest and my favourite as well, for in all these years I have never failed to enjoy staying there. And in any case, grim and ghostly or not, at least you, Ebba, will feel safe there, because I have decided that you shall lodge in the tower.'

'In the tower?'

'Indeed, in the tower, but not in a tower of serpents, because your Swedish maid is going to live underneath and Holk above you. I think that should reassure you. And every morning when you go to the tower window, you will have the most beautiful view over the lake and the town and the courtyard and everything surrounding you and if all my wishes come true, you are going to be very, very happy in your historic keep. And I have already decided what I shall give you for Christmas.'

Whilst talking, they had already passed well beyond the north-east corner of Lake Fure and as they drove along the almost straight causeway, with its clumps of mountain ash still bearing their clusters of red berries, gradually they drew near to their destination. Their first indication was not the castle itself but the little town of Hillerød, situated on the outskirts, and when they were almost there and already

driving between the mills and barns of the village, a
slight flurry of snow began to fall; but a sudden
breeze as quickly drove the snow-flakes away and
when the Princess's carriage reached the market-
place, the weather suddenly cleared and a patch of
blue sky was seen above the pale evening glow; and
against this glow were silhouetted the lofty towers of
the castle of Fredericksborg, mirrored, silent and
fairy-like, in a small lake that lay between the town
and the castle. Beyond the castle was the park and
some of its trees came right down to the edge of the
lake on both sides, magnificent plane trees whose
leaves, blown by autumn gales, lay thickly scattered
over the still surface of the water. Meanwhile the
second carriage had also arrived and Holk, who had
wisely chosen to sit beside the coachman, jumped
down and went to the Princess's carriage door to tell
her how idyllic and rustic he found the market-place
and how beautiful the castle, a remark which mani-
festly pleased the Princess who would certainly have
made a gracious reply, if at the same moment another
man had not come out of a near-by house and gone
up to her carriage door.

This other man was Schleppegrell, the pastor of
Hillerød, an imposing man in his fifties whose portly
stateliness was greatly enhanced by his long, flowing
clerical robe. He kissed the Princess's hand with more
gallantry than devotion and ceremoniously expressed
his pleasure at seeing his patroness again.

'You know how indispensable you are,' said the
Princess, 'and I have only stopped on your horribly
draughty market-place, where it is blowing a gale
from all directions at once, as far as I can see, I have
only stopped to make sure that you come and visit us

this very evening. . . . But I am forgetting to introduce you gentlemen . . . Pastor Schleppegrell, Count Holk.'

The two men bowed.

'And you must be forbearing and well-disposed, my dear Pastor. Count Holk is a genealogist and thus something of an historian and as such, and as an excellent questioner, he will give you the opportunity of learned conversation. You always have the best conversation when there is someone asking questions and someone else replying to them. You know how inquisitive I am myself; I would not exchange my curiosity for anything. And do bring your dear wife with you. The only time I like to drink tea in Hilleröd and Fredericksborg is when my dear friend from the vicarage has poured it out. Yes, Ebba, that is the truth and you must accept it and not be jealous. But I see that I am falling into another sin of omission . . . Pastor Schleppegrell, Fräulein Ebba von Rosenberg.'

The pastor greeted the young woman and promised not only to come but to bring his wife; and the party then left the market-place to continue their way up to the castle, after Holk, in obedience to the Princess's command, had taken the front seat in her own carriage for the short remaining stretch. Here, he found himself sitting next to Ebba opposite Countess Schimmelmann, and felt sufficiently stimulated to make a further attempt at conversation.

'Pastor Schleppegrell has a very stately appearance and yet, at the same time, a sort of cheerfulness that prevents him from being overbearing. I have rarely seen a man so calm and self-assured when talking to royalty. Is he a Democrat? Or a general Dissenter?'

'No,' laughed the Princess, 'Schleppegrell is not a

general Dissenter, although he is in fact the brother of a real general, General Schleppegrell, who was killed at Idstedt. Perhaps it was just at the right time, because it was de Meza who took over from him.'

'Ah,' said Holk, 'that explains it.'

'No, my dear Holk, I am afraid that I must contradict you once again. That doesn't explain it at all. What you call his self-assurance springs from quite another reason. When he was twenty years old he came to court as a teacher—a teacher of religion, in fact—to several young princesses and the rest you can imagine. He has seen too many young princesses to be impressed by old ones. What is more, we owe a great debt of gratitude to him and to his wisdom and discretion because on three occasions the situation arose that, had he wished, he could have become a member of the family. Schleppegrell was always very sensible. Nor, by the way, do I have the heart to blame those princesses particularly. He really was a very handsome man and a good Christian—and he knew how to say no. Let anyone resist such a combination of virtues if they can.'

Holk was amused, Ebba too, and a smile even flitted across the features of the Countess. They saw that the Princess was in the best of humours and took this as a good augury for the days to come. Then, while they were still talking, the carriage drove over two narrow bridges into the castle courtyard and stopped in front of the castle door.

CHAPTER 20

SERVANTS with hurricane lamps were already waiting and hurried forward as the Princess mounted the broad horseshoe staircase towards her suite of apartments, not very extensive, in the middle of the castle and flanked by the two towers which stood at the acute angle formed by two projecting wings joined together by a colonnade. On the first landing, on which a small rococo sofa had been placed, the asthmatic Princess rested for a moment and then dismissed the ladies and gentlemen of her suite with the injunction to make themselves as comfortable as possible in their tower rooms. At seven o'clock, she added, turning towards Holk, tea would be served as usual; Pastor Schleppegrell and his wife would be coming somewhat earlier to inform her of all the latest happenings in Hilleröd, which she was greatly looking forward to hearing: small-town gossip was always the most interesting, for it made you laugh so much and to be able to laugh at your dear fellow beings was really the greatest enjoyment in your old age. With these gracious words they parted, and half an hour later anyone passing through the courtyard could easily have recognized which of the rooms had been occupied by the new arrivals. On the first floor of the main building, in the rooms occupied by the Princess herself, there could be seen only two dimly-lit Gothic windows while the two side-towers shone brilliantly from top to bottom. Everything had been arranged more or less according to the Princess's instructions: on the ground floor lodged the maids, on the first floor the two ladies-in-waiting, with

Pentz and Erichsen above Countess Schimmelmann and Holk above Ebba.

Seven o'clock was approaching and as the castle clock struck the half-hour, the Schleppegrells came across the moat from Hilleröd, preceded by a maid with a lantern. Soon afterwards Holk, too, made himself ready. In the hall of the tower that he was occupying, he met Karin, Ebba's maid from Stockholm and almost one of her friends. She informed him that Ebba was already with the Princess. From the hall to the main body of the castle was not far, and a minute later Holk was climbing the stairs to enter the high gallery that served as reception and drawing-room when the Princess was in residence. This gallery had only a narrow frontage on the courtyard as on the park at the back of the castle; but it was, nevertheless, a large room. In the middle of one of the side-walls was a tall Renaissance fireplace above which hung a picture, larger than life, of King Christian IV, who had always been very fond of Fredericksborg and, like the Princess, had preferred this gallery to any other room in the castle. To the left of the fireplace were baskets filled partly with big logs and partly with pine-cones and juniper branches, while to the right, apart from an immense poker, lay a pile of resinous pine-torches for lighting departing guests through the dark corridors. All the decoration of the gallery was still half medieval, like the gallery itself, on whose panels, in addition to the portrait of King Christian, were hanging huge pictures brown with age. At the very back stood a sideboard and, in place of the usual high chairs, a number of modern arm-chairs were arranged round the hearth.

Holk bowed as he approached the Princess and said how beautiful the gallery was and what a wonderful Yuletide they would be able to celebrate there, for nothing was lacking, not only the pine-torches but the pine-cones and juniper as well. The Princess replied that she was intending to hold just such a celebration; Christmas in Fredericksborg was the best day of the year and, after adding that she had already arranged a kind of pre-Yuletide celebration for tomorrow, she invited Frau Schleppegrell to take her seat beside her. The pastor's wife was a short, stout woman with red cheeks and black hair piled up on top of her head, extremely plain but quite indifferent to the fact, being one of those happy people who are completely unconcerned about themselves and, least of all, about their personal appearance. Ebba had sensed this at once and taken an immediate liking to her.

'Do you not find it difficult to leave your children for a whole evening, Frau Schleppegrell?' she asked.

'We haven't any children,' replied the pastor's wife with such a guffaw that the Princess asked what was the matter. There followed such general amusement that even Schleppegrell had eventually to join in, albeit rather wryly, since the laughter was primarily at his expense. Noting this, Holk felt that he ought to change the conversation and, in a jocular and apparently casual tone, he asked about the portrait over the fireplace. 'I notice that it is of King Christian and so it's difficult for anyone to be particularly interested in it, because his portrait must be *de rigueur* almost everywhere. May I ask who painted it? I should have guessed a Spaniard, if I had known that we had a Spanish painter in Copenhagen at that time.'

Schleppegrell was about to reply when Ebba broke in: 'If we are going to start talking about art and pictures, it is absolutely forbidden to begin with a picture of King Christian, even if it is by a Spaniard, which I venture to doubt, like Count Holk, whose opinions I frequently share—at least in artistic matters. So I propose that we leave the unavoidable king alone. Personally, I should prefer to know who those two are.' She pointed towards the opposite wall. 'The old man with the pointed beard and the grand lady with the white hood.'

'The man with the beard is Admiral Herluf Trolle from whom King Frederick II bought this castle, or rather exchanged it with him and then named it Fredericksborg after himself. Not one single stone of the old castle was left standing and nothing was taken over except these pictures here on the right and the left commemorating the great naval victory of Oeland in 1559 under Admiral Herluf Trolle and, in addition to those murals, the two portraits between them, one of Herluf Trolle himself and the other of Brigitte Goje, his dearly beloved wife, who because of her Protestant piety was almost more celebrated than her husband.'

'Which is not surprising if she really was so devout,' said Pentz emphatically, 'because although I am sure that actresses and mistresses of the great are the most popular figures, immediately after them come the devout and I am not certain if they are not sometimes even slightly ahead.'

'Yes, sometimes,' laughed Ebba. 'Sometimes but not often. And now, pastor, what is this about

Herluf Trolle's naval battle? I'm afraid that it must
have been fought against my dear compatriots the
Swedes, although to judge by the costume, it took
place in a pre-Rosenbergian era and so my patriotism
is not too closely involved. And a naval battle at that!
In naval battles, friend and foe alike are always
drowning and a charitable cloud of smoke hangs over
everything so that a plus or minus quantity of dead,
which people call victory or defeat, can never
properly be ascertained. And especially where, in
addition to the gun-smoke, you have a three hundred
year old coating of dust and grime.'

'And yet,' said Holk, 'it seems to me that everything is still more or less recognizable and if we can
perhaps look more closely . . . but where can we find
the necessary light to do that . . .?'

'Here,' said the Princess, pointing to where the
pine-torches were lying. 'There will be a certain
amount of smut but that will only increase the
illusion and if our pastor and cicerone is in good form
today, then we shall surely be able to fight this naval
battle all over again. So, Schleppegrell, to work and
do your very best, we owe that much to an historian
of Holk's calibre. And we shall perhaps even convert
him from his Schleswig-Holsteinism to Danism.'

Everyone agreed and Pentz ironically applauded
with two fingers. Schleppegrell, himself a passionate
picture-lover, took one of the large torches and having
lit it, went over to the left-hand side of the picture
on which there could be discerned, in a dim yet harsh
light, the sails of a number of vessels, flags, pennants,
gilded figure-heads and the white crests of waves
but no trace of fighting or gun-smoke.

'But surely that is not a battle!' said Ebba.

'No, but the preparations for it. The fighting is still to come, on the other side, immediately to the right, beside Brigitte Goje.'

'Oh,' said Ebba, 'I understand: a double battle-painting, beginning and end. Now, I am all eyes and ears. And each time your torch passes in front of Herluf Trolle's flagship, you must give him—or me— half a minute for a curtsey so that I can impress him on my mind, even in the heat of battle.'

'You will hardly succeed in doing that,' said the Princess. 'Herluf Trolle is hidden in too much gun-smoke or has sunk in the general gloom and you will have to be satisfied with his proper portrait. But now you must begin, Schleppegrell, and give us good measure, not so short that we want a great deal more and not so long that we start casting anxious glances at each other. Holk is the expert but, thank Heaven, not the sort to embarrass anyone; he knows that art is difficult.'

During these kind words, Schleppegrell had once more approached the circle of people gathered round the fireplace and said: 'Your Royal Highness commands and I obey. What we can see here' and he pointed to the second half of the great wall-painting, which was not illuminated even by the reflection from the fire, 'what we can see here is the decisive moment when the *Immaculate* blew up.'

'The *Immaculate*?'

'Yes, the *Immaculate*. That was, in fact, the flag-ship of the Swedes, who just at this period stood at the zenith of their power, in spite of their mad king, Eric XIV. And so our ships sailed against the Swedes and their powerful fleet, superior to ours in size and possessing other large vessels in addition to the

Immaculate. Our commander was the great Herluf
Trolle. And when he came out of the bay of Kjöge
into the open sea, he steered sharply east towards
Bornholm where he suspected the Swedish fleet to
be hiding. However, it was no longer at Bornholm but
off Stralsund under Admiral Bagge. And as soon as
Jacob Bagge had perceived that the Danes were
searching for him, he weighed anchor and sailed
north-east against the enemy; and close off Oeland
the two fleets met and a three-day battle was joined,
the like of which the Baltic had never seen. And on the
third day, it seemed as if the Swedes would be vic-
torious. Then Herluf Trolle, whose own ship was
in sorry shape, summoned his second-in-command
Admiral Otto Rud and gave him the order to board
the *Immaculate* at all costs. Delighted to receive such
an order, Otto Rud sailed towards the enemy, but
hardly had his ship, which was only small, thrown its
grappling-irons, than Admiral Jacob Bagge had all
sails set on the *Immaculate* in order to tow the small
Danish ship attached to him into the midst of the
Swedish fleet. That was a difficult moment for Otto
Rud but he still did not delay his assault with the
boarding-party and when a number of our men had
crossed, one of them shot a fire-shell into the armoury
and a fire broke out which reached the powder-room
and the *Immaculate* blew up with friend and foe and
Klaus Flemming took over the command of the
Swedes and led the rest of the fleet back to Stockholm.'

There was a short silence and then Holk said:
'But the real hero of that story seems to me to be Otto
Rud. However, I should not like to argue about it
and no doubt Herluf Trolle had some part in it; what

I should like to know is, what became of him and how
he met his death.'

'As befitted a hero, he died the following year from
a wound received in an engagement off the Pomeranian coast. The wound was not in itself a fatal one
but it was during that remarkable war in which everyone who received a wound, whether slight or serious,
died from it. At least, that is what the history books
say.'

Pentz suggested poisoned bullets but Ebba rejected
this (Sweden was not a country of poisoners!) and
added that she would rather hear something about
Brigitte Goje, for the pastor had already said that
she was almost more famous than her husband.
'I don't see why we are always concerned with husbands or even with their naval battles; the story of
their wives is usually much more interesting and
perhaps even in this case. What was the story of
Brigitte?'

'She was very beautiful.'

'That seems to go with the name,' said Ebba, with
a glance at Holk. 'But beauty doesn't stand for much
when you're dead.'

'And by her very beauty,' continued Schleppegrell,
unperturbed, 'she became the pillar of the new faith,
so that some say that without Brigitte Goje, Denmark
would have remained wrapped in Popish darkness.'

'How terrible. And how did it happen?'

'It was a time of religious strife and the Danish
nobility and high clergy were opposed to our people,
who at that time were already following the new doctrine. Above all Joachim Rönnov, Bishop of Röskilde,
wished to extinguish the flame and exile the weaker
and poorer Lutheran clergy, in spite of the fact that

they were already numerous. Then Brigitte Goje went to the bishop and pleaded that the oppressed Lutherans be allowed to stay and, moved by her beauty, he withdrew his edict and his heart and soul were so touched that he asked Brigitte's father, Moga Goje, for his daughter's hand in marriage.'

'Is that possible?' said the Princess. 'A Catholic bishop!'

Schleppegrell smiled. 'Perhaps he wanted to borrow this much at least from the new doctrine, just as they did in England. In any case, we have accounts of the wooing of this beautiful young woman as detailed as if they were accounts of the wedding ceremony itself.'

'And did it come to marriage?'

'No, it came to nothing and she eventually married Herluf Trolle.'

'She was right. Wasn't she, Ebba?'

'Perhaps, your Highness, and perhaps not. I am not really one for bishops, but when they are exceptional bishops like this one of Röskilde, then I am not sure whether they don't rank higher than heroes. A bishop who wants to marry seems to me to have some amenable qualities, quite apart from his episcopal grandeur, and I wonder if he might not have been the sort of man to bring about a reconciliation between the churches.'

The tiny pastor's wife was delighted at this remark and came up to whisper a small declaration of her affection in Ebba's ear. But before she could do so, the scene was transformed as tables, already laid, were carried in through a low side-door at the far end of the gallery and, immediately afterwards, double-branched candelabra were placed on them, brightly illuminating the half of the gallery that had hitherto been totally in darkness and considerably enhancing the splendour, not only of the room, but especially of the huge wall-paintings, with the two portraits in between.

It was Pentz who first noticed this. 'Look how Brigitte Goje is smiling, Holk. All Brigittes have something strange about them, even when they are devout . . .'

Holk laughed. The day had passed when such a remark would have embarrassed him.

CHAPTER 21

THE company remained together until eleven, but, in spite of this, Holk insisted on accompanying the Schleppegrells for part of their way home. This offer was gratefully accepted and Holk went with them to where the path went round the end of the lake. He had left Erichsen to accompany Ebba, much to her amazement.

From the point of the lake back to the castle was not very far, but far enough to justify Holk's astonishment when, on climbing the tower-stairs to his room, he found Erichsen and Ebba still in lively conversation at the door of her room. But his surprise was not of long duration, for it was quite obvious that Ebba had only detained the poor baron in order to make it plain to Holk that she was not accustomed to finding herself neglected for anyone and least of all for the provincial Schleppegrells. 'Ah, we meet again,' she said addressing the count as, with a polite smile, he tried to go past her and Erichsen. 'Oh dear, those Schleppegrells . . . and particularly the pastor! As a young man, the Princess assured me, he used to win every heart with his apostle's head and now, in his old age, he does it with Herluf Trolle. I can't really consider it an improvement.'

With these words she made a bow and went into her room, where Karin was awaiting her.

It was morning and the sun was shining brightly through the window, as it does only on November mornings; but the night had been very stormy. A south-easter had made the lightning-conductor, which ran down the side of the tower, rattle furiously all night, but even more disturbing had been the moon which, despite the storm, had shone straight on to Holk's bed, although it stood in a deep recess in the wall. He could have protected himself from its strange effect by drawing the blinds, but that went even more against the grain; he wanted at least to be able to see what it was outside that was depriving him of his sleep. Towards morning, he fell into an uneasy slumber disturbed by frightening dreams. Blown up with the *Immaculate*, he had just seized a piece of mast to save himself when Ebba emerged like a mermaid from the other side, tore him from the mast and hurled him back into the water. At this point he awoke. He recalled his dream and said to himself: 'She would have been quite capable of it.'

He was about to follow up this train of thought when he was prevented by the arrival, with his breakfast, of an old gardener who acted as a house-servant whenever the Princess had guests in the castle and who apologized, as he laid the table, for being so late.

Fräulein von Rosenberg had already expressed her disapproval, he said, and rightly so, but it would soon be different, things were not yet properly organized. While talking, he handed Holk his newspapers and a letter. Holk took it and saw that there was no postmark. 'No,' said the gardener, 'it didn't come through the post. Pastor Schleppegrell sent it by hand and another one for the Fräulein.' And the old man departed.

'Ah, from Pastor Schleppegrell,' said Holk, when he was alone. 'Splendid. I'm curious to know what he has to say.'

But his curiosity could not have been over-strong, for he put the letter on one side while he finished his appetizing breakfast and then picked it up again and sat down at his writing-table, in a rocking-chair that hardly seemed to match the other furniture in the room.

My dear Count,

Your kind interest in my friend Herluf Trolle has encouraged me to send you a fragment of a ballad concerning this hero which I found some time ago and have translated from the old Danish. It is hardly necessary for me to ask for tolerance on behalf of this ballad, because whenever we read something with love, we are bound to read with indulgence. At about eleven o'clock, my wife and I intend to fetch you and Fräulein von Rosenberg (whom I am informing at the same time as you) for a walk in the park together, perhaps towards Fredensborg. We shall hardly be able to go more than a third of the way but it is the first third that is particularly lovely, lovelier at this season than perhaps at any other. We shall be back at twelve noon, so that we may appear punctually before

our gracious mistress the Princess to partake of her festive lunch, for it will undoubtedly be a minor feast.

Your devoted and respectful
Arvid Schleppegrell

Enclosed with the letter was a pink sheet of paper
covered with verses in a feminine hand. 'Ah, presumably the handwriting of my tiny friend the
pastor's wife. She seems to be one of those kind
people who believe in making themselves useful by
doing favours, because I can hardly imagine that she
nourishes a personal passion for Herluf Trolle. But
be that as it may, I'm curious to know how Pastor
Schleppegrell has christened his piece.' He picked
up the pink sheet and glanced at the title, which
read: *The Burial of Admiral Herluf Trolle.* 'Excellent,
at least we know what it's all about'; and he pushed
his rocking-chair up to the window and read:

> *Ein Bote mit Meldung ritt ihnen voraus.*
> *Und als in den Schloßhof sie schritten,*
> *Brigitte stand vor dem Trauerhaus*
> *In ihrer Frauen Mitten.*[1]

'Ah, that must be Brigitte Goje, his pious wife
whom we heard all about yesterday; pious and pretty
and as hard as a stone towards the Bishop of Röskilde.
But let us see what Schleppegrell has to say about
her in his ballad.'

> *Am Eingange stand sie, grüßte den Zug,*
> *Aufrecht und ungebrochen,*
> *Und der Erste (der das Bahrtuch trug)*
> *Trat vor und hat gesprochen:*

[1] A courier rode ahead with the message and as they came into the
courtyard, Brigitte stood before the house of mourning surrounded by
her women.

'Was geschehen, wir sandten die Meldung dir,
Eh' den Weg wir selber gingen,
Seine Seel' ist frei, seine Hüll' ist hier,
Du weißt, wen wir dir bringen.

An der pommerschen Küste vor Pudagla-Golm
Um den schwankenden Sieg uns zu retten,
So fiel er. Nun Herrin von Herlufsholm
Sage, wohin wir ihn betten.

'Betten wir ihn in den Toten-Saal
Von Thorslund oder Olafskirke ?
Betten wir ihn in den Gjeddesdal
Unter der Trauerbirke ?[1]

'Betten wir ihn in die Kryptkapell'n
In Röskilde, Leire, Ringstede ?
Sage, Herrin, wohin wir ihn stell'n
Eine Ruhestatt für ihn hat jede.

'Jeder Kirche gab er, um was sie bat,
Altäre, Türme, Glocken,
Und jede, wenn sie hört, "er naht",
Wird in Leide frohlocken.

'Eine jede ladet ihn zu sich ein
In ihrer Pfeiler Schatten . . .'
—Da sprach Brigitte: 'Hier soll es sein,
Hier wollen wir ihn bestatten.

---

[1] She stood at the entrance and greeted the procession, upright and steadfast, and the first man, the pall-bearer, stepped forward and spoke: 'We have sent the tidings before us on the way. His soul is free, his body lies here, you know whom we are bringing. On the Pomeranian coast off Pudagla-Golm, when victory was uncertain, he fell to ensure it. Now mistress of Herlufsholm, tell us where we are to lay him to rest. Shall we lay him to rest in the burial vault of Thorslund or Olaf's church? or in the valley of Gjeddes beneath the weeping-birch?'

'Wohl hat er hier keine Kirche gebaut
—Die stand schon viel hundert Jahre—
Hier aber, als Herluf Trolles Braut,
Stand ich mit ihm am Altare.

'Vor demselben Altar, auf selbem Stein,
Steh' er wieder in aller Stille,
Nichts soll dabei gesprochen sein,
Als, Herr, es geschehe Dein Wille.

'Morgen aber, eh' noch der Tag erstand,
In seinen Kirchen allen,
Weit über die See, weit über das Land,
Soll'n alle Glocken erschallen.

'Und zittert himmelan die Luft
Als ob Schlachtendonner rolle,
Dann in die Herlufsholmer Gruft
Senken wir Herluf Trolle.'[1]

Holk pushed the sheet back into the envelope and
repeated softly to himself: *'Dann in die Herlufsholmer
Gruft senken wir Herluf Trolle . . .* Hm, I like that.
I like it very much. There is no real content and it is
just a situation and not a poem but that doesn't

---

[1] Or shall we lay him to rest in the chapels in the crypts of Röskilde or
Leire or Ringstede? Say, Mistress, where shall we lay him? Each church
has a resting-place for him. He gave each church what it desired, altars,
towers, bells, and each one when they hear 'he is approaching', will
rejoice in its grief. Each one of them will invite him into the shadow of its
columns. Then Brigitte spoke: 'Here must we bring him. True, he has
built no church here, for one has been standing here for many a hundred
year, but I stood with Herluf Trolle as his bride here at the altar. Before
the same altar, on the same stone, let him lie here in peace and silence; no
word shall be spoken save that God's will be done. But tomorrow, before
the day dawns, in all his churches, far and wide over sea and land, all the
bells shall ring out and when the air resounds to heaven as if with the
thunderous roar of battle, we shall lower Herluf Trolle into his grave at
Herlufsholm.'

matter. It has a certain tone and just as the colouring makes a picture, at least my brother-in-law has assured me so more than once, in the same way the tone makes a poem. And Alfred is probably right as usual. I shall make a copy of it today and send it to Christine. Or better still, I shall send her the sheet of red paper straightaway and the fact that the poem comes from a pastor's house will be a special recommendation for her. But I must first remember to ask the little woman to write her name and above all her status on the paper, otherwise the whole thing may misfire. The pink paper is suspect enough, in any case, and that handwriting as stiff as a laundry-list, well, who could say where that comes from? Court ladies also have strange handwriting sometimes.'

Looking at his watch, he perceived that it was approaching eleven o'clock and so he interrupted his reflections. If he was going to be dressed and ready by the time the Schleppegrells appeared, he would have to hurry. What would the paths be like, incidentally? Shortly before midnight, rain had fallen, and even if the south-east wind had dried up a good deal of it, he knew from his park at Holkenäs that paths are usually difficult after rainy weather. He chose his dress accordingly and hardly was he ready than the Schleppegrells appeared in the courtyard. He called to them not to trouble to come up; he would fetch Ebba and be with them at once. Less than five minutes later, they all met at the front entrance and passed through the castle to leave by an equally imposing back entrance giving on to the park. Here they met Erichsen, who was just returning from a ninety-minute constitutional but expressed his readiness to join them for another walk, an offer which was admiringly accepted. Erichsen therefore gave his arm to Ebba, while Holk followed with the little pastor's wife, with Schleppegrell himself in the lead. As at their first meeting, he wore a voluminous, shapeless cloak, which covered him from shoulder to toe, and a soft felt hat; he carried a heavy oak stick which he brandished vigorously, when he was not throwing it up and catching it again.

Although Holk would have greatly preferred to be walking beside Ebba, he showed Frau Schleppegrell every attention and asked her, in case he should not have the opportunity of doing so himself, to express to her husband his delight at receiving the ballad; adding that he was hardly less indebted to herself, since he had no doubt that the copy had been in her hand.

'Yes,' she replied, 'We must help one another, that is really the best thing in marriage. Helping and supporting each other and, above all, showing consideration and trying to see the justice of the other's point of view. After all, what is right? It's always changing and varying. But with a good husband, it is never wrong to defer to his wishes.'

Holk made no reply and the little woman went on talking in this way, little realizing what thoughts and reflections she was arousing in his mind. The sun which, earlier on, had been shining so brightly, had now gone in, the wind had changed and a grey haze covered the sky; but such a light made the clumps of trees stand out with wonderful clarity across the wide park meadows. The air was mild yet fresh and on the slope of a sheltered terrace, various flower-beds planted with late asters could be seen; but everywhere in the hollows of the meadows there were large and

small ornamental lakes, beside which stood chalets
and summer-houses with fantastically shaped roofs
from which the leafless branches of various creepers
were hanging down. Almost every tree was bare; only
the plane trees still retained some of their foliage but
each stronger gust of wind loosened some of their long
yellow leaves, scattering them over the meadow and
the paths. At no great distance from the castle ran
a broad moat, crossed by a number of rustic birch-
wood bridges. There was no bridge, however, at the
point where Schleppegrell now reached the moat
but, instead, a ferry-boat with a rope stretched from
one bank to the other, by means of which the punt
could be effortlessly pulled across. Once across, it
was but a short distance to a small hillock from which,
as Schleppegrell assured them, they could see equally
well northwards to Fredensborg and southwards to
Fredericksborg castles. This project, however, had
to be abandoned for lack of time and they returned
by a shorter route to the castle.

Holk had not left Frau Schleppegrell's side
throughout but after they had recrossed the moat,
they changed companions. Erichsen now gave his
arm to the pastor's wife, and Holk and Ebba, who had
till now had no opportunity of talking together,
followed, lagging further and further behind.

'I was afraid that I had been sacrificed to your
latest passion,' said Ebba. 'A dangerous pair, the
Schleppegrells. The husband yesterday, today the
wife.'

'Ah, my dear Ebba, you are trying to flatter me by
casting me in the role of a Don Juan.'

'And with such a Zerlina! In fact, with Zerlina's
great-aunt. What was she talking to you about? She

seemed to be going at full speed all the time, as far as I could see . . .'

'Well, it was about all sorts of things; about Hillerōd and its life in the winter and that the town was divided into two halves, the military and the civil: one might almost imagine oneself in Germany. On the whole, a charming little woman, full of *bon sens* but also extremely simple and narrow, so that I can hardly understand how the pastor is able to bear her and even less how the Princess can spend hours chatting with her.'

Ebba laughed: 'How little you know! Everything seems to prove to me that you only have contact with princesses once in a blue moon. Believe me, there is nothing too petty to interest a princess and the more scandalous the better. Tom Jensen has gone off to India and married a native and all his daughters are black and all his sons white; and Brodersen the chemist is said to have poisoned his wife with nicotine; the second gamekeeper fell into a limekiln as he was climbing out of his sweetheart's window last night—I promise you that such things interest our Princess more than the whole Schleswig-Holstein question, in spite of the fact that some people assert that she is the life and soul of the movement.'

'Ah, Ebba, you say that because you are a born cynic and like exaggerating everything.'

'I accept your comments because I would rather be like that than the opposite. All right then, I'm a cynic and a *mauvaise langue* and anything else you like. But that still doesn't alter in the slightest what I have just said about princesses. The more intelligent and witty the great are and the better developed their feeling and eye for the ridiculous, the more quickly and surely they come to realize that bores are as nice and as amusing as interesting people.'

'And you dare to say that yourself, when you are the living proof of the opposite! What is it that has won you your place in the Princess's affections? The fact that you are intelligent and knowledgeable, full of ideas and can talk, in short, that you are more interesting than Schimmelmann.'

'No, it is simply that I am different from her and she is just as indispensable to the Princess as I am or Erichsen or Pentz or perhaps even . . .'

'. . . Holk.'

'I did not say so. But shall we stop and have a rest for a moment, even though we are a long way behind? Here's a delightful spot where we have an excellent view of the castle from the back. Just look how everything stands out so wonderfully, the main roof and the steep roofs of the towers on both sides, in spite of the fact that everything is the same colour of grey.'

'Yes,' said Holk, 'everything does stand out splendidly. But it's the light itself that is causing it and castles oughtn't to be built with such a special light in mind. Those two splendid red brick towers in which we are living should have been built higher before putting on the pointed slate or shingle roof. As it is at present, it looks as if you could go straight from the lowest dormer-window of the tower on to the big cross-roof and take a walk out along the gutter.'

Ebba merely nodded, not tempted to follow Holk in his disquisition on these structural and lighting problems, and they both began to step out, as they thought that they noticed the pastor waiting for them to catch up. As they came nearer, however,

the knot, laid the napkin down beside him and said: 'Very well then, if you order me to; there is another version which is said to be more accurate. The king used to go walking in the castle garden with Christine Munk who was his wife without being his wife, unfortunately a rather frequent occurrence in our history, and Prince Ulrich and Princess Fritz-Anna were with them both and the king was more gracious and affectionate than he had ever been before. But Christine Munk, for reasons that no one has ever yet discovered or even surmised (and perhaps there were none), was very silent and glared around so grimly and sourly that it caused great embarrassment. And the worst of the matter was that this bad temper of Christine's lasted a long time and was not over by evening, when the king wished to retire to bed, for he found the door bolted and barred and was obliged to spend the night elsewhere. And since such a thing had never happened to him before, because Christine was not only one of the best-tempered but also one of the most affectionate of women, the king decided to perpetuate the memory of this remarkable day by having his name and the date carved on the stone where this mysterious conjugal quarrel began.'

'Well,' said the Princess, 'that is certainly rather more complicated but still far from requiring me to be invoked as a bogy of prudery, as my dear Schleppegrell seems to have done this morning. And apropos of prudery, yesterday I was reading in a French book that prudery when one is no longer young and beautiful is like a scarecrow that has been left standing after the harvest. Not bad: the French understand such matters. But to return to our subject, as far as the story of King Christian's exclusion from his bedroom is concerned, I should be only too glad if all our stories of kings and princes were equally harmless, for nowadays they seem to deal mainly with the opposite process. I am sure that Count Holk shares my view. Tell me, Count, what do you think of the story?'

'To tell the truth, my dear Princess, I find it rather petty and somewhat trivial.'

'Trivial?' echoed Ebba. 'Now there you must let me join issue with you. The paying of the wages on Saturday was trivial, but not this. A grim and sour woman is never trivial and when her bad humour goes so far as to exclude her husband from her bed (I regret to have to mention this but history demands that the truth be unveiled, not hidden), then it is most definitely not trivial. I call my gracious Princess as witness and shall seek refuge in her protection. But men are like that today; King Christian had the event engraved in stone as something remarkable to go down to distant posterity and Count Holk considers it trivial and rather petty.'

Holk saw that he was being driven into a corner and realized at the same time that the Princess was clearly in a mood to support Ebba. He therefore hummed and hawed a little and tried to adopt a half serious, half ironical attitude, pointing out that in such matters one must distinguish between the private and the historical viewpoints; from the private point of view, such an event was something most regrettable and almost tragic, but for a king thus to be shut out of his wife's bedroom was something quite inadmissible which should never have taken place and if history nevertheless recorded it, then it was losing its grandeur and dignity and degenerating into what, rightly or wrongly, he described as 'petty'.

'Bravo, Holk,' cried the Princess. 'A most elegant evasion. Now Ebba, it's your turn.'

'Yes, Your Highness, I shall do as you say and if I cannot do it as a German, then I shall try to do so as a pure Scandinavian.'

Everyone was amused.

'As a pure Scandinavian,' repeated Ebba. 'Of course, on my mother's side, which is the decisive factor here. The father is never really of any importance. And now to our thesis. What was Count Holk saying? Well, from his Schleswig-Holstein point of view, he may be right in his preference for grandeur, for his protest against the petty can only mean, of course, that he prefers the grandiose. But what is this grand style exactly? It merely means ignoring everything that really interests normal people. Christine Munk interests us and her ill humour interests us and the results of that ill humour on that remarkable evening, that interests us still more . . .'

'And Fräulein Ebba interests us most of all in her saucy mood today . . .'

'Although I feel rather less saucy at the moment than I do normally. I really am being quite serious. In any case, I assert with all possible seriousness and sincerity, and I am prepared to have a vote taken in every girls' school in the country, that King Henry VIII with his six wives will carry the day in any competition concerning the grand manner, not because of his couple of beheadings, you can find those anywhere, but because of the complicated little bagatelles that preceded those executions. And after Henry VIII comes Mary Stuart and after her comes France with its plethora of heroines from Agnès Sorel onwards up to Pompadour and du Barry, and Germany lags far behind. And last of all, there comes Prussia with a complete blank in this sphere. This no doubt explains why a few women writers of genius have, in desperation, been forced to attribute half a dozen love affairs to Frederick the Great merely because they felt that, without something of the sort, it was not possible for him to be considered great.'

Pentz nodded in agreement, while Holk shook his head.

'You seem to have doubts, Count, and perhaps, above all, doubts as to my sincerity, but I am speaking nothing but the truth. The grand style! Bah, of course I know that people ought to be virtuous but they are not, and if you accept this, on the whole things are better than when morality is a mere façade. Loose living only harms morals but the pretence of being virtuous harms the whole man.'

As she was speaking, a wax angel fell from one of the Christmas trees standing round the table just where Pentz was sitting. He took it up and said: 'A fallen angel; signs and portents are occurring. Who can this be?'

'Not I,' laughed Ebba.

'No,' confirmed Pentz and the tone in which he said this made Ebba change colour. But before she could retaliate for this impertinence, a pattering of feet was heard behind the screen of firs and cypresses, orders were given in a whisper and children's voices started singing. It was a song specially composed by

Schleppegrell for this pre-Christmas celebration
which now rang out through the gallery:

> *Noch ist der Herbst nicht ganz entflohn,*
> *Aber als Knecht Rupprecht schon*
> *Kommt der Winter hergeschritten*
> *Und alsbald aus Schnees Mitten*
> *Klingt des Schlittenglöckleins Ton.*
>
> *Und was jüngst noch, fern und nah,*
> *Bunt auf uns herniedersah,*
> *Weiß sind Türme, Dächer, Zweige*
> *Und das Jahr geht auf die Neige*
> *Und das schönste Fest ist da.*[1]
>
> *Tag du der Geburt des Herrn*
> *Heute bist du uns noch fern*
> *Aber Tannen, Engel, Fahnen*
> *Lassen uns den Tag schon ahnen*
> *Und wir sehen schon den Stern.*[2]

CHAPTER 23

THIS small pre-Christmas celebration, which ended
in conversation round the fireplace, with Grundtvig
as the principal topic, lasted until dark and the company finally dispersed after being together for more

---

[1] Autumn has not yet quite gone but winter now comes striding on
already, like Santa Claus, and forthwith the tinkle of the sleigh-bells
rings out from amidst the snow. And everything that we last saw in all
their colours near and far, towers and roofs and boughs are now white
and the old year is on the turn and the loveliest feast is nigh.

[2] Day of our Lord's birth, you are distant still today but pine trees,
angels and flags lead us to expect you soon and we can even now see the
star.

than six hours. The Princess withdrew to her rooms and Holk once again accompanied the Schleppegrells, this time, however, as far as the town itself, and returned to his tower-room, after having given his word to visit the pastor's house next time he was free in order to see Schleppegrell's collection. Returning to his room, he wrote several letters, to Asta, Axel, and to Fräulein Dobschütz. He had received a note from the latter on the previous day, just before the departure of the court for Fredericksborg; in it she informed him that Christine would not be writing, as she was unwell. It cannot be claimed that this information caused Holk much disappointment. Although he was aware of his wife's love of the truth, he said to himself: 'She must be in a bad temper and calls it being unwell. If one wants, one can always become ill and enjoy the privilege of being able to justify any whim.'

Next morning was again bright and cloudless; the air was still and Holk, who was to report for duty at noon, was sitting by the window looking over to Hilleröd church with its weather-cock glittering in the sun. All the houses lay still and silent, the roofs spick and span, and but for the smoke rising from the chimney-pots, one might have thought that the whole town was under a spell. No trace of any people. 'How happy one would be to live amid such quiet,' he said to himself; and then, realizing that Holkenäs was just as quiet, he added: 'Yes, as quiet but not as peaceful. How I envy the pastor the life he leads! He has his parish, his prehistoric tombs, his excavations in the peat, quite apart from Herluf Trolle, and he lets the world go on its way. Hilleröd is his world. It's true that no one can know what his inner life is like. He seems so restful, so limpid, so completely at peace, but is he? Even if it is true that three princesses fell in love with him one after the other, or perhaps all together, his present idyllic existence seems to me a doubtful sort of happiness as the outcome of it all. Marrying a princess is an even more doubtful happiness, I know, but when you have been prudent enough to avoid it and then have only the provincialism of Hillerød as sole reward for your pains, you must often feel a sort of yearning for the past. An excellent little woman, that dumpling of a wife but quite unsuited to help a man like Schleppegrell to forget the past. After all, everyone has his particular form of vanity and pastors are said not to be deficient in this respect.'

He continued musing in this strain for a while and, while doing so, went once more over all the events and experiences of the past twenty-four hours: the walk towards Fredericksborg, the ferry with the cable to cross the moat, the wonderful view of the back of the castle with its steep roof and its towers and finally the stone inscription and his conversation with Ebba. 'Ebba never speaks with any affection for the Princess, which is another proof that wit and gratitude make bad bed-fellows. If she wants to say something caustic, then she says it, and any sense of obligation is buried and forgotten. I don't want to bring up the Stockholm affair again, it's better to let the matter rest, although there may well be grounds for gratitude there as well; but even now, when the Princess is spoiling her so thoroughly in all that she says or does, Ebba merely takes everything for granted, not only as something quite normal, but almost as if she feels herself superior to the Princess. But she is not superior, it's merely that the Princess is less sophisticated in her way of speaking. For example, when we were talking about old Grundtvig yesterday, how excellent were all the remarks she made, from the wealth of her wide experience—which reminds me that I might use them as a postscript for my letter to Julie, since it turned out to be a trifle thin, in any case.'

He sat down at the desk beside the window and wrote on the side that was still blank: 'A short postscript, my dear Julie. Amongst other subjects of conversation yesterday was Grundtvig. Schleppegrell was trying to make him out to be a plaster-saint, in which he was supported, ironically of course, by Pentz and Fräulein Rosenberg. But the Princess took it all quite seriously and said: "Grundtvig is an important person whom we have a right to be proud of, as Danes. But he has one fault: he always tries to hold aloof and dissociate himself from the rest of mankind, even including the Danes, and though people say that his opinion of Denmark is so high that he seriously believes that God speaks Danish, yet I am certain that if that opinion were ever to be generally accepted, from that day forth he would endeavour to maintain and prove conclusively that God doesn't speak Danish but Prussian. Grundtvig can't bear to find anyone agreeing with him!" This gives an excellent idea, my dear Julie, of the tone of our conversation at table and in the evening and I add this little postscript to my letter with all reservations, because I know how great is Christine's interest in pastoral anecdotes and theological controversy. And the question as to God's private language surely comes under that heading, I think. Once again, my heartiest greetings. I shall write to Christine to-morrow, if only a few lines.'

He had just placed this letter, and those to Asta and Axel, in their envelopes when there was a knock on the door. 'Come in!' But the knock was merely repeated and Holk went to see who it was. Outside stood Karin, looking embarrassed, although em-barrassment was the least of her accomplishments. She handed Holk some papers and letters which the postman had, in his hurry, left below with Fräulein Ebba, to save time. Fräulein Ebba sent her compli-ments and was planning to take a walk with Baron Pentz as far as 'the stone'; the Count would know which stone she meant. Holk smiled, made his excuses, and sat down again to see what the latest post had brought. He pushed aside the newspapers as being not very promising, in view of the momen-tary political calm, and examined the addresses on the letters. They were all easily recognizable: one was from Petersen, another from his gardener, and the last from his brother-in-law Arne, as the Arnewieck postmark testified.

'From Alfred? What can he want? He usually interprets his free hand as major-domo broadly enough not to bother me with any queries. And it's a good thing that he does and, in general, is the sort of man that he is, for I've no desire while I am here to be worried about wool-prices and how many fat sheep are to be shipped to England. That's his business or Christine's and both of them know more about it than I do; the Arnes have always been big farmers, which is more than I can say of the Holks; I've never really done much more than play at farming. So what does he want?' Realizing the pointlessness of further conjecture, he took the letter and slit open the envelope with a small ivory paper-knife, slowly because he had a premonition that the letter contained nothing very agreeable.

He read:

Dear Helmut,

As you know, I have deliberately refrained from bothering you in Copenhagen with any business matters from Holkenäs, nor has it hitherto been necessary, since your own easy-going nature makes it easy to be in charge in your stead. You not only have the happy gift of agreeing with everything that others want to do, but the even happier one, in an emergency, of allowing two and two to make five. Let me therefore say straight away, in advance, that I am not writing to you on any pressing matters of management and even less do I wish to go over with you again all my special plans, with which you are in general already familiar: Shorthorns rather than Oldenburgers (milk production has gone too far) and Southdowns rather than Rambouillets. Why worry about wool? An out-dated conception which may suit Lüneburg heath but not us. The London cattle-market is the only one worth considering for such produce as ours. Meat, and yet more meat! But no more of that. I am writing to you on more important matters, about Christine. As Fräulein Dobschütz will already have informed you, Christine is ill, whether seriously or not depends on how you view it. She doesn't need sending to Carlsbad or to Nice but she is none the less ill, ill in her mind, and it is you, my dear Helmut, who are responsible. What

kind of letters do you imagine that you have been
writing for the last six weeks, or perhaps I ought
rather to say, that you have *not* been writing? I can't
understand you. From the beginning of our friendship, I have always accused you of not knowing anything about women and I must now repeat it, not as
a joke but in bitter earnest: you really do not understand women at all and least of all your own wife, my
dear Christine—I hardly dare write our dear
Christine in view of your present attitude. At this
juncture, I can imagine you becoming impatient
and accusing me of being the chief cause and insti-
gator of all the peculiarities of conduct that you have
been perpetrating with such enthusiasm and de-
liberation since your departure from Holkenäs. If
you wish to judge me and my advice purely according
to your own lights, then I cannot deny that you have
a certain justification in your accusations. It is true
that I once advised you to adopt the course that you
have now adopted. But, my dear Helmut, I must
point out to you, as strongly as I can, the truth of *est
modus in rebus*. Do I have to draw your attention to
the fact that in all our actions, it is moderation that
must decide and that the wisest advice—forgive me
for seeming to put mine into that category—the
wisest advice can be turned into the reverse if the
person following it fails to maintain the right balance
and loses all sense of proportion? That is what you
have done and are still doing. I begged you to be on
your guard against Christine's wilfulness and to
resist as strongly as possible the urge to dominate,
which not only underlies her religiosity but is continually being fostered by it. No doubt I also advised
you, *en passant*, to try jealousy and to make her aware

that *any* possession is always hazardous and the best husband in the world may have a moment of weakness. Yes, my dear Helmut, I did speak to you in those terms, not out of lightness of heart but, if I may be allowed the expression, by reason of a certain academic appraisal of the situation and I have no regrets for what I said nor do I want to withdraw any of it. But what have you actually done in applying these suggestions, which I still maintain were correct? Pin-pricks that might have done good have turned into real wounds and the pins into poisoned arrows and, what is worse, instead of reluctance, which might have hinted that the execution of your scheme was involving struggle and effort on your part, instead of that, your letters revealed only indifference and an attempt—not always successful, because it was so obviously forced—an attempt to conceal this indifference under a cloak of town and court gossip. I have read your letters, which didn't take me very long, for there weren't many of them and none of them could be accused of excessive length; but at least half of them were concerned with the fabulous beauty of the, to say the least, somewhat peculiar Frau Brigitte Hansen and the other half with the witticisms of the equally peculiar Fräulein Ebba von Rosenberg. You barely devoted twenty lines to your wife and children, just a few questions, the answers to which, it was quite plain, hardly interested you at all. I believe, my dear Helmut, that it's enough simply to have made you aware of all this. You are too honest to deny the truth of the charges that I have made in this letter and too kind and too generous not to want to remedy them at once. The arrival of such a letter at Holkenäs will be the signal for Christine's

recovery; you must let me hope that it will not be
long delayed . . .

> As always,
>> Your loving and affectionate brother-in-law,
>> Alfred Arne

So powerfully was Holk affected by the contents
of this letter that he abandoned any thought of reading the other two: Petersen's was probably in a
similar vein. What is more, it was now time for him to
present himself before the Princess and he feared
that, in any case, he might have difficulty in con-
cealing his emotion. He would certainly have failed
to do so if, when he had appeared, everything had
been as usual and the Princess's eye as sharp as it
normally was. Fortunately this was not the case, for
she, too, had meanwhile received a letter which was
greatly preoccupying her mind and which robbed
her of the power to be concerned by Holk's own
behaviour.

CHAPTER 24

THE letter received by the Princess was from the
gentleman-in-waiting Baron Blixen-Fineke and ran
thus:

'I beg most obediently to inform Your Royal Highness, in all haste, that His Majesty the King, who
returned to Copenhagen today from Glücksburg,
has the intention of spending the next few weeks in
Fredericksborg Castle, probably until the New Year;
in any case, he hopes to celebrate Christmas there.

Only a few persons of his immediate entourage will accompany him; perhaps Colonel du Plat, certainly Captain Westergaard and Captain Lundbye. I thought it proper to apprise Your Royal Highness of His Majesty's decision.

> I remain,
> Your Royal Highness's most humble
> and obedient servant,
> Blixen-Fineke'

Her first thought on reading this note had been to leave the field free before the arrival of the King and return to Copenhagen within the next twenty-four hours. Once the King had arrived, such a retreat would be much more difficult, if not impossible, since, in view of the excellent personal relations between nephew and aunt, it would be too obvious that the Princess merely wished to avoid being under the same roof as the hated Countess Danner. So a rapid decision was essential and the question 'departure or not' was the problem occupying the Princess and her suite, particularly Ebba, who saw more hope than fear in the possibility of an immediate return, for however finely developed her feeling for nature and however pleasant she found Schleppegrell, in spite of an occasional revulsion against his perpetual antiquarianizing, all in all the capital was considerably more to her taste; there you could hear the news at least six hours earlier and in addition have a box at the theatre every evening. The vast gallery at Fredericksborg was certainly a magnificent specimen of its style, and the play of light and shadow on the walls and ceiling was pleasantly romantic and a little uncanny, but one could hardly continue staring at Herluf Trolle with the same interest for six hours from dusk till bed-time and even less at the big naval battle and the explosion in the *Immaculate*.

Had it been Ebba's choice, therefore, an immediate return would have been rapidly decided; but the Princess, who through sheer superstition was not anxious to leave a place that she had become accustomed to regard as her Christmas residence, remained hesitant in a manner quite out of character and was therefore glad when Holk remarked: 'With your permission, Your Highness, is it quite definite that the countess will accompany the King? As far as I know, the King has always shown nothing but the greatest consideration for your Highness and not only knows but also respects your feelings. It's true that he does not allow himself for that reason to be swayed in his affections nor indeed is it in his power, if people are right when they talk of a sort of witch's spell which Danner has cast over him, but surely it's possible for him to retain his affection for the Danner woman and still leave her behind in Skodsborg. He can then visit her every day, which perhaps suits him better than having her with him from morning till night. Surely the time must be past, even if it ever existed, when he felt the need to throw her loving glances at all hours of the day.'

'Who knows,' laughed the Princess. 'You see, my dear Holk, this spell is a sort of intermittent fever and there are said to be days when he is free from it. But I don't see it like that at all, a real spell never fails or comes to an end. Anyway, pass me Blixen-Fineke's letter again, Ebba my dear, I want to read what he says carefully. He is a man who is very punctilious in his choice of words.'

Ebba passed the letter and the Princess read: '. . . only a few persons of his immediate entourage will accompany him; perhaps Colonel du Plat, certainly Captain Westergaard and Captain Lundbye . . .' 'Holk is right; Blixen-Fineke knows too well how matters stand not to have given at least a hint. The countess will clearly not be coming and my nephew and I are on excellent terms: he is a very kindly soul and the nicest man in the world. In any case, there's no need to think about leaving today. In all probability, Berling will be writing and he will express himself less diplomatically than Fineke.'

And in fact, the following day, a letter did come from the gentleman-in-waiting Berling, confirming the impending arrival of the King, but at the same time offering complete reassurance with regard to the countess. In accordance with her own wish, the countess was taking up residence in Skodsborg and would receive the King's visits there. So all hesitation was now at an end and it was decided to stay; but even had the opposite decision been taken, an insuperable obstacle would have stood in the way of its execution, for the Princess now fell ill. The nature of her illness remained obscure but whatever it was (there was talk of a hidden non-malignant nervous fever), Dr. Bie from Hillerød called three times a day and partook regularly of the luncheon served for those attached to the Princess's court and of most other meals as well. This Dr. Bie was the brother of Frau Schleppegrell whose shortness, stoutness, and shrewd, friendly eyes he shared, as well as the favour of the Princess. He carried a gold-topped cane and wore gold-rimmed spectacles, which he regularly removed whenever he wished to see anything; he took one's pulse in a loud voice, like a piano-teacher counting the beat, and he enjoyed chatting about Iceland and Greenland, where he had been ship's doctor for fourteen years and to whose inhabitants he was in general very well disposed. 'In Copenhagen people usually laugh at the Icelanders; but how about Are Marson, who discovered America five hundred years before Columbus, and Eric the Red and Ulf Squinteye and all his gallant band? Heroes and sages every one, and Icelanders every one of them. I'm only sorry that your Royal Highness has never visited the island. It is quite a strange feeling to eat an egg boiled in a geyser, perhaps at the very moment that it is spitting fire as well. The idea that Icelanders read our papers twelve months later, day for day, is merely a piece of conceit on the part of the Copenhageners; the Icelanders have their own newspapers and every other day an English or an American boat puts in and if there is an election for a town or even just a parish councillor, it's quite as interesting as when they elect the new mayor of Copenhagen. Ah, your Highness, I am tempted to say that we should stop making all these differences between villages and palaces; wherever they live, people go on loving and hating and it makes very little difference whether a singer can hold a trill for a whole minute or a fiddler play the "Valiant Soldier Lad", at least as far as I am concerned.' With remarks such as these he could be certain of enlisting the Princess's highly amused approval and when Pentz and Ebba asked whether her Royal Highness would really not prefer her own private doctor, Dr. Wilkins, who in any case had nothing to do and ought to be reminded, now and again, that he was drawing his salary for a mere sinecure, the Princess refused, saying: 'No, I am not yet at death's door and if I were, I don't think Wilkins, who reads everything and knows practically nothing, would be likely to save me. Bie is doing everything a man can do for me and after I have been listening to him for half an hour and sat beside him in his reindeer sleigh or eaten raspberry fool with the missionary Dahlstrom, then I have had exactly what is meant by the expression "a doctor's healing presence"; *medico praesente*, I believe they call it. No, Bie must stay. And what would his sister say to such an insult, my dear little pastor's wife who considers him as famous as Boerhave and is firmly convinced that a letter addressed to Dr. Bie, Europe, from the North Pole or the South Pole, would arrive without fail at its destination.'

The Princess's illness, although not dangerous, dragged on. The King had meanwhile arrived and had taken up residence with his suite in the left wing of the castle. He restricted himself, as far as the Princess was concerned, to inquiring every day after her state of health. Otherwise, one was hardly aware of his presence, a fact partly due to his frequent visits to Skodsborg and partly to his other pastimes: he was a great lover of all outdoor sports. If he was not out with the hounds, he was deer-stalking and if he was not digging out badgers, then he was excavating barrows and between-whiles he went over to Vinderöd and Arreseedal, where he kept his yachts, to go sailing on the large lake of Arre.

Holk had known Captain Westergaard and Captain Lundbye very well in Schleswig and Flensburg, where they had been temporarily in garrison, and he now renewed his acquaintance with them, which gave him from time to time a few hours pleasant chat, but as soon as he was alone again, his thoughts went at once to what was happening in Holkenäs and he was overcome by a feeling of embarrassment. Things could not continue as they were. Not only had all correspondence between him and Christine ceased but Petersen's and Arne's letters had remained unanswered. He would, in any case, have to answer the latter, for a week had already passed since its arrival; if he did not, then he risked offending the one man who had always been his best friend and counsellor and, perhaps too often, his advocate in his earlier minor clashes with Christine.

He was not on duty today, the weather was bright and clear and Dr. Bie, on his way from the Princess, had called on him and entertained him with some amusing Hilleröd gossip and a medical story or two. Holk was anxious not to waste such an opportunity, for being in a good mood was half the battle. And after all, what was all the trouble about? Christine was a woman with less geniality than was desirable and more principles than were necessary. This was now an established fact that nobody, not even Christine herself, would deny. Holk continued to address himself on these lines for some while and when he had finally succeeded in persuading himself that, seen in perspective, the whole affair was merely a mole-hill that had been made into a mountain and that there was really nothing to worry about at all, he finally sat down at his desk and wrote:

Dear Alfred,

Many thanks for your letter of the 23rd, all the
more as, after so many proofs of your friendliness
towards me, I know full well that in emphasizing all
your misgivings with regard to my sins of commission
and omission, you are only following what you take
to be the path of duty. But, my dear Alfred, let me ask
you frankly if it is your duty? In acting on this
occasion as Christine's advocate (you used to be
mine) and in expatiating on your client's rights
against me, haven't you, perhaps, invented an injustice that doesn't, in fact, exist? All your accusations against me are based on my own letters. Well
those letters are now all in Holkenäs and the details
are not all fresh in my mind any more, but when I try
to recall their contents from memory, I can find
nothing that would justify all your insinuations.
There are the Hansens and there is Fräulein von
Rosenberg and in describing her, I may, as the saying
goes, have used more parsley than was warranted by
the chicken; but any exaggeration ought to have been
interpreted rather as proving my innocence or as
springing from my tendency to let absurdity condemn itself. I do recall having spoken in one of my
letters of a half-fabulous audience given to the lovely
capitana by the Emperor of Siam and in another of
the piquant and certainly somewhat broad-minded
Fräulein von Rosenberg as an amanuensis of David
Strauss; but I must ask you, my dear Alfred, if
these are expressions that justify Christine's being so
upset and, even more, all the reproaches contained
in your letter? A moment ago, I mentioned my
innocence which ought to be placed to my credit
but I am prepared to admit, on the other hand—

and that's the only admission that I am prepared to
make—that in my correspondence with Christine,
I have never been able to strike the right note. As
soon as one finds oneself suspected, it is very difficult
to maintain the right tone and attitude and all the
more difficult since, however innocent one may be,
one is always vulnerable to attack by certain misgivings and even self-reproaches, once doubt has
been cast on your intentions. How many doubts
assail us, how many misgivings creep up on us, until
we begin to have doubts about everything! But it
was Martin Luther, whose name occurs only too
frequently in our home, who once said—I know this
because I happen to have studied his pamphlets—
'We cannot prevent wicked birds from flying over
our heads, we can only prevent them from nesting
there.' Yes, Alfred, that is the whole point. Christine,
with all her virtues, lacks the one virtue of humility
and as she was educated and brought up with a special
sense of righteousness, from which she seems continually to expect salvation and enlightenment, the
thought naturally never strikes her that she may be as
mistaken as anyone else. She has sent Asta to
Gnadenfrei and Axel to Bunzlau and these two
actions show that any possibility of weakness or
error is quite excluded from her mind—weaknesses
and errors to which others who go off to Copenhagen instead of to Herrnhut are, of course, only too
prone. And now that I have conducted my defence
and towards the end even changed from defendant
to plaintiff—perhaps more than I might have
wished—I must conclude by leaving my case in your
hands, in the knowledge that with all your wisdom
and, above all, the love you have both for Christine

and for me, everything, God willing, will be for the best.

As always,
Your affectionate brother-in-law,
Helmut Holk.

Putting down his pen, he took the sheet of paper to the window to read through, line by line, what he had just written. He found much to criticize and when this or that displeased him, he muttered to himself: 'almost as dogmatic as Christine'; but the conclusion about the special sense of righteousness pleased him and even more the passage about his having been robbed of his sense of innocence because as soon as anyone was once under suspicion, however innocent, he was vulnerable to attack by misgivings and even self-reproaches. His eye dwelt as if spellbound on these words, until finally his satisfaction waned and all he could see in them was the confession of his own wrong.

CHAPTER 25

THE fine weather which had lasted for almost the whole month, despite its reputation, came to an end as November turned into December and violent gales set in from the north-west, only to be followed by showers of rain which then would frequently give way again, after a few hours, to another gale. This change of weather was, naturally enough, reflected in the life of the castle; the walks which often extended to Fredensborg and as far south as Hilleröd, now came to an end and the almost official gatherings in the large Herluf Trolle gallery were replaced by small reunions which were held 'over here or over there', in other words, in the two towers and took place on alternate evenings in the rooms of the two ladies-in-waiting. The Princess had personally been anxious that this should be done and Countess Schimmel-mann, however stiff and ceremonious in other ways, was an extremely affable hostess, so that her *soirées* rivalled Ebba's. The company consisted always of the same people: first, the Princess's entourage, then the two Schleppegrells and the King's two equerries, one of whom, Lundbye, played the part of the courtier and man of the world while the other, Westergaard, was the free-thinker—social *nuances* which only served to enhance the charm of their company. They all met daily, alternating between the left- and the right-hand towers, and just as the company was always the same, so the entertainment, too, always took the same form, being limited to play-readings, poetry recitals, and charades.

Now and then, if only to oblige Pentz and Countess Schimmelmann, after supper a game of whist was allowed which led to a little, quite harmless, gambling. Ebba always won because, as she said: 'I'm always unlucky in love.' They were often cheerful to the point of hilarity and while there were naturally complaints about the continuing stormy and rainy weather and even more about the Princess's illness which refused to be cured, they all agreed at the same time that it was to these so-called misfortunes that they owed their enjoyment.

So matters continued until the second Sunday in Advent when the weather changed again and the sharp north-easterly winds that now set in at once brought bitter cold, which froze all the ponds and puddles on the very first night and, on the following day, even the tiny lake in front of the castle. After the lake, it was the turn of the dyke in the park which connected the two lakes of Arre and Esrom and when, another week later, the news came that the great lakes themselves were frozen hard, at least at their edges, and when Dr. Bie had given his word that an excursion in bright frosty weather was exactly what was best calculated to remove the Princess's 'castle malaria' (his own diagnosis), it was decided to organize a skating and sleighing party to Lake Arre for the next day.

This day was even sunnier and fresher than any previous, and shortly before two o'clock they all met at the now familiar cable-ferry, which was already frozen into the ice. There were first of all the Princess herself, with Holk and Ebba, the Schleppegrells, and the equerries. Pentz was an absentee because of his age, the pastor's wife because of her *embonpoint*, while Erichsen and Countess Schimmelmann had not cared to expose themselves to the rather sharp north-east wind. But even these four had not wished to deprive themselves of all part in the excursion and had gone on ahead, in a closed carriage, to await the hardier half of the party in a small hotel close to the spot where the park dyke flowed into Lake Arre.

Beside the ferry, which had been transformed by an advance party of servants into a tent to shelter and accommodate the party, there stood an elegant sleigh and when the Princess had been installed in it, wrapped in all sorts of furs to protect her from the cold, the accompanying skaters had only to decide who should lead the way and who should be entrusted

with the honour of steering the sleigh over the ice.
It was quickly decided that, as the local expert,
Schleppegrell should lead the procession and that
Holk should steer the sleigh, while Ebba should
follow close behind with the two officers. They then
set off in that order and, being all skilful skaters as
well as elegantly and suitably dressed, they made a
fine sight as they glided away over the smooth ice.
Most impressive was Schleppegrell, who today was
looking more like a heathen Wotan than a Christian
apostle; the collar of his cloak was billowing in the
wind high above his broad-brimmed hat, while to
increase his speed he thrust his pointed stick with
ever increasing vigour into the ice. The Princess was
overjoyed at the sight of her fantastic 'path-finder', as
she expressed it to Holk; but with her highly developed sense of beauty—and despite her lack of
any feeling either for order or for elegance—she
would have been still more delighted had she
occasionally looked back at those following her.
Ebba, with her dress tucked up and in high skating
boots, was wearing a glengarry whose ribbons
fluttered in the breeze, and as she stretched out her
hand now right, now left, to her partners beside her,
her progress seemed like a dance in which, in spite of
her wide sideward sweeps, she moved forward faster
and faster. The distance to be covered was not far
short of a mile but in less than half an hour they
came within sight of the hotel, standing on high
ground, from which a pale wisp of smoke was rising,
while behind lay the broad expanse of the other part
of the lake, gleaming and glittering as far as the ice
extended and then blue and shimmering where the
ice-free water stretched out towards the sea. As soon

as Schleppegrell sighted their goal, he brandished his stick triumphantly and, increasing their not inconsiderable speed still more, in a very short while they reached the hotel, on whose terrace Pentz and Countess Schimmelmann were already waiting with the little pastor's wife. They all waved at the approaching party. Only Erichsen had, as it transpired, retreated with a box of throat-pastilles into the hotel. Holk, with one hand resting on the back-rest of the sleigh, raised his hat with the other and in a second they came to a halt beside a small wooden jetty leading to the hotel. Pentz had come up meanwhile, and offering the Princess his arm, he assisted her up the bank, followed by the two captains. Only Holk and Ebba remained standing by the jetty as they watched the others going ahead and then they looked at each other. There was something very like jealousy in Holk's eyes and as Ebba's seemed to reply with a half-mocking challenge which said: 'Nothing venture, nothing win', he seized her hand violently and pointed far out to the west where the sun was sinking. She gave an almost arrogant nod and then, as if the others' amazement were only an additional spur, they sped away together towards the place where the narrow gleaming strip of ice between the receding banks was lost in the wide expanse of Lake Arre. Nearer and nearer they drew to the danger zone and it seemed almost as if they were both trying to make for the open sea, straight across the belt of ice now only a few hundred yards wide. Their eyes met and seemed to be asking: 'Shall we?' And the answer was, at least, not a refusal; but just as they were about to pass a line of small firs marking the final limit of safety, Holk suddenly swung towards the right, pulling Ebba with him. 'We've reached the limit, Ebba. Shall we go beyond it?' Ebba drove the point of her skates into the ice and said: 'If you are thinking of going back, that means that you want to, and that's good enough for me. In any case, Erichsen and Schimmelmann will be expecting us, though perhaps not the Princess.'

CHAPTER 26

AN hour after sunset, when, as Pentz put it, Holk and Ebba had returned to civilization, from their Polar expedition, the party took their seats in a covered *char-à-bancs*, well provided with rugs, to return to Fredericksborg. On the way, the 'romantic escapade' was eagerly discussed, in spite of the presence of the two protagonists, and the tone of the discussion left no doubt that everyone considered it as something relatively harmless, a mere high-spirited prank that Ebba had forced on poor Holk, who had had to accept willy-nilly. Most of the party expressed themselves in these terms and only the Princess, contrary to her usual custom, failed to share this attitude of amused approval and said very little, a fact which struck no one but the equerries who, noticing her silence, were reminded of some earlier remarks of the Princess, made half-anxiously, half-disapprovingly. 'Ebba likes playing with danger,' had been her opening words, 'and it's all very well for her to do so, because she has the knack of avoiding it at the last moment. I'm sure that she has a life-belt under her furs all ready for any emergency. But not everybody is as clever and far-sighted as that and least of all our dear friend Holk.' She had made these remarks half-jokingly when taking coffee, while Holk and Ebba were still outside, but in spite of her jocular tone she was obviously serious.

They arrived back at the castle towards six o'clock and at once took their leave of the Princess, who still liked to spend her evenings in her rooms. The others went their separate ways, calling to each other as they did so: 'Until this evening!'

'Which tower?' asked the two captains, who had been on duty the last few evenings and thus not been in the Princess's suite.

'Ebba's tower. Eight o'clock at the latest. Anyone arriving later has to pay a forfeit.'

'What forfeit?'

'We shall see.'

And they all went to their rooms after Schleppe-grell had promised to bring his brother-in-law, Dr. Bie.

The two Schleppegrells and Dr. Bie, having the furthest distance to go, were naturally the first to arrive. It had started to snow slightly and, all flecked with white, they came into the hall at the bottom of the tower whence a spiral staircase led first to Ebba's and then to Holk's rooms, on the next floor. No one had bothered to discover what happened on the third and fourth floors, not even Karin who, since it had turned cold, had been chiefly concerned with keeping as warm as possible, first of all for her own sake and secondly for the sake of a young gardener's boy with whom she had formed a very close and intimate connexion within the first twenty-four hours of her stay in Fredericksborg. She had had a good deal of experience in such matters and she was well aware that warmth was a most valuable auxiliary to love. Today as always, therefore, she had taken care to ensure a comfortable atmosphere and when the guests from Hillerød felt themselves caressed by the prevailing temperature, Dr. Bie patted her hand and said: 'Well done, Karin. You Swedish girls know all about that. But how do you manage to keep the hall so well heated? I'm almost tempted to sit down here on the staircase and spend the evening with you.'

Schleppegrell, knowing his brother-in-law's easy-going ship's-doctor's manner only too well, threw him a glance warning him not to be too familiar but Karin, who liked being on good terms with everyone and most certainly with old naval surgeons, pointed to a place in the wall behind the staircase, the centre of which seemed to be glowing. Going nearer the doctor saw that a huge stove was built into the wall, with its front opening into Karin's own room while its back, made of bricks into which had been let a large iron plate, was heating the lower hall and half the staircase as well. 'Splendid,' said Bie, 'splendid. I must have a word with the castle management and see if they make another one like it. An iron stove with double heating, so to speak, for the hall and the room as well. Over on the other side, with Countess Schimmelmann who has no Karin to help her, of course, it's always bitterly cold; everything is freezing, including the Countess, by the way. And then we are supposed to cure her of her everlasting catarrh, not to speak of chilblains and her red nose. It's a good thing that Countess Danner isn't here. It's true that she has her own doctor and we must not forget her greater natural heat, either. Otherwise she wouldn't be the sort of woman she is.'

Schleppegrell was clearly not in agreement with his brother-in-law's suggestion for structural improvements to the castle and while they were climbing the stairs, he said: 'I'm all against it, Bie. Leave the towers as they are.'

'Ah,' laughed Bie. 'The historian's scruples again. You think that if people have been freezing in a tower for two hundred years, they must go on freezing for ever. You call it respect for tradition and the Church has a still grander name for it. As for me, I like to be warm.'

'Yes,' said Schleppegrell, 'that's the privilege of all Arctic explorers. The nearer the Pole, the nearer the stove. And you said that you intend to go and see the castle management to recommend the installation of another stove? Well, in that case, you must let me go with you and while you arrange for another double stove—which is made half of iron, by the way—I shall arrange for this one to be taken out. You can't realize what you are doing, with all these pine-cones and fir-wood everywhere and the floors and partitions worm-eaten and dry as tinder.'

While talking, they had reached the top of the stairs and went into Ebba's room where everything was prepared for the occasion: lamps and candles were burning and the table, already laid, had been pushed into the large bay-window. Everything was spacious and orderly but before ten minutes had passed, the whole room was humming with activity, and order was only restored when most of the party had seated themselves at two hastily improvised card-tables, Countess Schimmelmann with Pentz and Lundbye on the left, Frau Schleppegrell with Erichsen and Westergaard on the right. Holk and Bie would have liked a game and that would have made it possible to play four-handed whist without a dummy, but they could not play because Schleppegrell never touched a playing-card on principle and they could not leave him all to himself. It is true that there remained Ebba; but as hostess, she had to keep her eye on all her guests and although the supper had already been prepared in advance, there was still a great deal to do and there was no end to the instructions given to Karin and the gardener's boy, who had been called in to help.

Seeing that they had no chance of a game, Holk and Bie retired to a corner formed by a projecting column in the wall, next to the bay-window. Here they were soon engrossed in private conversation and the ever-inquisitive Holk naturally managed to bring it round to the subject of Iceland.

'You know, doctor, I really do envy you your experiences as ship's doctor there, not only because of scurvy and all the amputations that you must have had to deal with, but for ethnographical reasons.'

Bie, who was little more than a superior medical orderly, had probably never heard the word 'ethnographical' in his life and, in any case, had never worried about its meaning; he was thus somewhat taken aback and would have found it difficult to reply if Holk, entirely absorbed by his own curiosity, and quite unaware of Bie's problem, had not continued: 'And if Iceland were a country that did not concern us particularly, we should perhaps not be so interested; but the Icelanders are our half-brothers and pray for King Frederick every Sunday just as much as we do, and perhaps more. For they're a serious and religious people. And when I think that we live from one day to the next and really know nothing about things we ought to know, I feel ashamed and rather inclined to blame myself. For example, as my old Pastor Petersen at home has often assured me a hundred times, what would the whole of Germano-Scandinavian literature be like, but for Snorre Sturleson, the pride of the Icelanders? Nothing at all. And so I should like to ask you, doctor, during your stay on the island, did you find that all those things were still known and loved and sung and talked about by everybody, I mean the women and girls at their spinning-wheels and the men when they were out seal-fishing?'

Schleppegrell had been listening to all these questions with the greatest embarrassment, not for himself, but for his brother-in-law; but the latter had meanwhile recovered his poise and replied with great good humour: 'I'm afraid that my brother-in-law knows all about that much better than I do, without ever having been there; people who've never been to places always know more about them. All that I know about the Icelanders is that their beds might be better, although they have eiderducks on their doorstep, so to speak. And the feathers really are good and you really are warm inside them and that, to be honest, is always the most important thing up there. But their weak point is their bed-linen. One could put up with the fact that their thread is as coarse as twine; the real trouble is their lack of cleanliness. It's all too obvious that, up there, ice is commoner than water and the laundry women are only too glad to put their hands back into their fur gloves. It must be admitted that it's not a clean country. But there is some splendid salmon. And then the drink! Some people are always talking of Icelandic moss[1] but I can assure you, Count, that I've never found better whisky anywhere, either in London or Copenhagen or even in Glasgow which is, after all, the home of the best whisky.'

This conversation about Iceland continued for a while and Schleppegrell, at first embarrassed, was finally gently amused to see all of Holk's unrelievedly earnest questions skilfully parried by Bie. Ebba came up to them now and again, laughing to see the conversation continually going round in circles, and then quickly went back to the card tables where, to the great advantage of Frau Schleppegrell or Countess Schimmelmann, she picked up the dummy hands and put them down again so often that Pentz, who was losing steadily, finally had to protest. Nothing could have been more welcome to Ebba and leaving the cards, she went over to the fireplace and built up the fire with coal and juniper branches, though not too much, as the large number of lights alone had ensured that nothing could be felt of the cold outside. Also, although it had been freezing all day, the snow had raised the temperature, while the wind had risen, as could be noticed each time Karin, cheerful and competent, came through the doorway with the various trays.

It was now ten o'clock, the game was over, the card-tables pushed to one side and the supper-table, laid on three sides only, so that no one need sit with their back to the blazing fire, stood ready in the centre of the room. Countess Schimmelmann had the place of honour in the middle of the table, with Holk and

---

[1] A lichen with supposed therapeutic properties.

Pentz on either side; then, to left and right, the four
remaining men, while Frau Schleppegrell and Ebba
sat at the ends, so that they could survey the whole
table and, if necessary, renew the provisions. The
atmosphere of the party was already gay but it now
became even gayer, largely owing to the lively and
varied talents of Dr. Bie as an entertainer. He was
not only a good raconteur and toast-master but above
all a virtuoso in the art of laughing, which enabled
him to accompany not only his own but also other
people's stories with veritable salvoes of uncritical
guffaws, thereby making everyone else laugh too,
even if they did not know what they were laughing at.
Even Countess Schimmelmann, to everyone's delight, deigned to show unmistakable signs of enjoying herself, although this did not prevent the general
hilarity from increasing noticeably as soon as she
withdrew punctually at eleven o'clock. There was,
indeed, one further factor in the increasing gaiety
and this was the Swedish punch which though
not appearing regularly on all occasions, was being
served today from a huge silver bowl. Everyone sang
its praises, especially Bie who, after reaching his fifth
glass without undue delay, rose in his seat to give
a toast, with the permission of the ladies. 'Yes, ladies,
a toast. But to whom? Naturally to our charming and
hospitable hostess, in whom our sister-land of
Sweden, a seafaring people like ourselves, has
reached, if I may say so, its supreme expression. As
we all know, beauty was born out of the sea, but in the
North Sea there was born northern courage—
Swedish courage. Although I was not myself a witness of that splendid deed of Nordic courage this
afternoon, I have heard all about it. And surely, to

hover on the brink of death, one false step and you're in Davy Jones's locker for good, isn't that one of life's greatest thrills? And such a life is a Norseman's life. Where the ice begins, there the heart burns with the fiercest flame. So let us drink to the Nordic lands and their brave and beautiful daughter!'

Glasses were raised and, not for the first time that day, the 'Lake Arre escapade' became the subject of general pleasantry. Pentz, who had little confidence in either Holk or Ebba, was particularly enjoying making fun of them and lovingly enlarged on what would have become of the couple had an ice floe, with a fir tree on it, broken free and carried them away into the open sea. They might perhaps have landed in Thule. Or perhaps not, and then they would have had nothing on their iceberg but a Christmas tree, without any nuts or raisins. And then Holk would have killed himself and offered his heart's blood to Ebba, not forgetting the inevitable references to the pelican. In olden times such things had been known to happen.

'In olden times,' laughed Ebba. 'Yes, such things did happen in olden times. I don't claim to know much history, I leave that to others, and I know still less about ancient history than any other sort, but you only need to know a little about the Trojan war to have great respect for the olden days and their courage—even greater respect than for that Nordic courage that Dr. Bie has just been praising in such glowing and for me, flattering, terms.'

Here, Westergaard and Lundbye chimed in together to point out that, where the most important form of heroism, the heroism of passion, was concerned, times never changed and that they personally would guarantee that love could still perform the same marvellous feats as in former days.

At this, the company immediately split into two camps, those who were of the same opinion (including the little pastor's wife, whose face was now glowing all over); and those who flatly denied the truth of what the captains said, the latter headed, of course, by Ebba. 'The same marvellous feats,' she repeated ironically. 'That's not possible because such feats were the product of something that has been lost, a sort of sublime recklessness. I use that word because I want to avoid the word passion, although one of you has already used it; but we can talk of recklessness without feeling compelled to blush when we say it. And now I should like to ask you all, and I shall begin with the two captains, which one of you would be willing, for the sake of Helen, to start a Trojan war? Who would be ready to kill Agamemnon for the sake of Clytemnestra?'

'We would, we would,' and Pentz, waving a fork, even added: 'I'm Aegisthus!'

Everyone laughed but with growing vehemence Ebba continued: 'No, gentlemen, the truth is, that sort of recklessness no longer exists. Of course, it must be admitted—and it is up to you to make use of this against me—even in antiquity there were isolated cases of weakness. I remember, many long, dull years ago, when I was still in short skirts, I remember seeing Racine's *Phèdre* with the celebrated actress Rachel in the title role; she had just come from St. Petersburg and was taking in poor old Stockholm on the way. Well, the said Phaedra loves her stepson, that is, someone not really of the same family and therefore having no reason at all to consider any question of incest; and yet this stepson refused to say yes, and spurned her although she was beautiful and a queen. Perhaps the first example of decadence, the first small voice of our modern weaklings.'

'Oh no,' protested Lundbye, 'not modern. Modern taste would condemn that sort of pusillanimity out of hand', and Pentz added: 'What a pity that we haven't a Phaedra handy to settle the argument straightaway; perhaps we might manage to fetch one from Skodsborg . . .' But he broke off in the middle of his sentence as he noticed that the two officers were looking at him very sharply, to let him know that, in their presence at least, he must not mention irreverently the name of Countess Danner which was on the tip of his tongue.

Almost at once, they rose from table and prepared to take their leave; and Holk, as the sole other inhabitant of Ebba's tower, felt in duty bound to accompany the guests as far as Karin's hall, which was being used as a cloak-room. He remained here until they had all left and then, saying good night to Karin, he suggested opening the windows and the door, as the stove seemed to be giving off too much heat; and then quickly went upstairs again.

As he came upstairs, Ebba was standing in her open door and the lights were still burning. Holk felt some doubt whether she had merely been waiting for all the guests to depart, or for him to return. 'Good night,' she said and with a mock-solemn bow seemed to be on the point of going back into her room. But Holk seized her by the hand and said: 'No, Ebba, you mustn't go like that. You must listen to me.' And following her into her room he gazed at her with eyes full of a turmoil of passion.

But she gently released herself from his grasp and, alluding to the conversation of a few minutes ago, said: 'Well, Helmut, what role are you playing now? Paris or Aegisthus? You heard that Pentz has volunteered for one of them.'

And she laughed.

But her laugh only increased Holk's confusion, which she continued to enjoy for a moment and then, half-pityingly, she said: 'Helmut, you really are more German than the Germans. . . . It took ten years to conquer Troy. That seems to be your idea, too. . . .'

CHAPTER 27

AN hour later there was a knock at the door. Holk started up; but Ebba, less afraid of being discovered than of appearing ridiculous by anxiously trying to avoid discovery, went quickly to the door and opened it. It was Karin.

'What's the matter, Karin?'

'Something serious. My room is full of smoke and luckily a piece of soot fell down the chimney and woke me. I've opened the door and windows and made a draught, but it doesn't seem to help, it seems to be coming out of the walls and floor-boards.'

'What can it be?' said Ebba, who at first had thought that it was merely curiosity that had brought Karin up to her room. 'The wind must be blowing down the chimney. I'll come and see but I must put some more clothes on and fetch a light, you must have groped your way up in the dark.' She went back to her room, letting the door shut behind her, but in less than thirty seconds she was back with a light in her hand and went downstairs, followed by Karin. The maid had not been exaggerating; smoke and fumes were filling the staircase and before either of them was half-way down, they were finding it almost impossible to breathe. 'We must dash through quickly,' said Karin and set off across the hall, through the floor of which small flames were already beginning to spurt. Immediately afterwards she could be heard shouting 'Fire' in the courtyard. Ebba was about to follow Karin to safety when she remembered Holk and, hastily deciding not to leave him in the lurch, she hurried upstairs again to her room. He was no longer there. 'The fool, he wants to save my reputation, and perhaps even his own, and now he'll kill himself and me with him.' Saying this, she ran quickly up the second flight of stairs to see if he was in his own room. He was standing in the doorway. From the courtyard, they could hear Karin still crying for help and other voices were now joining in. 'Quick, Helmut, or we are lost. Karin is safe. We must try, too'. Without waiting for an answer, she seized his arm and dragged him with her down the two flights of stairs. Fast as they were, the fire was even faster and what had been possible two minutes ago was now no longer so. 'We're lost!' said Ebba and seemed on the point of collapsing on the stairs. But Holk grasped her, half-fainting, and with the strength of despair carried her up the spiral staircase from floor to floor until at last they were standing together beneath the rafters of the roof of the tower. Here, the light from an open dormer-window enabled them dimly to discern where they were in the jumbled disorder of the room. Laboriously feeling

his way past the roof-timbers towards the opening,
Holk stepped out into the open air, pulling Ebba
after him. For the moment, they were out of danger
and, had the almost vertical roof of the castle had a
gentler slope, they would have been completely safe;
but the roof was so steep that it was not possible to
climb along it and the best they could do was to hold
on to the lightning-conductor, bracing their feet
against the strong gutter. Fortunately, the wind was
blowing the smoke and fumes away from them in the
opposite direction. But all this was but a respite: how
would it help them if they were not noticed from
below or if the wind were to change and set fire to the
roof against which they were leaning?

'Will you try?' asked Holk, pointing to the
lightning-conductor by which, with sufficient deter-
mination, it might still have been possible to lower
themselves to the ground. But Ebba shook her head
helplessly. 'Then let's see if we can work our way
along the roof as far as the next mansard and climb
in through there.' Cautiously, leaning back all the
time, they slowly edged along the steep slope, bracing
their feet against the gutter. It was a bare ten yards
and everything seemed to be going well, but hardly
had they gone half-way than Ebba said: 'It's no
good, my legs won't carry me any more.' Holk
thought of shouting and waving but he soon realized
that it would be useless, because in order not to over-
balance, he had to remain leaning back and this
excluded any possibility of being seen from below.
Their only hope now lay in Karin, who presumably
would not only be trying herself to discover where
they were but would also have warned the others;
and it was this that now actually rescued them from

their fearful predicament. A quarter of an hour must have passed when they noticed that some persons had gone round the end of the lake and, almost at once, they heard cries from the Hilleröd side, where it was possible to have a better view of the roof. Although they could not understand the shouts, their encouraging tone left no doubt that those shouting were certain of rescuing them. A short while later, they heard behind them what sounded like the blows of axes and hammers and, immediately afterwards, they spied heads peering out of a hole in the roof, trying to see where they were. The first time, they misjudged the distance but this was easily remedied and, after a short delay, strong arms reached out from inside the castle and lifted first Ebba and then Holk into safety. In triumph, they were carried downstairs and into the courtyard. The first person to address them was the King himself.

Although having returned from Skodsborg to Fredericksborg at midnight, only an hour before the outbreak of the fire, it was he who had been leading all the rescue operations and had been the most active and successful in bringing his precious antiques to safety; indeed, it was largely owing to him that anything was saved at all. His two equerries were beside him.

'So it's you, Holk,' he said as soon as he noticed him. 'And like a gallant knight, you have rescued your lady too. I must make sure that this famous deed becomes known in Skodsborg.' And despite the gravity of the occurrence, there was a touch of mockery in the casually spoken words.

Westergaard and Lundbye were anxiously bustling round Ebba. 'Where is the Princess?' she asked.

'At the station,' was the reply. 'A special train is being provided for her. She says that she feels like a cat on hot bricks here.'

The pun was quite unintentional and everyone took it as such. Only Ebba saw the unwitting humour of the remark and unable, even at such a moment as this, to resist a witticism, she said: 'On hot bricks, indeed! The Princess has much less right to say that than Holk and I!'

CHAPTER 28

ANXIOUS to take advantage of the special train, Ebba wanted to go to the station at once but she was still in such a state of weakness that Holk, as well as the young equerries, urged her against it. Eventually, she allowed herself to be persuaded and was taken over to the left wing of the castle which was untouched by the fire. Here the castle chapel was being used as temporary accommodation and round the altar itself, where all the candles were lit, there were sitting, or rather camping, the wives and children of officials and servants, the children decked out in all sorts of clothes, including communion robes from Catholic times which had been brought out from the vestry. There was nothing left for Ebba to put on; all that could be found was a couple of pillows to protect her at least from the bitter cold of the stone floor. But it was not enough and after Holk had vainly searched for something better in the small caretaker's lodge nearby, he suggested to Ebba, who was becoming increasingly chilled, that it would be better, after all, to risk going to the station. An old servant showed them the nearest way and so they set off, reaching the station just in time to hear the clock strike six. The Princess had left more than an hour before and the next train from Elsinore was not expected for another thirty minutes. At the station itself, everything was at sixes and sevens and there were no more seats in the waiting-room, which was full to overflowing with people from Hilleröd, young and old, who all wanted to get to Copenhagen as quickly as possible to report on the horrible events of the night—the most sensational of which were, fortunately, pure inventions. In one tower, it was being said with complete assurance, everyone had been burnt to cinders, three people from the court and a gardener as well. Ebba, who was having great difficulty in remaining on her feet, was forced to hear all this and she would have been hardly better off here than she had been in the icy chapel, if one of the station staff had not hit upon the good idea of opening up for Ebba and Holk the separate room reserved for the royal court. Here, it was not only warm and roomy but they found Pentz and Erichsen as well, who had remained behind in order to be able to report to the Princess the fate of those thought to have been trapped, a last-minute arrangement made when the Princess had already climbed into the compartment with Countess Schimmelmann. Holk and Ebba were naturally greeted with the greatest relief by the two gentlemen-in-waiting, who had feared the worst; and even more heartfelt, when she rushed in immediately afterwards, was their greeting of Karin, who had till now been sitting crouched in a corner of the adjacent waiting-room. 'Never mind,

child,' said Ebba, trying to joke. 'What is there to
make such a fuss about? First it was rather too warm
and then rather too cool, that's all.' But Karin, fond
of jokes as she was, found it impossible to respond to
Ebba's humour and was unable to stifle her tears
and sobs as she kept kissing her mistress's hand. As
may be imagined, Pentz was full of questions,
principally addressed to Holk, but, before the latter
could reply, a whistle was heard in the distance,
signalling the approach of the Elsinore train. A
minute later, it drew in at the platform and in spite
of the lack of coaches, it was found possible to arrange
for a special compartment for Ebba, where she was
able to lie down covered by plaids and coats. Karin
sat with her, while the three men climbed into an
adjacent coach.

At eight o'clock the train came to a halt in the
Copenhagen railway station, carriages were ordered
and Pentz drove with Ebba and Karin to the palace,
while Erichsen and Holk went to their own homes.
Holk knocked and the door was opened by the
beautiful Brigitte, who said: 'Thank God, you have
come back, Count Holk.' But some disappointment
was plainly mingled with her relief, not surprisingly,
since immediately after the arrival of the special train,
rumours of the horrible death of Count Holk and
Fräulein von Rosenberg had begun to circulate,
a story sensational beyond the dreams of mother or
daughter. And now the Count was alive, after all,
and perhaps—or indeed certainly—Fräulein von
Rosenberg as well. It was obviously impossible to
rely on anything any more; it was always the most
exciting things that turned out to be false. But

Brigitte concealed her feelings and repeated: 'Thank God, Count Holk. We were so afraid for you. And for that lovely Swedish girl . . .'

As she spoke, her eyes never left Holk's face and her extraordinary intuition—extraordinary in one direction, at least—enabled her to realize everything that had happened, particularly what most intimately concerned Holk and Ebba, as clearly as if she had been present.

'Yes, my dear Frau Brigitte,' said Holk, who only heard, or chose only to hear, the sympathy in her voice, 'yes, it was a dreadful experience that I wouldn't wish my worst enemy and least of all myself and . . .'

'. . . such a lovely girl.'

'Well, if you like; but she's not quite as lovely as you always seem to assume, and in any case not half as lovely as others whom I won't name. But we must talk about that another time and decide the question then. At the moment, I am dog-tired, dear Frau Hansen, and I want to catch up with all the sleep that I have lost. Please tell everyone that I'm not to be disturbed, even Baron Pentz, if he calls. But wake me at twelve. And then I should like some lunch.'

Holk slept soundly until he heard a knock on his door warning him that it was time to get up and dress, which he hastily did. He still felt in a dream and all that had happened seemed like some play passing through his mind; but when he went to the window and looked down into the street, all the events of the night came suddenly into clear focus. At this moment, Brigitte appeared with lunch and as she wanted Holk to begin telling his story, she not only laid the table

very slowly but even went so far as to ask direct
questions, a thing which she would normally never
have done. But on this occasion, Holk remained
impenetrable, replied only briefly, and through his
whole attitude gave her to understand that he would
prefer to be alone, which not only greatly amazed the
beautiful Frau Hansen but gave her an even lower
opinion of the young Swedish woman. None of this
escaped Holk's notice; but since he felt it prudent
not to put the pretty Brigitte into a bad temper, he
asked her to excuse his vagueness and to remember
that he was still suffering from the effects of his
terrible experience.

'Yes,' said Frau Hansen. 'Terrible; it must have
been terrible with the responsibility and wanting to
help and not being able to. And with everybody
looking on and perhaps wearing only a very thin
dress . . . if she was wearing a dress . . .'

She said all this with such a serious expression on
her face and in such an emotional tone that when she
had left, Holk was once again left wondering if he
ought to consider it all pure malice and shameless
play-acting on her part. Yet perhaps there was some
real sympathy in her, for, after all, that type of person
is always very good-hearted. But whatever it was,
he was in no mood to pursue the matter further and
hardly was he alone than he was once more assailed
by all the thoughts and fancies which Brigitte's
appearance had merely interrupted. It seemed hardly
possible that it was not twenty-four hours ago that
they had set out on the excursion to the hotel on Lake
Arre. So much had happened since then! First, their
escapade together out to the broken and crumbling
ice and then the return and the teasing and Ebba's

arrogance at supper . . . and then when Karin came and the flames spurted from the floor and walls and how they finally stepped out on to the castle roof, with death and destruction below them, and how this step had eventually led them to safety.

'Yes, to safety,' he said to himself. 'With everything hanging by a thread, as it did then and as it always does. What was it that saved us? The fact that, on the very first day, we walked by the lakes and summer-houses as far as the ferry in the park and on that very day, the sun happened to be shining and I looked back at the castle which was bathed in light; and because everything was so clear and bright, I could see quite plainly how the lower end of the tower-roof joined on to the bottom of the castle-roof. Yes, it was that which saved us. A pure chance, if there is such a thing. But no, there is no such thing; it had to be so, some providence had arranged it. And I must accept that and use it as the foundation for all that I now intend to do. When someone is in trouble and doubt, he is waiting for some sign to show him what he is to do; and I have been given a sign, by the fact that a higher providence brought us out of danger. If all my feelings had been wrong all this time, punishment would have overtaken us and Ebba and I would have fallen unconscious and been suffocated and never found our way to safety. And if I understood Christine's last letter properly, she also feels that this will be the best thing for us to do. All those happy days we spent together mustn't be forgotten, of course not, and by remembering them we can lessen the bitterness of parting, but part we must and I think it is our duty to do so, because we have become complete strangers to each other. Ah, all that

I

bickering and nagging! I'm longing for a new life, one that doesn't begin and end with religious tracts, I want harmony in my home, not a harmonium, joy and mutual understanding and air and light and freedom. That's what I want and that's what I have always wanted, ever since the first day I arrived here, and now I've been given the sign that I'm going to be allowed to have it.'

He broke off for a moment and then he started all over again. His thoughts were all revolving around one idea and he had only one purpose in mind: to still an inner voice that refused to be silenced, because, while believing that he had proved everything to his own satisfaction, in his heart of hearts he was still haunted by the thought that his proofs were worthless and if he had been able to step outside himself and listen to his own arguments, he would have realized that he was studiously avoiding two words: God and heaven. He was appealing to neither because, dimly yet quite certainly, he felt that he was fighting in the defence of an unjust cause and he did not dare to misuse the name of God by involving Him in the question. Had he been able to see himself from outside he would have been able to realize all this, but this gift had been denied him; and so he continued to float along on the stream of his specious arguments, following his dreams, lulling his conscience to sleep, writing himself one certificate of good conduct after another. And why not? After all, he was an easy man to live with, as he said to himself, if only one set about it the right way; but Christine had never known how to do it nor did she want to; yes, she was the victim of all her fine Christian talk, that was quite definite, or at least he wanted it to be

definite, and suddenly filled with a longing to bring
his good cause, his just cause, to a speedy conclusion,
he finally lost all sense of judgement and reason. He
would go and see Ebba this very minute and then
take her to the Princess, confess everything to her
and then beg first for forgiveness and then for her
consent. And tell her, too, that Christine had already
written in the same terms or at least hinted at it.
There could be no question of opposition from anyone in Holkenäs, their separation was as good as
accomplished, just one tiny formality and he would
ask the Princess to approve the step that he proposed
to take and agree to consider his relationship with
Ebba as an unofficial engagement.

He felt relieved as this plan took firm shape in his
mind; Ebba must be told of it within the hour; he
could see no obstacles or, if he did, he brushed them
aside.

It was striking two from the tower of the Town Hall
as he made his way towards the palace. Two or three
times he was delayed by meeting acquaintances who
had heard of the danger from which he had escaped
as if by a miracle. Holk spoke to them, but each time
broke away quickly, pretexting 'duty with the
Princess'.

Ebba lived above the Princess's rooms in the palace
itself. Holk tugged at the bell; no one answered.
Finally, Karin appeared but what she had to tell Holk
did little to satisfy his urgent desire for a speedy
solution to his problems. He was told merely that,
after a fever lasting many hours, Ebba had just fallen
asleep and must not be awakened. 'All right, I shall
call again later. And don't forget, Karin, to tell your
mistress that I called and asked after her.' Karin

promised with a smile. She had no idea of all that was going on in Holk's mind and saw him only as an impetuous lover eager for further proofs of affection.

Holk went slowly downstairs and it was not until he was passing through the long corridor, off which the Princess's rooms lay, that he suddenly remembered that he had omitted to fulfil what should have been his first duty. But was it his first duty? Certainly not for him. In his present mood, the health of the Princess was for him largely a matter of indifference and her only purpose, as far as he was concerned, was to give her blessing to his project and make him and Ebba happy. And suddenly (for he was convinced that Ebba had the same idea), he was seized with the desire to make sure, that very day, that the Princess would give her assent. And so he went into one of the ante-rooms, only to be told by one of the gentlemen-in-waiting on duty that Her Royal Highness was keeping to her bed. Yet another disappointment, for if the Princess was kept to her bed, there could naturally be no question of any decision—which he considered the equivalent of approval. How tiresome, nothing was going as he had hoped. Pentz and Erichsen were in the next room, but he did not want to see them and left quickly, to go for a walk as far as the citadel and then to stroll for an hour in Ostergaade. At five, he was back in the palace asking once again for Ebba. 'The doctor had been', he was told, 'and had prescribed two things: medicine and a night-nurse. Fräulein Ebba had a high fever again and it was hardly surprising after the danger she had been through . . . and everything else. . . .' These last three words were half whispered, almost involuntarily, by Karin, loth to deny herself the pleasure of letting Holk guess her thoughts.

Holk's patience was now being sorely tried. He had hoped to see his fate settled within the hour and now he was meeting obstacle after obstacle. Ebba ill, the Princess ill. In his own mind, he was sure of Ebba and thus far there was no difficulty; but the Princess? He could not imagine how he could spend all those waiting hours, hours that might turn into days and, when he went over in his mind all the entertainments that pleasure-loving Copenhagen offered, he was horrified to realize how much he loathed them all. The Alhambra and Tivoli, Harlequin and Columbine, the Thorwaldsen Museum and Klampenborg, all of these, and the beautiful Frau Brigitte as well, had lost their attraction for him; and even when he thought of Pentz, he felt a shudder run down his back: that was the last thing that he could bear; he would rather suffer Erichsen's banalities and Countess Schimmelmann's stiff formality than Pentz's puns and *bons mots*. . . .

He slept little that night and his head felt heavy, partly through excitement, partly because he had caught cold; and he was glad when the morning sun reddened the roofs across the way. Breakfast came and the papers and, in these papers, detailed accounts of the fire at the castle. He read everything, was amused and, at least while he was reading, almost succeeded in forgetting his troubles. The actual events had been very much embroidered to his credit; according to two almost identical reports, he had tried to let himself down by the lightning-conductor, in order to fetch help for the unfortunate young lady; but when he reached that part of the tower that was on fire, it had been impossible to slide further down the iron bar, which was already red-hot; and so, with a courage and strength equalled only by his agility, he had clambered up again. He read this and thought to himself that he must certainly be the hero of the hour. The hero! And yet how unheroic he was now! Indeed, he felt on the brink of a nervous breakdown and in real danger of falling ill himself, and perhaps even becoming deranged in his mind, unless he could finally succeed in settling today what he had been vainly trying to arrange yesterday. It was unlikely that Ebba would have recovered yet, but the Princess might be well again and that was really even more important. What she had suffered since the day before yesterday was, after all, relatively slight and if, as was very probable, she had left her bed, she would have to listen to him and tell him her decision. 'And her decision must mean endorsing my happiness, because she is kind and broad-minded.'

Yes, that was what he must do, and at ten o'clock he was once more at the palace where, to his great joy, he learned that the Princess had passed a fair night. Through the same chambermaid as he had spoken with before, he inquired whether it might please Her Royal Highness to grant him an audience, and immediately afterwards, he was shown into her presence, for she had stated that she wished to speak with him urgently.

The room was the one in which he had had his first audience with the Princess on the day after his arrival. The large portrait of King Christian was still there and, on the opposite wall, that of the deceased landgrave with its frame and crêpe greyer and dustier than ever. Hunched on the sofa under the portrait of the king, sat a decrepit old lady, looking very little like a princess and nothing of an *esprit fort*. It was plain that even if she was practically recovered from her illness, she had by no means recovered from the shock and excitement of those last hours at Fredericksborg. She seemed exhausted and her eyes were tired and lustreless.

'That was a bad night, my dear Holk. You can see that I am still suffering from the effects of it. And yet it was nothing compared with what you went through. And Ebba as well. A miracle that you were saved, as I have been told, by your own presence of mind. I wanted to see you so that I could have the opportunity of expressing my gratitude to you. Such things are unforgettable. Particularly by Ebba herself. She will never be able to forget what you did for her and I am sure that she will be obliged to you for the rest of her life.'

These words could hardly have been better chosen to encourage Holk to say what was already trembling on his lips and, for a moment, he was about to unburden his heart to her and reveal all his plans. But however encouraging the words, her attitude and the tone in which she uttered them were not so in the least. Everything about her was listless and, however anxious Holk was for certainty, he saw quite clearly that this was not the best but the worst possible time to make his confession. In this completely senile old lady sitting underneath the solemn portrait, there was no longer the slightest trace of the free-thinking princess who normally delighted, or at least was interested, in amorous escapades and *mésalliances*, divorces, and marital squabbles. The only lesson that could now be read in her haggard face seemed to be that boldness and excess had little to offer as a rule of life; that keeping a promise and obeying the law were the only things really to be recommended and, above all, that a genuine, not a reluctant, marriage, was the only safe haven. Holk would have liked to find something else in the Princess's expression but it was so plainly impossible to do so that, instead of making his confession, he merely asked for several days' leave of absence. In doing this, he had no clear plan in mind and if asked why he wanted it, he would not have known the answer. But the Princess who, from the beginning of the interview, had had only the one desire, to withdraw as soon as possible into her private study, was only too glad not to ask any indiscreet questions and graciously granted his request. And then, with a kindly nod of her head, she ended the audience, if audience it could be called.

CHAPTER 29

WHEN Holk had asked for leave, one thing only was clear in his mind: something must be done; and now that leave had been granted, the question at once arose: what was to be done now? A meeting with Ebba—although he was sure of her agreement; arrangements for the future—that would have been the most obvious course; but Ebba was ill and when he called again, Karin gave the same reply: she could see no one. And so he faced a true testing-period, days during which there would be nothing to do but wait. And in his present state of mind, that was the most difficult thing of all. Finally, he accepted the situation and decided to shut himself up and see nobody, read newspapers, write letters. But to whom? He saw at once that there was no one to write to. . . . Petersen, Arne, the children—all impossible. Fräulein Dobschütz—even more so. There remained only Christine herself. 'Christine. Yes, that would be the best thing. She must know eventually and the sooner the better. . . . But why write to her? Must I really write, as if I haven't the courage to go and see her? But I do have the courage, because it's my right to have what I want. People don't live together just in order to be perpetually squabbling and always going in different directions. Christine has driven me away by her coldness. Yes, that's the right word and it was her ever-increasing coldness that was worse than quarrels and violence. A woman must have some warmth, some temperament, life, sensuality. What can one do with an iceberg? And even if it's the most transparent kind of iceberg, that sort of ice is the coldest and I won't be frozen. Yes, that's right, that's a good gambit but it must be face to face. I shan't write, I shall say it to her face. Her own letter has offered me a golden opportunity. And once I'm free and back here again. . . . Ah, how I long for life, warmth, joy. I've been spending my days surrounded by shadows from the underworld—the worthy Dobschütz for example; but I'm still young enough to want flesh and blood.'

He rang. The widow came.

'Dear Frau Hansen, I want to go over to Holkenäs for the day . . .'

'Ah yes, for the Christmas presents. That will please the Countess, now that she is so much alone and with the children away, too, as you told me.'

'Yes, to Holkenäs,' said Holk. 'Do you know how

the steamers are running? I mean those between Glücksburg and Flensburg. I should prefer to leave this morning, or perhaps this evening. Then I could be there early tomorrow. Perhaps you could send someone down to the harbour to inquire, my dear Frau Hansen? But it must be someone reliable, because I don't want any mistake.'

Frau Hansen said that she would go herself and in less than an hour she returned from her errand with the news that there was no further ship that day, but tomorrow evening the *Holger Danske* was going and would be off Holkenäs at ten o'clock in the morning.

'That's the day after tomorrow. What's the date today?'

'The 21st, the shortest day of the year . . .'

Holk thanked her for her trouble and was glad in his heart that it would not be Christmas Eve when the ship would be tying up at the Holkenäs jetty.

On the 23rd, the coast of Angeln came into sight and as ten o'clock approached, the castle of Holkenäs could be seen from the deck, perched on its dune. A vague mist was shrouding its outlines and, for a moment, it started to snow. But the flurry of snow-flakes soon ceased and the mist, too, had almost lifted when the ship's bell began to ring and the smart steamer came alongside the pier. Holk walked down the gangway on to the jetty, the steward brought his luggage down after him and in less than five minutes the *Holger Danske* was steaming on towards Glücks-burg. For a few moments, Holk followed the ship with his eyes and then, flinging his coat between his two bags, since it would have impeded his climb up to the terrace, he set off along the jetty. Now and again, he stopped and looked up at Holkenäs. Now that the fog had momentarily lifted, the castle stood out clearly in front of him but it seemed deserted and lonely and the thin spiral of smoke which rose from it suggested that it was only half alive. The many shrubs in front of the veranda were bare and leafless, save for a few cypresses and the veranda itself was enclosed by boards and hung with matting to protect the rooms behind from the north-east as far as possible. Everything was silent and sad but, like the afterglow of earlier happiness, a certain peace seemed still to surround it—a peace that he was coming to disturb. Suddenly he was appalled at what he intended to do; assailed by doubts, the voice of conscience that he was endeavouring to still refused to be completely stifled. But for good or evil, it was now in any case too late to retreat: it *had* to be. How Ebba would have laughed at him and spurned him if, on his return to Copenhagen, he had said to her: 'I wanted to do it and couldn't.' And so he walked on again and eventually climbed slowly up to the terrace. On reaching the top, he called to one of his old servants who happened to be there, one who had lived for years as a pensioner in a nearby cottage, and asked: 'Is the Countess in the castle?' 'Certainly, master,' replied the old man, almost scared. 'I shall go and inform her ladyship of your arrival.' 'No, leave it,' said Holk. 'I shall go myself.' And then he turned and walked towards the back of the castle which looked out over the park and gardens sloping away from the sea.

When he reached there, everything seemed warmer and more comfortable and Holk, stopping

only for a moment to look around him, mounted the
three marble steps which led between two pillars to
the door of the summer drawing-room. . . . And now
he went into the room itself where, although the
children were not there, everything seemed to have
been made ready for Christmas. On the corner table,
where previously Christine used to sit and sew
with Fräulein Dobschütz and Asta, there stood the
Christmas crib with all its figures, one which had
often been used over the years but was still in good
condition; and in the opposite corner stood a large
Christmas tree, as yet undecorated but so tall that its
top nearly reached the ceiling. From all this, it
seemed that someone must have been busy here quite
recently but no one was to be seen. Had she run away
to avoid him? Before he could answer his own
question, he saw that he had been mistaken, at least
as far as running away from him was concerned, for
from the dark corner behind the Christmas tree
stepped a woman in black. It was Fräulein Dobschütz,
carrying a bowl of gold- and silver-coloured nuts in
her hand, with which she had probably just been
beginning to decorate the tree. She gave a sudden
start as she recognized the Count. 'What has happened? Shall I call Christine?'

'No, my dear Julie,' said Holk. 'Let us leave
Christine for a while. What she has to hear will be
soon enough. I have come here sooner than I expected
and I should have preferred to choose another day
than this. But I am not staying long.'

Fräulein Dobschütz knew how things stood and
how, over the last few weeks, Holk had increasingly
humiliated and offended his wife; but what she had
just heard was much more than this and went much

further. What could be the meaning of these words that seemed to say so much and yet said nothing? And as he spoke them, Holk stood with a half defiant, half embarrassed, expression on his face, as if he had come to accuse someone and himself as well.

'I should prefer to go and inform Christine that you are here.'

He nodded, as if to say, very well, if you wish, it makes no difference whether it is now or later. Then he walked over to the crib, picked up one or two of the figures and looked round to see if Dobschütz had meanwhile left the room or not.

Yes, she had gone and now, for the first time, he let his gaze wander slowly round the room, looking at everything, large and small, almost with indifference and, as he did so, he could also see out over the park drive on which hens were walking because there was no one to stop them. Then he walked back again to the open grand piano, at which Elizabeth and Asta had so often sat and played duets or sung their songs, one of them on the last day—or was it the last but one?—before his departure. And all at once it seemed to him that he heard it again, but far, far away.

He stood thus, dreaming, half forgetful of what he had come to accomplish, when he thought he heard the door open. Turning, he saw that Christine had come in. She was standing, holding Fräulein Dobschütz's hand, as if for support. Holk went towards her. 'Good morning, Christine. You see that I have returned earlier than I had expected.'

'Yes,' she said, 'earlier.' And she gave him her hand and waited to see what he would do, some sign to show her how things stood, because she knew that in spite of all his weaknesses, he was honest and could not dissemble.

Holk held her hand in his and tried to look her in the face but he could not bear the gaze from the calm eyes that met his and in order not to lower his own, turned them away again, while she continued to remain silent. 'Shall we not sit down, Christine?'

They both walked to the corner table. Julie followed but remained standing while the Countess sat down opposite Holk, who drew up a chair. The Christmas crib stood between them and across the crib their eyes questioned each other.

'Please leave us, Julie,' said the Countess after a pause. 'We had better be alone. I think my husband has something to tell me.'

Julie hesitated, not because she wanted to witness the painful scene that was obviously about to follow but because of her love for Christine who, she feared, might need her help and support. But finally she left.

Holk seemed at first to be contradicting his wife's statement that he had something to say, for he remained silent, playing with the figure of the Christ child which, without thinking, he had taken from the lap of the Virgin Mary.

Christine looked at him and almost felt sympathy for him. 'I shall make it easy for you, Helmut,' she said. 'What you cannot bring yourself to say, I shall say for you. We were expecting you on New Year's Eve or New Year's Day and you have come for Christmas. I don't imagine that you have come to see the crib or for the sake of the Christ child that you are playing with. You have something else on your mind than Him and it can only be whether your hope of happiness is called Brigitte or Ebba. It is really one and the same thing. You have come to do what I suggested to you as a last resort, to tell me that it was I who wanted it to be so. Yes, I did want it to be so because I can't bear half-heartedness in any relationship. Among my many special kinds of selfishness, I possess that of not wishing to share with anyone. I want the whole of a man, the whole of his heart, and I don't wish to be a man's wife for the summer while others take it in turn to be his wife during the winter. So tell me openly that you have come to talk of separation.'

It was unfortunate that the Countess could not control her feelings. Had she spoken more mildly, she might have been able to turn Holk, indecisive as he was, away from his plan and made him recognize his mistake, for in spite of everything, he had not yet stifled the voices of conscience and justice, and all that he needed was the strength to listen to them. Had Christine succeeded in giving him this extra strength, he might even now have changed his mind. But her tone betrayed her and awakened in Holk all those feelings that had irritated him for so long and which, since he had known Ebba, had made him so ready to consider himself the wronged party.

And so, as soon as Christine had stopped speaking, he threw the Christ back into the crib, not caring where it fell, and said: 'I think you said that you wanted to make it easy for me. Well, I'm indebted to you for being willing to keep faith with what you had promised—in your usual supercilious way. Let me confess to you that I was deeply moved when I saw you appear a moment ago and come towards me leaning on Julie. But I'm not moved any more. You don't have the power to heal or console or lighten anyone's burden or even to spread flowers in anyone's path. You have no light or sun. You lack anything feminine, you're bitter and morose . . .'

'And self-righteous . . .'

'And self-righteous. And above all, so stubborn in all your beliefs, in everything that you say and do that, for a while, one begins to be convinced oneself and goes on being convinced until one day the scales fall from one's eyes and one is angry with oneself, above all at the thought that anyone can see God's lovely world as a narrow, fenced-in enclosure covered by a shroud. Yes, Christine, such a world does exist, and it is lovely and bright and spacious and that is the world that I am going to live in, a world that may not be paradise but at least is a reflection of it, and in this bright and cheerful world, I want to hear the nightingales singing and not see golden eagles, or condors if you like, soaring solemnly heavenwards all the time.'

'All right, Helmut, let us say no more about it. I don't want to exclude you from your paradise any longer, because what you have just said about its being a mere reflection means nothing: you want a *real* paradise on earth and, as you expressed it rather peculiarly, you want to hear the nightingales singing in it. But sooner or later, they will stop singing and then you will hear the sound of only one bird, softly and more and more bitterly. It will not be bringing you joy and when it comes, you will find yourself looking back on an unhappy life. I'm not going to mention the children to you, I cannot bear to bring them into a conversation such as this; a man who will not listen to his wife, a wife who has claims on his love because her love was only for him, such a man will be just as indifferent to the feelings that the mere names of his children ought to arouse in him. I shall go now. My brother will look after my affairs from Arnewieck, not in any way to resist, or even protest against your plans, Heaven forbid, but merely to settle what has to be settled and, above all, whether the children are to be yours or mine. If I know you well enough'—she gave a bitter smile—'you will not raise any difficulties on that score; there were times, I think, when the children meant something to you but those times are past. Times change and what used to give you joy has now become a burden. I shall do my best to spare your new *ménage* any special strains, including the strain of being a stepmother. And now good-bye and I hope that you will not be too heavily punished for all that you are doing.'

While speaking, she had risen to her feet and without trying to avoid him, brushed by him to go towards the door. Her whole attitude now betrayed no sign of any of the weakness she had shown on entering the room; the indignation in her heart gave her the strength to bear everything.

Holk rose too. A world of conflicting feelings was surging inside him but the predominant feeling now, after all that he had heard, was one of bitter resentment. For a long while, he walked up and down and then went over to the balcony window and again looked out on to the park drive, strewn with leaves and pine-cones, as it sloped gently downwards and finally curved left towards Holkebye. The sky was overcast again and, suddenly, a violent flurry of snow began to fall, the flakes dancing and whirling until the wind abruptly dropped and they continued to fall, heavily and thickly, to the ground.

Holk could only see for a few yards but, densely though the flakes were falling, he recognized the figures of two women who, coming from the right of the castle, turned into the drive and started to walk towards Holkebye.

It was the Countess with Fräulein Dobschütz.

They were alone.

CHAPTER 30

WHEN he saw Christine going down the drive and disappearing into the flurry of snow, Holk was touched, but only in his heart, not in his mind. His decision was firm: his past happiness now lay behind him, so much was certain, and he added: 'perhaps through my fault but certainly through hers as well. It's she who wanted this, it's she who has vexed and tormented me, first by her overbearing pride and then through her jealousy, and now she has told me to go. And she didn't show any restraint, on the contrary, she surpassed herself and instead of her usual arrogance, she put on a pitying air and then she left. I may have wronged her in the past, during these last few weeks I certainly have, but it was she who started it, it was she who alienated me more and more and now that's the end of it all. Yes, it's the end of the story but not the end of my life. No, on the contrary, it's the beginning of something else, something better, more cheerful, and if, in my new existence, some bitterness still remains over the past, I must not let it embitter my life for ever. How I long to see a laughing face! Oh, that everlasting look

of the Mother of Sorrows with her heart pierced
by a sword when, in reality, it was only pin-pricks.
It was unendurable and in any case, I was tired
of it.'

The old retainer, who had meanwhile fetched the
luggage from the landing-stage, now came to ask
whether the Count wished to eat. 'No, Dooren,
not now. I shall ring.' And alone again, the question
once more arose as to what he ought to do. 'Shall
I stay here and put a dozen candles on the Christmas
tree that I have just prevented Julie from decorating
and then light the candles tomorrow and try to bring
myself luck as a Christmas box? Impossible. And
I can't stay here just to play the part of the affable
and generous landlord, up here in the castle and down
in the village, and give all the girls of the village
a silver dollar stuffed in an apple and ask Michael
after his Anne-Marie or Anne-Marie after her
Michael and whether the wedding is to be at Easter
or Whitsun. And even if I did want to do something
like that, it would take a whole day or even two,
because here they don't give their Christmas presents until early in the morning. Two days, that's
impossible, how would I possibly spend them? It
would be an eternity and I'm not in the mood to
check account books in between and talk about
parsnips and turnips. And what about Petersen? He
would appeal to my conscience and still all to no
purpose. And then Christine will presumably be
there, too; I expect she'll stay down in the village
and send a message to Arnewieck and Arne will come
and fetch her. I've no desire to be still here then, or
even in the neighbourhood. No, I prefer to go to
Flensburg, there may perhaps still be a boat for

Copenhagen today. Even if there isn't, I can't stay here; I must get away.'

He pulled the bell-cord. 'Tell John to harness the horses. The gig and the ponies. I'm going to Flensburg.'

It was just striking three o'clock when Holk drove into Flensburg and a moment later stopped in front of the Hillmann Hotel, where he used regularly to stay on his frequent visits to the town. The landlord was somewhat surprised to see him until he was told that the Count, of whose position at court he was aware, had only been on short leave in Holkenäs.

'When is the next boat to Copenhagen, my dear Hillmann?'

Hillmann fetched the time-table of arrivals and departures of all the steamers and ran his finger down the list: 'That's right, Iversen's ship is due to go tomorrow but traditionally the 24th is a holiday and Iversen lives with his daughter and has grandchildren, so he certainly won't break with that tradition; he'd sooner be under a Christmas tree than on deck on Christmas Eve. But he's a good skipper, one of the old school who's worked his way up from cabin-boy. He'll be sailing on the 25th, the first day of Christmas, at seven o'clock in the evening.'

'And arriving?'

'And arriving in Copenhagen early on the second day of Christmas. That means about nine o'clock or perhaps an hour later.'

Holk was not much pleased by all this and it was only when he thought of Holkenäs that he was heartily glad at spending such a long period, more than two days, in Flensburg. He took a room on the second floor that looked out over the Rathaus square and after eating a late lunch, with a healthy appetite, for he had scarcely eaten anything since the previous evening, he left the hotel to go for a long walk round the bay of Flensburg. At first, it was twilight, but then the stars came out to shine in all their wintry splendour, reflected in the broad expanse of water. With every minute, Holk felt his burden grow lighter and if he still did not feel completely at ease, any uncertainty that remained now concerned the future, not the past, and was more like excited expectancy. In his mind's eye, he imagined all kinds of agreeable events that would be taking place, certainly no later than May. By then, everything would be settled: the wedding date fixed, and he saw himself in Hilleröd church thronged with people. It was Schleppegrell who would deliver the wedding sermon and his good wife would be overcome by his eloquence while Dr. Bie was overjoyed that, with the help of a beautiful Swede, a Schleswig-Holstein heart had been won over to Denmark. In the pew reserved for the court, the Princess was to be seen, with Countess Schimmelmann beside her and Pentz and Erichsen behind them both. And then they would take their leave of Hilleröd and all the guests and travel in a special train to Copenhagen and the same evening to Korsör and Kiel and spend their first night in Hamburg. And afterwards there was Dresden and Munich and Lake Garda, with an excursion to Mantua where, strange as it might seem, she was anxious to visit the ditch under the ramparts where the Tyrolean patriot Hofer had been executed, and then on and on, southwards to Naples and Sorrento. There the journey would come to an end, with Vesuvius on the right and Capri on the left; he wanted to forget the world and all its sorrows and live only for himself and his love. Yes, it would be in Sorrento, where there was a superb bay like the bay here in Flensburg but brighter and more splendid and when the sun ushered in each new day, it would be a real sun and a real day.

All these images passed through his mind and whilst he saw them tangibly before his eyes, the water of the bay flowed solemnly and sombrely past him, despite the rays of light reflected in it.

He returned late to his hotel and spent the next day reading and chatting with Hillmann. But when evening came, he felt once more the urge to go out and walk through the streets and alleys of the town and where the shutters were still open or not tightly closed, he peeped inside and in front of more than one house, when he saw the happiness inside and a child in its mother's arms and the father reaching out his hand towards his wife, he was suddenly seized by fear of what was to come and more than once he found himself seeing all that he had lost instead of what he hoped to gain.

What a Christmas Eve! But it went by and it was now Christmas Day and though the hours passed slowly, seven o'clock came at last, and the ship's bell rang and Holk was standing beside the old captain; and when, an hour later, the ship came into the open channel, Iversen was busily spinning a yarn and telling all sorts of tales, old and new.

It was a good crossing and the wind was mild as they stood beneath the stars until after midnight and calculated that they would arrive in Copenhagen half an hour before they were due. They congratulated themselves on this and, soon afterwards, the few passengers turned in to their bunks. But then the weather changed and when they were level with Möen at five o'clock, or assumed that they were, the sea-fog had become so thick that they had to damp down the boilers and drop anchor. As usual, the silence awakened the sleepers and when they came on deck a quarter of an hour later and tried to look towards the coast of Zealand, they were told by the quartermaster that the ship had anchored.

'How long for?'

'Well, it may be till noon.'

Noon came and went before the fog eventually cleared and the ship was able to set off again. A whole day had been lost and there was no question of being able to go to the Princess's palace that day. The street lamps were alight all round the harbour when they moored alongside the wharf soon after five o'clock.

At his lodgings, Holk was welcomed by old Frau Hansen and not, as was usual, by her daughter; she led the way upstairs and lit the lamps without asking after anything other than the weather and if he had had a good crossing. She made no sort of inquiry as to the health of the countess or whether he had spent a merry Christmas and when Holk for his part asked, first, after the health of her and her daughter and then of the Princess, she replied in a strangely innocent tone, in the use of which she was, if possible, almost superior to her daughter: 'The young lady has left her bed.' The words came out in such a strange way that even Holk was surprised, but he was at that moment preoccupied with far too many other things to take up her remark and so he let it pass, and merely asked for the papers and a cup of tea. 'I'm frozen after standing all that time on deck.' Frau Hansen brought both. The newspapers were only half-size, because of the holidays. Holk perused them quickly and then went early to bed. He went to sleep at once, for the last few days had taken toll of his nerves.

He was up again early. Frau Hansen (for Brigitte was not showing herself today, either) brought the breakfast and perhaps because she felt that she had gone too far the previous evening, she showed the utmost nonchalance and produced all her gossip with such artless good humour that Holk found himself not only forgetting his annoyance at the slyness of her previous remarks but also, to his great surprise, relieved of much of his gloom. Everything, even subjects of the greatest delicacy became, through Frau Hansen's narrative gift, something thoroughly amusing and thoroughly natural and when she had gone he was left with the feeling that he had been listening to a sermon on the art of living that was not perhaps very moral but all the wiser because of this. When he tried to sum up what he had just heard, it amounted to something like this: 'Yes, Count Holk, it always was and always will be so: things can be taken seriously but they can also be taken lightly and someone who has the art of taking them lightly, knows how to live and anyone who always takes things seriously, does not know how to live and worries over things that don't exist. . . .'

'Yes, Frau Hansen is right,' thought Holk when he had finished his meditations on what he had just heard. 'Take things as they come, everything as it comes, that's the best way and that is what people like best. The first step to success is laughter.'

Twelve had not yet struck as he left his lodging in the Dronningens-Tvergade and set off towards the palace. It was the third day of Christmas, the weather had cleared up and a wintry sun shone over the streets and squares of the town. 'The young lady has left her bed'—these were the words that Frau Hansen had spoken to him yesterday evening and there could be no doubt as to their veracity; but it was also most improbable that this young lady, after such a violent attack of fever, would yet have returned to duty and so, without inquiring further at the Princess's apartments, he went straight up to the second floor where Ebba had her rooms. Karin opened. 'Is she at home?' 'Yes.' And Karin led the way, followed by Holk.

Ebba was seated in a chair at the window, looking out on to the square which showed no trace of life; now not even the autumn leaves were whirling about any more. As Holk came in, Ebba stood up and walked towards him in a manner that was friendly, but tired and somehow sedate. She took his hand and then sat down on a sofa some distance away from the window, at the same time asking him to draw up a chair near to her.

'I'm expecting the doctor,' she began quietly, speaking in a rather strained voice. 'But I'm in no hurry to see him and so I'm very glad that you have come. It means that I shall be able to talk of other things; it's so boring always having to answer questions about one's health, not only for the doctor but for the patient as well. . . . You must have spent Christmas at home on the other side of the water. I hope that you found the Countess as well as you expected and that you had a pleasant holiday.'

'It was not a pleasant holiday,' replied Holk.

'Then I can only hope that it wasn't your fault. I have heard so many nice things about the Countess; the Princess who called to see me yesterday was full of her praises. A woman of character, she said.'

Holk forced a smile. 'A woman of great character— yes, the Princess is fond of that expression, I know, and uses it to suggest that not everyone possesses it. She may be right in that. But it's easy for princesses to enthuse about character when they are rarely in a position to meet people who do possess it. Such people may have a hundred good qualities, in fact they certainly have, but they are awkward people to know and that is the last thing that princesses are likely to find pleasant.'

'Everybody says that you are a very chivalrous person, Helmut, and I would be the last to deny it because I haven't any grounds for doing so; but you're not being very gallant towards your wife. Why are you trying to belittle the Princess's praise of her? As a rule princesses are not very free with their praise and one ought to add to it rather than detract from it. My feelings are the same as the Princess's. I'm full of admiration for the Countess and if admiration is too strong a word, then I should perhaps say that I am full of sympathy for her.'

Holk could contain his impatience no longer. 'The Countess will doubtless be most grateful to you for that. But I think that her gratitude will be rather less than her amazement. Ebba, what sort of game is this that you're playing? First the Countess and then more Countess and then character and then admiration and then, to crown it all, sympathy. Do you expect me to believe all that? What has happened? What's the reason for this change in you? Why such formality all of a sudden, why all this reserve? Before I went away, I tried to speak to you, not because I wanted to be sure that you loved me, I felt certain of that or at least thought I could be certain of it, no, it was simply that I had an urge to see you and find out how you were before I went over to Glücksburg. So I left and while I was there, I suffered a great deal and I was forced to fight and say things that, frankly, you ought to realize as well as if you had been there listening to it all.'

Ebba tossed her head and Holk went on: 'You're being haughty and tossing your head, Ebba, as if you wanted to say: I know every word you spoke and I disclaim every one of them.'

She nodded.

'Well then, if I've guessed correctly, let me ask you once more, what is this all about? You know that I was captivated by you from the very first day and that I have staked everything—perhaps more than I should—on winning you. And I did all that and I'm standing here in front of you today, whether guilty or not, only because you led me on—deny that if you can. Every word you uttered went straight to my heart and your eyes spoke the same language, and they both said, your words and your look, that you would be unhappy for the rest of your days that you had not slipped off the crumbling ice and died in the sea, if I were ever to abandon you. Deny that, Ebba—those were your very words.'

While Holk was speaking, Ebba had been leaning back with her eyes closed. Now that he had stopped, she sat upright again, took hold of his hand and said: 'My dear friend, you're quite incorrigible. I remember telling you at the very beginning of our acquaintance and later on as well, in any case, more than once, that you were on the wrong track. Nor will I take anything back, on the contrary. All those things that I used to mention merely to tease you and irritate you a little when I was feeling impertinent, I shall now repeat in deadly earnest and even as an accusation. You try to be a courtier and a man of the world and you are neither the one or the other. You're half-hearted in both and you're always sinning against the most elementary rules of the game—particularly at the present moment. How can anyone, where a lady is concerned, refer to words that she was foolish enough—or perhaps kind enough—to utter in an unguarded moment? All that remains now is for you to mention certain *happenings* and you'll be the perfect gentleman. Don't try to interrupt, I've worse things to say to you yet. Except for the small matter of constancy, Mother Nature has endowed you with everything needed to make a good husband and you should have been content with that. In any neighbouring territory, you're completely at a loss and you only go from one blunder to another. In love, what counts is the moment and we experience that moment and enjoy it, but anyone who wants to perpetuate it or base any claims on it—claims which, if they were recognized, would destroy every better, in fact, any really legitimate claim—any man who can do that and just as his partner is being intelligent enough to have second thoughts, solemnly stands on his rights, as if they constituted a right to marriage, such a man's love is not heroic but stupidly quixotic.'

Holk jumped to his feet. 'Now I know. It was all a game, a mere farce.'

'No, my dear Helmut, only if by being too solemn,

which God forbid, you try to take something seriously which should be taken lightly.'

Holk stared blankly in front of him without a word and once again he realized that she had hit the mark. 'Very well, then,' continued Ebba, 'you have already committed the stupidest blunder of all and I refuse to accept any responsibility for it. I've never made myself out to be better than I am and nobody can say of me that I ever seriously pretended anything untrue. Words are only words; that much, even you must have known. Yes, Helmut, life at court is futile and boring, here and elsewhere, and because it's so boring, you either have to be as priggish as Schimmelmann or—how shall I put it?—as un-priggish as Ebba. And now, instead of stripping all the greenhouses in the country to strew flowers in my path or singing the praises of your lady like a trouba-dour—before going on to try your luck elsewhere—instead of doing that, you want to make me swear everlasting love on the strength of a single word, or not very much more, and turn a mere game into bitter earnest, all at the expense of a woman who is worth much more than both of us and whose feelings you are outraging just because you fancy yourself in a role for which you're quite unsuited. Once again, I refuse to accept any responsibility. I'm young and you're no longer young and so it wasn't for me to preach morality to you and, since I was bored, keep you anxiously on the path of virtue—that was none of my business, it was yours. I disclaim any guilt on my side and even if there was any (I suppose there may have been just a little), well, I've no desire to magnify it ten- or a hundred-fold and turn a peccadillo into real sin, one which I myself would recognize as such.'

Holk felt his head spinning. So this was the happiness of which he had dreamt! While he had been contemplating this step, he had certainly been filled with a vague feeling of anxiety at the thought of what the world, his children (whom he would be bound to alienate), and perhaps, sooner or later, his own heart would have to say. That had been in his mind but nothing else. And now a snub, a complete and unqualified rebuff, his proposal refused, his love spurned, with a peremptory firmness that excluded any possibility of a further attempt. If only he could have found relief in a sudden outburst of indignation! But even that solace was denied him, for as she stood there, loftily tearing his character to pieces, he found her more entrancing than ever.

'And so everything ends,' he said after a short pause, 'with my complete humiliation, to which is added for good measure all the bitterness of being ridiculous—and all *pour passer le temps*. Everything has been calculated to pander to your vanity, and I must accept and submit to your latest caprice. But in one thing, Ebba, I'm not going to accept your verdict: I refuse to recognize that it was my duty to doubt the genuineness of your feelings; on the contrary, I felt that I could believe in them and I still think so. You have simply changed your mind and in the meantime—it's not for me to try to explore your reasons—you have decided that you prefer to call it all just a game. Well, if it was one and nothing more and you say so, then all that I can say is, that you played it very well.'

He bowed and left the room. Outside stood Karin, eavesdropping. Contrary to her usual custom, she said not a word but her attitude as she accompanied

Holk along the corridor showed plainly that she disapproved of her mistress's conduct. She was, indeed, fond of the Count, on whose kindness and, no doubt also, on whose weakness she may well have been building many a plan for the future.

CHAPTER 31

ALMOST eighteen months had passed; it was the end of May and the London squares were offering the charming prospect that is usual at Whitsun time. This applied in particular to Tavistock Square: the carefully watered turf was fresh and green behind its iron railings, the lilacs were in the full splendour of their blossom, and the yellow panicles of laburnum hung over the railings into the wide streets round the square.

It was indeed a charming prospect and Holk, too, was enjoying it as he sat in his first-floor room of the beautifully kept old corner-house, with its balcony running all along the double front overlooking the delightful square. Holk had loved this district of London ever since the time when, as a young attaché to the Danish Legation, he had lived there twenty years before; and he had taken it as a sign of good omen that on arriving in England the previous November he had succeeded in finding suitable lodgings there.

Yes, Holk had been in London since November, after travelling all over Europe and visiting all the most famous beauty spots where, year in, year out, many thousands of people seek distraction, only to find at the end that the dullest place at home is still

better than the liveliest place abroad. After taking
written leave of the Princess and sending a full and
friendly letter to Arne, appealing to him not to desert
him in his hour of need, he had gone first to Brussels
and then to Paris, but found such little contentment
there that by Easter he was already in Rome and a
few weeks later had arrived in Sorrento, that same
Sorrento in which he had dreamt of spending happy
days with Ebba. . . . These happy days had not been
realized but the depression which had been weighing
on him was cured at last by meeting a friendly
English family with whom he shared an annexe at the
Hotel Tramontana and he had once more discovered
what it means to live and, more important still, to be
concerned with other people's lives. In this way the
weeks went by, with drives to Amalfi and excursions
to Capri while sailors sang their full-throated,
nostalgic songs; but the hot season, which began
earlier than he had hoped, drove him north into
Switzerland where, although he normally loved it, he
was unsuccessful in finding any place to suit his
present mood: Lake Geneva was too dazzling, the
Rigi too much of a caravanserai, Pfäffers too much
like a hospital. So feeling drawn, if not homewards,
at least towards somewhere in the north, he decided
to try London, to which he was attached by pleasant
memories of his youth and where his friends, who
had left Sorrento at the same time as he, had been
urging him to come and visit them. So to London he
went, where he had been for the last six months; and
surrounded by customs and a way of life which were
more or less akin to those of Schleswig-Holstein, he
found himself feeling as much at home as any home-
less person can expect. The social conditions suited

him, therefore; but many other things, too, helped him to forget, for a few hours or days at least, his growing sense of loneliness. He rediscovered his passion for the theatre, which even in his youth had made his time as attaché so agreeable; and at the Princess Theatre, which was very close to Tavistock Square, he was to be seen regularly, sitting in the stalls whenever Charles Kean, who was at that time making history with his Shakespeare revivals, was playing one evening in *A Midsummer Night's Dream* or *The Winter's Tale* and the next in *The Tempest* or *King Henry VIII*, with a hitherto undreamt-of magnificence. In the course of that winter he entered into personal relations with Charles Kean and in that celebrated actor's house, the haunt of so many distinguished artists and writers, he finally made the acquaintance of Charles Dickens and found himself drawn into all sorts of theatrical and literary circles whose lively behaviour and extreme good humour he found uncommonly sympathetic, without in any way having to neglect his Sorrento friends, who were country gentry. He had become particularly enthusiastic about Dickens himself and on the occasion of a 'whitebait party' in Greenwich he drank a toast to his new-found friend, of whose work, he said, it was true that he knew only *David Copperfield* but that work alone sufficed to make its author the greatest of all living writers. When at the end of his speech, he was challenged by the others present, amid laughter, to read other works of Dickens, he stated that he felt compelled to refuse because even Dickens would find it hard to better *David Copperfield*, so that any further reading could only lead to a diminution of his admiration.

Parties such as these, at which ladies famous in the artistic world of London were regularly to be seen, such as the beautiful and much-courted Miss Heath and, above all, Miss Atkinson, whose Lady Macbeth was a performance of genius—such parties were more than a mere distraction for Holk and with such agreeable company he would not merely have escaped from his loneliness but been uplifted in mind and spirit, had he only been able to feel himself a free man. But this was exactly what he lacked: the little patch of earth to which he felt attached body and soul, where he had been born and had spent so many happy years, that single patch of earth was closed to him and presumably would remain closed unless he succeeded in making his peace with society, which again presupposed a reconciliation with Christine. But according to all that he heard from home, such a reconciliation was unthinkable, for although, on the one hand, the Countess insisted that the children should fulfil all their obligations to their father with the utmost conscientiousness and would make sure, for example, that every one of his letters received a respectful answer (for, driven by this feeling of loneliness, he often wrote), on the other hand, every attempt to bring about a reconciliation had been in vain. With characteristic bluntness, Christine had opened her heart to her brother on this question, avoiding for once her usual lofty moralizing tone.

'All of you,' she wrote, 'have become accustomed to considering me as something abstract and doctrinaire, and in the past I may have had more than my fair share of that, in any case more than men like to find in a woman. But I can assure you that, first and foremost, I am still a woman and because of that, after all that has happened, I have been left with something still preying on my vanity; please notice that I don't claim that it is anything more than wounded *amour-propre*. But to put it bluntly, Holk is not yet properly cured. If he had married that young woman over in Copenhagen and sooner or later had realized that he had made a mistake, then perhaps it would have been all right. But it didn't happen like that. She simply did not want him and so, as far as I am concerned, the unpleasant possibility still remains that, had she been prepared to have him, the affair might have had quite a different ending. It's quite likely that my turn would not have come again. So, in this tragi-comedy, I have played something of the part of a *pis-aller* and this I find disagreeable.' Holk had been informed of the gist of this letter and the feelings expressed in it were never far from his mind, in spite of the fact that old Petersen and Arne both took pains to encourage his hopes of a successful outcome to the matter. 'You must never give up hope,' wrote Petersen to Holk. 'I know Christine better than any of you, even better than her brother, and I assure you that, apart from any question of Christian charity, which after all teaches forgiveness for the sinner, she still loves you truly as a woman; so much so that she is embarrassed because she still feels a certain affectionate weakness for you. I can see this quite plainly from the letters which I receive now and then from Gnadenfrei. Things are more favourable to your case than you imagine or deserve and it would spoil my last few days on earth if it were otherwise. In any case, at eighty, one knows what things are like and I guarantee, Helmut, that I shall live to join your hands in a new marriage with Christine. That will be my last act as pastor and then I shall retire and wait till God calls me to Him.'

Petersen had written this letter at the beginning of April and if Holk personally had little trust in its overconfident tone, yet there were still times, as today, when he found himself counting on it. So, filled with cheerful thoughts, he was sitting on the front balcony of his house under the branches of a splendid old plane-tree which might well have already been standing there a hundred years before, when the quarter was first built. The tall sash-windows, reaching to the floor and open at the bottom, gave free access between room and balcony and the fire in his drawing-room, more for appearance than for warmth, as well as his morning cigar, increased his feeling of present well-being. Beside him on a bamboo stool lay a copy of *The Times* which, contrary to his habit, he had pushed to one side, diverted by the charming glimpse of spring outside. Now he picked it up and began as usual at the top left-hand corner with the personal column where, picked out in sharp and elegant type, the personal announcements of London society were to be found: births, marriages, and deaths, one after the other. When Holk reached the marriage column, he read: 'Miss Ebba von Rosenberg, Lady-in-Waiting to Princess Maria Eleanor of Denmark, married to Lord Randolph Ashingham, formerly Second Secretary to the British Legation at Copenhagen.'

'So that's that,' said Holk, paling in spite of himself, for he did not feel especially moved. He would perhaps have been more deeply affected by this announcement had he come upon it suddenly and unexpectedly, but this was not the case. Towards the

end of the winter, Pentz, who used to write to keep
him *au courant*, at the end of one of his longer letters,
had spoken of this marriage as more or less imminent:
'And now, my dear Holk, a small piece of information
which will interest you more than all these stories of
the Hansen household—Ebba Rosenberg yesterday
gave notice to the Princess of her engagement which,
however, in order to facilitate the settlement of
certain difficulties, must be kept provisionally secret.
The happy man is no less than Lord Randolph
Ashingham whom you will remember, if not from
Vincent's then perhaps from a *soirée* at the Princess's.
It was at the very beginning of the '59–'60 season.
Lord Randolph, who is rumoured to own a whole
quarter of London (perhaps the very quarter where
you are living at the moment), as well as forests of
fifty million pine trees in Fifeshire, has been thinking
over this matter for a good year—perforce, I may
say, because all sorts of scruples were being put
forward by a much richer uncle from whom he has
expectations. These scruples, in fact, still exist. But
Ebba would not be Ebba if she could not succeed
in convincing the highly eccentric uncle of her
virtues in the realm of *le chic* and in society, and so
the engagement will be announced very shortly. It's
only a question of time. Incidentally, it seems that
the two of them, his lordship and Ebba, need have no
fear of mutual recriminations; he, like so many of his
kind, is said to have been an extinct volcano by the
age of fourteen and is only marrying Ebba in order
to have someone to tell him little stories to keep him
amused and from this point of view he has chosen just
the right person. Every day she will say something—
and I suppose, later on, do something—which will

strike his lordship, and perhaps one day she will set light to the fifty million pine trees and take the opportunity of showing herself and her beloved spouse in the right light. And now, *tout à vous, beau Tristan*, Yours, Pentz.'

The two lines in *The Times* were therefore only a confirmation of Pentz's letter. 'It's a good thing,' said Holk, after a while. 'Now the slate is wiped clean. Her ghost was always haunting me and I could never quite rid myself of it. Now she has done it herself; everything is finished, everything gone and even if Christine is still lost to me and will remain so, at least the thought of her can now occupy the place in my heart where it belongs.'

He took up the paper again and tried to immerse himself in the correspondent's report from Berlin which, it seemed, was dealing in some detail with the doubling of the strength of the army and with the opposition party that was resisting it. But today he had no patience for such things and he was soon glancing over the top of his paper. The clock of nearby St. Pancras' Church, whose steeple reared up before his eyes, had just struck nine and through Southampton Street, which formed his side of the square, cab after cab was rolling by from Euston Square station towards the centre of the town. He broke off one of the plane-tree leaves that was hanging down by the window and played with it and, hearing some sparrows chirping, he took a few crumbs and scattered them over the balcony. At once the sparrows flew down from the branches, pecking and squabbling, but a moment later they fluttered off again, as a sudden series of loud knocks announced that the postman was at the door. Holk, whose birthday it was tomorrow, listened eagerly and soon afterwards Jane came in and handed him four letters.

The four postmarks, Gnadenfrei, Bunzlau, Glücksburg, and Arnewieck, left no doubt as to the writers of the letters; and they brought little news, or so it seemed at first. Asta and Axel sent their best wishes in stiff, formal and certainly rather short letters and even Petersen, who was usually full of news, was content this time merely to send birthday greetings. Holk was rather disappointed at this but recovered his good humour on opening Arne's letter and seeing from the very first line how affectionate and friendly it was. 'Yes,' said Holk to himself, 'he never changes, he will always be the same. And yet it is he who should be most angry with me, as the brother of his beloved sister. Yet that is the reason and explanation, after all, for he loves his sister and almost idolizes her, but he has lived long enough to know very well, in spite of being a bachelor, what it must be like to be married to a St. Elizabeth.[1] . . . If only she were a St. Elizabeth, who was gentle and forgiving. . . . But enough of that,' he added, interrupting himself. 'I'm only becoming embittered when I should be trying to put myself into a conciliatory mood. I had better read what he's written.'

Arnewieck, 27th May, 1861.

Dear Helmut,

Your birthday is due and I must see to it that you have my good wishes. If they arrive a day early, as I imagine they may, you must take it as a sign of my eagerness to wish you the best of luck. But there is

[1] A thirteenth-century German saint known for her good works as well as for her devotion.

no need for me to make a recital of all the things that
I wish you. They all add up, as always, to the one
hope that your reconciliation with Christine shall not
be long delayed. I know very well that you have little
confidence in the possibility of this and try to explain
your lack of confidence by Christine's character. And
perhaps there is an inner voice whispering into your
ear that she is justified, which only strengthens your
disbelief. But now things are much more favourable.
You used to suffer from your wife's dogmatism and
I warned Christine, in a friendly fashion, long before
there was any serious conflict, not to try to force you
to toe any narrowly sectarian line or impose on you
any sort of asceticism quite foreign to your nature.
Any criticism of Christine implicit in such an attitude
was justified and, if I may repeat myself yet again,
I have no desire or reason to withdraw any of it. But
the antidote is supplied by the very strictness of the
doctrines from which we have all had to suffer.
Whether her love for you—which still exists and,
often against her will, appears in many of her letters—
whether that love is strong enough to make her forgive you is a question that we must leave unanswered
and I cannot say one way or another; but what she
might be incapable of doing for love, she might find
herself impelled to do out of a sense of duty, if only
the matter can be put into the right hands. I empha-
size: into the right hands; all the suggestions put
forward by good old Petersen in his letters (he,
incidentally, continues to remain confident) have
had up till now very little success and, in any case,
have certainly not managed to win her over. But
where our rationalistic old friend has failed—in spite
of the fact that Christine is so fond of him and

disapproves only of his religious attitudes—I think that Schwarzkoppen, who was appointed Superintendent-General four weeks ago, might find it easy or at least not too difficult if he chooses the right moment. I have been seeing Schwarzkoppen almost every day during the last week and I have now addressed an urgent request to him to take the matter in hand before he leaves us and the neighbourhood, and since his religious convictions and his personal feelings coincide where you and Christine are concerned, I don't, for an instant, doubt that he will succeed where Petersen has hitherto failed. Schwarzkoppen has always been the highest court of appeal for Christine and particularly now when he is leaving his post as principal of the seminary to become a major luminary of the church. He has been appointed to Stettin in his home province of Pomerania and will be leaving us at the end of September to take up his new post on October 1st. I won't write any more now and, above all, won't trouble you with any estate matters, on which I shall be writing to you another time. I see Countess Brockdorff frequently now, sometimes in her own house, sometimes at the Rantzaus, but also, occasionally, here in Arnewieck, when we have the meetings of the mission here, at one of which I was recently a most unworthy chairman. Christine refused my invitation for Whitsun, ostensibly because Julie has not been well since the spring and needed attention. The real reason is no doubt that she does not wish to return to places and people that can only awaken painful memories. In her eyes Gnadenfrei has many advantages, not the least of which is that of being able to hide from the world. But I console myself with the thought that her need to retreat from the world will slowly disappear and that we shall very soon see her return to us and find happiness once more, a happiness only interrupted by a moment of madness—a fit of madness that became a guilty act. What would I not give if our Whitsun procession this year were to see you back here and the whole arcade at Holkenäs decorated with green may-trees and the old coat of arms over the entrance bedecked with roses! That that time will come, and soon, is the dearest wish of your

Alfred.

Holk put down the letter and, drawing a deep breath, looked happily out over the square, all green and blooming. Joy was in his heart; and in his mind, possibilities were taking shape of which he had hardly dared expect the realization; buried hopes were resurrected and became almost certainties; and the couple who, inwardly and outwardly, had for so long been divided, again took possession of their castle by the sea, and past happiness and good fortune flourished there once more.

CHAPTER 32

AND Holk's dreams came true or seemed to come true.

It was Midsummer Day and over the whole of Angeln the sun was shining in a blue sky and nowhere more brightly than over Holkenäs castle.

Lines of carriages were halting all along the drive and Holk's coat of arms above the entrance was decorated with a wreath of ivy intertwined with red and white roses. Arne had wanted myrtle, but Christine had insisted on ivy.

Twelve o'clock now rang out from Holkebye village and hardly had the sound of the last strokes died away than the huge bell, rung by two men, began slowly to toll, announcing far and wide that the celebration for which all their friends had gathered together, had begun. Soon the tall french-window leading out on to the park swung open and the many spectators who had taken up points of vantage along the flower-beds could see a procession forming in the hall, led by Holk and Christine, the Countess in white satin and with a crown of orange-blossom on her veiled head. Behind the couple whose marriage vows were about to be renewed, came Asta and Axel, then Arne with the dowager Countess Bockdorff and Schwarzkoppen with Fräulein Dobschütz, and many others with them; and finally all those who had asked to join in the festive procession and whose presence was especially welcome to Holk and Christine, since many of them were little more than acquaintances. The servants brought up the rear and as the procession moved off towards Holkebye and passed along the gravel path under the avenue of pines, the route was lined by girls from Holkebye and the neighbouring villages carrying baskets and strewing flowers in their path; some of them, unable to resist their feelings, flung their baskets aside and ran towards Christine to seize hold of her hand or even kiss her dress. 'They are treating me like a saint,' said the Countess, trying to smile. But Holk, to whom these words were whispered, saw that all this was causing her more sorrow than joy and that, true to her nature, this exaggerated homage was for her rather a source of anxiety and grief and even of dread for the future. But the whirling life around her made her forget these gloomy reflections and as she could now clearly hear more and more bells joining in, as if all the churches in the land were eager to celebrate this strange festival of reconciliation, all her sadness left her, for the moment at least, and her heart opened up to their joyous peal.

They had now reached the low churchyard wall along which, as when Asta and Elizabeth used to sit there, tall nettles were once more growing and the sawn-up logs were arranged in high piles, and when the head of the procession had passed along the wall, they turned in through the gate and moved on between the graves towards the church which was standing with open doors, giving a full view of the lighted altar at the end of the central aisle.

There Petersen was standing.

He had been frail for many years and to his great age had finally been added the burden of illness. But when he had learned that 'if Petersen was not well by Midsummer Day, Schwarzkoppen would have to conduct the service', he had immediately recovered and when people tried to recommend caution and urged him to spare himself, he retorted that he was going to be the one to restore her happiness to Christine even if he had to do so from his death-bed. Everyone had been touched by this, his strength had been restored to him and he was now standing as straight and upright as nineteen years ago when, also on Midsummer Day, he had joined their hands together for the first time.

As the procession moved up the aisle, a hymn was sung and when it was over, Petersen gave a short address, avoiding any personal allusions and above all any reference to the 'sinner over whom there is more rejoicing in heaven than over ninety and nine just persons'. Instead, in a simple yet deeply moving prayer, he asked for the grace of God to descend upon the hearts of the reunited and then pronounced the blessing.

The organ burst forth again and the bell pealed out and the long procession of witnesses to this renewal of vows made their way back along the path beside the sea and when they reached the jetty, they turned up towards the castle.

The wedding feast was laid out on the front terrace, so that all the guests could look out over the sea, and as the time had now come for someone, if not to propose a toast, at least to say a few words, Arne stood up and turning towards his sister and brother-in-law, said simply: 'To the luck of Holkenäs.'

Everyone was strangely moved by these words which, indeed, had an almost melancholy sound and those sitting close to the bridegroom silently touched glasses with him.

But there was little real rejoicing and all the bystanders had an anxious foreboding that if there was to be any 'luck of Holkenäs' it was, at best, on that day only. By tomorrow, it would already have been buried.

CHAPTER 33

HOWEVER, the feeling of sadness that had dominated the splendid celebration appeared to be unjustified and the 'luck of Holkenäs' seemed, in reality, likely to revive. At least, such was the impression gained by all those who were not intimates of the castle. The Holks lived amicably together, entertained a great deal (more than before), and visited their neighbours, on which occasion Holk was never lacking in charm and good humour and only the more observant noticed that one essential was absent. It was not happiness but merely peace that prevailed and before the autumn neither Fräulein Dobschütz nor Arne had any further doubt that as far as Christine was concerned, she had nothing but the *willingness* to be happy. Indeed, she was willing enough. There was no longer any question of differences of opinion and if, as occasionally happened, Holk launched out on some genealogical excursion or plans for model-farming, the Countess never smiled in the supercilious way that had so often vexed and exasperated her husband; but this anxious avoidance of everything that might have disturbed their peace, the sudden interruption of the conversation when an awkward topic chanced to turn up, the very care and constant self-control, were so oppressive that the last few years before the catastrophe, even though the real happiness of the marriage belonged by then already to the past, seemed in comparison a relatively happy time.

With his sanguine temperament, Holk for a long time refused to face this truth and made a point of ignoring the reserve, almost the aversion, with which Christine met his advances. Finally, however, he became impatient and at the end of September, in a state of mingled disgruntlement and sympathy, he resolved to speak to Fräulein Dobschütz to ask her opinion and, if possible, her advice.

It was a bright fresh autumn day and gossamer threads hung glittering on the bushes, already in part

leafless. Asta had arrived from school the previous
evening and as soon as breakfast, which had just
started, was over, she was eagerly waiting to go down
to visit her friend in the village. 'I'll come with you,'
said Holk, and as Fräulein Dobschütz had already
promised to accompany Asta, they all three set off
from the terrace to take the shorter and prettier way
beside the sea. The broad expanse of water was
almost motionless and only occasionally a slight swell
carried a little foam right up to the foot of the dune.
Asta was delighted to see the sea again and kept
breaking off in the middle of an account of happenings at school as, now and then, a wonderful shimmer
of light slid over the still water or gulls' wings dipped
into it; but all at once she lost all interest in the sea
and its reflections, as she spied Elizabeth Petersen
coming out from the dunes on to the beach. She
hurried towards her and gave her a hug and a kiss.
Holk and Fräulein Dobschütz had been left somewhat behind, which suited the two girls very well as
they naturally had a thousand and one things to tell
each other as they went on ahead. Holk, too, was
pleased as it gave him the opportunity, for which he
had been waiting for some time, to speak freely to
Julie about Christine.

'I am glad that we are alone for a moment, my dear
Julie,' he began, 'because I've been wanting a talk
with you for a long time. What is wrong with
Christine? You know that I am not inquiring out of
mere curiosity or even less to complain and least of
all to blame her. There were times when you found
yourself having to hear such things and try to smooth
them over; but as you know, my dear Julie, such times
are past and will never return. There is never any

conflict over anything now and when I go walking
with Christine in the park, as I did before breakfast
this morning, and a squirrel runs across the path and
a swan glides over the lake and Rustan refuses to
budge even when a swarm of hens flies out before our
noses—then I think of a picture of Paradise that I
once saw in which everything was at peace: the lion
was walking with the lamb and God came and spoke
with Adam and Eve. Yes, Julie, my present life
reminds me of that picture and I could be satisfied
and perhaps I should be. But I'm not, on the contrary
I'm depressed and anxious. If it were only a question
of myself, then I wouldn't waste words if, in spite of
this peacefulness, I feel uneasy and unable to enjoy
myself. I should simply accept it as a punishment and
not grumble, perhaps even feel a sort of grim satisfaction. After all, a wrong requires penance and
penance can bring contentment because it satisfies
our sense of justice. So let me say once again, if I am
speaking to you now, it's not on my own behalf but
on Christine's and because every day makes it plain
to me that she would like to forget but cannot. And
now tell me what you think.'

'I think that you're quite right. Christine is trying
to forget but cannot.'

'And has she said anything to you to suggest that?
Has she given you to understand that everything has
been in vain?'

'No, not at all.'

'And yet you yourself are convinced of it?'

'I'm afraid so. But although I feel it so strongly,
you mustn't try to deduce from that anything more
painful or more definite than you need, or indeed
than you ought. Although I still enjoy Christine's

friendship—it could hardly be otherwise, because I am always trying to show her how much I love her— I no longer have her trust. She won't confide in anyone, not even in me. It makes me very sad because she always used to open her heart to me and when, on that dreadful, unforgettable day when we left the house and afterwards went through those terrible times together, first in the village and then in Arnewieck and Gnadenfrei, there was not a single thought or feeling that she didn't share with me. So close were we to each other that we were like two people with a single life. But from the moment Christine moved back here, all that came to an end. She is so sensitive that, having said to herself that a new life, full of joy and happiness, had begun or was about to begin, as soon as she saw—you must excuse me if I say this—as soon as she saw that this new life had failed and yet it seemed wrong to complain further and even ungrateful towards God, she became accustomed to keeping silent and even now I can still only guess at all that is taking place in her mind.'

Holk stood still, lost in thought and then said: 'My dear Julie, I had hoped that you would bring me consolation but I see that you've none to offer. If everything is as you say, then I can't see anything that can help us.'

'Time, dear Helmut, time. Mankind's guardian angel.'

'If only you may be right. But I don't believe it; time will not have time enough to do anything. I'm not a doctor and I certainly disclaim any competence in reading in someone's heart and soul. All the same, so much I *can* see, we're heading for disaster. People can live happily or they can live unhappily, and in both cases they may live to a great age. But this resignation, this melancholy smile—that cannot last long. Our life must be built on joy and once the light of joy has been extinguished, then night must fall and if that night means death, then it will still be for the best.'

A week later there was a small party at Holkenäs to which only a few intimate friends had been invited, amongst them Arne and Schwarzkoppen, in addition to Petersen and Elizabeth. Till dusk fell, they sat in the open because, in spite of the season, the air was mild and only when the lamps had been lit indoors did they leave the veranda and sit in the summer drawing-room to drink tea and have a little music. At school, Asta had become quite a polished pianist and since her return home she had been seeing Elizabeth almost daily and practising with her. This evening, a number of new pieces were going to be played in honour of Schwarzkoppen, who was leaving his post at Arnewieck in the next few days, and when the servants had ceased bustling about and the rattle of tea-cups and saucers had subsided, the two friends began hastily looking through their music-case until they had found what they wanted, only two or three pieces because Holk considered that music interfered with conversation. The first piece was a song from Flotow's 'Martha', followed straight away by Robert Burns's 'O bonnie was yon rosy brier' and when the last notes of this song had died away, amidst general applause, Asta announced to her audience, who had become more attentive, that there would follow a genuine folk-song, since Robert Burns was not really a folk-poet.

Schwarzkoppen disagreed with great vigour and
was supported by Arne who, in his avuncular capacity,
felt justified in adding that 'this was just the sort of
opinion you would expect from these modern
boarding-schools' and, once launched, he would
certainly have continued in the same strain with
further provocative comments, had not Holk interrupted at that moment to inquire the exact title of the
next song.

'It hasn't a title,' replied Asta.

'Nonsense. Every song has to have a name.'

'They used to have but now you take the first line
as the title and put a wavy line under it.'

'I can well believe that,' laughed Holk.

Eventually they stopped arguing and after a short
prelude by Asta, Elizabeth began to sing in her lovely
voice, admirably suited to the words and the music
of the song.

> *'Denkst du verschwundener Tage, Marie,*
> *Wenn du starrst ins Feuer bei Nacht ?*
> *Wünschst du die Stunden und Tage zurück,*
> *Wo du fröhlich und glücklich gelacht ?'*

> *'Ich denke verschwundener Tage, John,*
> *Und sie sind allezeit mein Glück,*
> *Doch die mir die liebsten gewesen sind,*
> *Ich wünsche sie nicht zurück . . .'*[1]

When the singing and, immediately afterwards,

---

[1] 'Do you think of vanished days, Marie, as you stare in the fire at
night? Do you wish for those hours and days to return when you laughed
full of joy and happiness?'

'I do think of those vanished days, John, and always they fill me with
happiness but those which were dearest to me, I do not wish them back
again.'

the accompaniment, had come to an end, everyone, including even Holk, rushed to the piano to compliment Elizabeth, who was embarrassed at receiving so much praise. 'Yes,' said Asta, proud of her friend's success, 'you've never sung it so beautifully.' Everyone wanted to hear the last verse again; but there was one person who did not join in this request because, in the middle of the general excitement, she had not failed to notice that, just as two years ago at the performance of Waiblinger's melancholy song, Christine had quietly slipped out of the room.

It was, of course, Julie who noticed this. She hesitated a moment, undecided whether to follow her friend or not but quickly making up her mind, she went upstairs to find Christine in her bedroom. She was sitting with her hands clasped together staring at the floor.

'What is it, Christine? What's the matter?'

Julie knelt down in front of Christine and taking her hand covered it with kisses and tears. But Christine pulled her hand away and said softly to herself:

> '*Und die mir die liebsten gewesen sind,*
> *Ich wünsche sie nicht zurück.*'

CHAPTER 34

A WEEK had gone by.

The air was mild and but for the Virginia creeper that was already taking on its autumn red as it twined luxuriantly round the columns of the castle terrace, one might almost have believed that midsummer had returned and that the splendid celebration of three months ago, in which the whole of Angeln had joined, was about to take place once again. Not only was the sun, almost summer-like, shining brightly over the castle and park, as on the day that the Count and Countess had renewed their marriage vows; but, as before, long lines of carriages gave a festive air as they brought the many guests to the castle. Bells were tolling far and wide and the village girls stood casting flowers as for the wedding procession. But today they were strewing white asters and the person who was passing on her way from the castle was dead. Solemn music accompanied the coffin behind which were walking Holk and the children and then the long cortège of relatives and friends. Petersen was standing at the entrance to the church and led the procession to the open grave beside the tumbledown old family vault. The choir was silent and every head was bared as the coffin descended and the earth closed over Christine Holk. A heart that had yearned for peace had found it now at last.

Julie von Dobschütz to
Superintendent-General Schwarzkoppen

Holkenäs, October 14th, 1861.

Your Reverence wished to know about our friend whose death was the first news that you received after taking up your office. I am glad to be able to satisfy your wish because, in spite of my grief, it is a consolation and an inspiration to be able to speak of our dear dead friend.

On the day that you last saw her, a thought must have been ripening in her mind which she may well have conceived long before. You may perhaps recall

the elegiac, almost melancholy, folk-song that Elizabeth Petersen sang that evening—Christine left the
room almost immediately afterwards and I believe
from that moment onwards, her resolution was
made. I found her deeply affected and I admit that
I was immediately seized with anxious forebodings,
forebodings which I could only succeed in calming
by recalling the Christian sentiments and religious
convictions of our dear deceased—those Christian
sentiments which bear us through life, for so long
as it is God's will.

The next day seemed to justify my belief. Christine told me that she had gone very late to bed but
she showed no signs of tiredness, on the contrary, she
had a freshness which I had not seen since her reconciliation with her husband. When she came down
to breakfast, she was more affable and friendly than
usual, indeed almost jovial, and she persuaded her
husband to join a shooting party in two days' time
to which he had just received an invitation from
Count Baudissin. Then, strangely enough, she talked
about clothes in great detail, though only in connexion with Asta who, she said, now that she was over
seventeen, must begin to think of 'coming out' and
as she said this I saw her eyes fill with tears.

The day went by and the sun was already quite low
when she invited me to go for a walk with her along
the beach. 'But we must hurry,' she added, 'or else
it will be too dark.'

We went off straightaway down the terrace and
when we were at the bottom, she said that she did
not want to walk along the beach as the sand was so
wet and her shoes so thin, so we went out on the jetty.
She deliberately avoided mentioning any serious

topic. When we finally reached the end-platform and the steps where the steamers tie up, we sat down on a wooden bench that the Count had recently had placed there and looked at the sun reflected in the sea, which was completely still, and at the magnificent colours of the clouds. 'How beautiful it is,' said Christine. 'Let's wait here to see the sunset. But as it's already getting cold, would you go and fetch our coats? But to save yourself the climb up to the terrace, just call up for them, Asta will certainly hear you.'

She said this with a touch of embarrassment, because it was not in her nature to tell a lie; but it would have struck me as strange had she not shown this embarrassment, because in her almost excessive kindness and goodness towards me, she was always most scrupulous about asking me to do favours for her. She saw, too, what was in my mind, but I still could hardly show her too plainly how anxious and worried I was and so I went back along the jetty and up to the terrace, because her suggestion about calling until Asta heard had obviously been an afterthought.

When I came back to the end of the jetty, I could see nothing of the Countess and I knew at once what had happened. I hurried back to fetch help, although I felt sure that it would be of no avail. The Count was stunned and did not know what to do. Finally, the alarm was given in the village and they searched the jetty and the beach until far into the night. Boats went out to search a shallow sandbank which lay some distance off the jetty but for hours there was no result and it was not until the following morning that some fishermen from Holkebye came up to the castle to announce that they had found the Countess. We all went down. Her face that for so long had borne the marks of silent suffering had been transfigured and she looked almost gay: so eagerly had her heart been longing for peace. A bier was brought from the church and to avoid the steepness of the terrace, she was carried over the dune and up the slope of the drive. The whole village accompanied her body in mourning, particularly the poor people to whom she had always shown such kindness and generosity, and some of them said bitter words against the Count that I hope he did not hear.

As for the burial and Petersen's funeral address which, as I can testify, would have satisfied the most orthodox, you will have read about that in the *Arne-wieck Messenger* which Baron Arne sent you and perhaps in the *Flensburg Gazette* as well.

I want only to add what you may consider proper concerning the state of mind of the Countess and what made her take the fatal step. As soon as we had brought her up from the beach, we went to her room to see whether she had left any farewell message. We did, in fact, find a number of sheets of paper on which a few words had been written showing that she had tried to say good-bye to her nearest and dearest— her husband and Baron Arne, as well as to me. On those addressed to the Baron and myself she had scribbled a few words such as 'Thank you . . .' and 'When you read these lines . . .' but they had been crossed out, and on the sheet addressed to Holk there was not even that. Instead, inside the sheet intended for him there was a piece of crumpled paper that had been carefully smoothed out again, on which was written the song that Elizabeth Petersen had sung

immediately before Holk's departure for Copenhagen and which had made such an impression on
her on that occasion, just as recently the folk-song
translated from the English which I mentioned
earlier. This latter song your Reverence will surely
still recall but the earlier one may have slipped your
memory, in which case, if you will allow me, I should
like to copy the first verse. This is how it goes:

> *Die Ruh' ist wohl das Beste*
> *Von allem Glück der Welt,*
> *Was bleibt vom Erdenfeste,*
> *Was bleibt uns unvergällt?*
> *Die Rose welkt in Schauern,*
> *Die uns der Frühling gibt,*
> *Wer haßt, ist zu bedauern,*
> *Und mehr noch fast, wer liebt.*[1]

The last line had been almost invisibly underlined,
and that gentle, almost timid underlining contains
the story of a whole life.

Your position and your faith will give you strength
to accept the death of our friend but I have lost all
that was dearest to me in life and what now remains
will be poor and empty. Asta asks to be remembered
to you as does Elizabeth Petersen and

Your most respectful
Julie von Dobschütz.

[1] See note on p. 52.

PRINTED IN GREAT BRITAIN
AT THE UNIVERSITY PRESS, OXFORD
BY VIVIAN RIDLER
PRINTER TO THE UNIVERSITY

DATE DUE

GAYLORD

PRINTED IN U.S.A.